Pretty Poison

★ ★ ★

Kim Vantrease

DANDELION WINE
PRESS

———————

2012

This book is for...

Red who always believed in me
and spent many nights alone making dinner
and doing laundry,
so I could "almost done"
my way to the end of this book,
and who
pushed me hard and helped
me find my place...

* * *

Amanda and Greg because of their
endless support and
a few long nights spent putting this together...

* * *

Sydney and Jared who nudged me along with their enthusiasm...

* * *

My two grandchildren, Lilly and Jason, who
inspire me and love me unconditionally...

* * *

Cara who has given me a
lifetime of adventure and books...

* * *

The wounded soul who has been
bullied, may you find your strengths
and conquer your sorrows...

* * *

Prologue

Ominous clouds that echoed her mood tumbled across the darkening sky while thunder rumbled in the distance warning of the progressing storm. Shards of lightning flickered in her reflection as Lola stood at the window sipping expensive champagne from a crystal flute. And long velvet drapes, the color of crimson, twirled in rhythm with the restless winds as howling gusts frantically roamed the room. With another blast of wind, she closed the window and moved across the room to the black sofa where her high school yearbook lay among the cushions.

She sat on the edge of the sofa, careful not to wrinkle her gown, and began sifting the pages that highlighted her miserable past. Hatred, spawned by reigning vengeance, seeped from her pores as she lingered on PAGE 42. "Poor, Sara Parkins, what ever will you do now?" she mocked bitterly and closed the book before tucking it inside her overnight bag with the champagne flute and a half bottle of *Dom*.

A solid chime rang inside the antique mantle clock, announcing the one-o'clock hour. *It's time*. Lola picked up her bag and cast one final glance around the room before heading toward the door.

Inside the grand foyer, she stood beneath a crystal chandelier that served as a crown to the evergreen walls. She lingered for a moment when a gilded mirror beckoned her attention one last time. Emotionless, she stared at the vacant soul inside her reflection. The pleading eyes of the desperate stranger looked back at her and tried to stop her, but Lola's will impeded all reason.

Chapter One

Late September in her senior year, Linda Wilson walked along a weathered path toward the doors of Miller Lake High School while clusters of students awaited the bell on the lawns in front of the old brick building. Her footsteps pounded heavily with trepidation as she approached her gateway to hell, mentally preparing for the morning deluge of insults soon to be delivered by Sara Parkins and her coterie. The malevolent stage was set with each performer awaiting her cue like a lion awaits its prey in tall grass.

"Here she comes," Debbie Harrison squealed excitedly, jabbing Joya Davis in the ribs with her elbow. Debbie's eyes sparkled in pleasure as their victim came through the door. "Was that an earthquake?" Sara's loyal minions shouted in unison.

"No! It's *Lardo Linda!*" Sara exclaimed, delighting in their joint malice.

Linda lowered her head, avoiding all eye contact, and pretended not to hear the taunting chorus of laughter that spewed from the gullets of the loathsome trio. The noxious blend followed her as she steered her way through a maze of roving students.

When Linda arrived at her locker she saw a sheet of paper flapping against the small door. Her eyes landed on the bold black letters, LINDA WILSON IS A LOSER! Everyone in the congested area commented as they walked past her. She yanked the offensive prop down and spun the combination dial when a familiar odor arose from the small chamber. Dreading what was on the other side of the door, she slowly opened it and found all of her books drenched in ketchup. Included, was her ten-page book report that she had finished a week early. Her entire lunch hour would be spent rewriting it she realized with a heavy sigh.

Tears threatened to drown her eyes, but were dammed by her enduring will. No, she declared in silence, she wouldn't reward her monsters with tears. She tried to smother her rising fury, but frustration festered, tempting a perilous degree. Furiously, she unfastened the jacket tied around her waist as the searing eyes of her antagonists were upon her, savoring their moment. Their penetrating whispers ricocheted off the sea of blue lockers, leaving Linda on the brink of rage and with the sleeves of her jacket, she wiped the reeking substance from her books and shoved them into her backpack.

"What is that smell?" Sara asked in feigned mystery, waving her delicate hand in front of her crinkled nose as she glided arrogantly past Linda's locker.

Linda resisted the urge to hurl her backpack at Sara's skull, slamming the locker door would have to suffice. "Someday, Sara, you're going to get what's coming to you," Linda mumbled under her breath before heading to class.

September drifted slowly into October where the leaves exchanged their green luster for the brilliance of autumn. Vivid reflections of nature's seasonal radiance painted the hills and valleys of the quaint New Hampshire town. Curious vines and sprawling trees, bursting with vibrant shades of scarlet, decorated the manicured lawns while fringes of gold roamed the stunning landscapes. It was Linda's favorite time of year.

With autumn came preparations for Miller Lake High School's homecoming dance and because of her artistic abilities, Linda had been invited by her art teacher, Mrs. Watson, to create the decorations for the dance. The opportunity was grand, filling Linda with hope. Her dance, as she perceived it, had to explode with panache, baring all of the magic, wonder and intrigue she could conjure. She planned to create the most memorable event for her peers knowing that they would positively acknowledge her fine contribution and, through her talent, she would weaken Sara's tainted influence and claim a respectable page in Miller Lake history.

If intellect were celebrated at Miller Lake High, Linda would be campus queen, however, such merit was hardly recognized by most students as they considered it an affliction. Mild obesity and intelligence banished Linda from esteemed ranking among her classmates, leaving her to exist in a world of loneliness and ridicule. She wore nothing from the fashion realm, only bulky earth-tone sweaters and generic blue jeans to disguise her unflattering figure, but nothing escaped the discriminating eye. Her soulful eyes, the color of whiskey, were stunning, yet only to remain in obscurity behind her glasses. A modern hairstyle would be pointless, she believed, so every morning before school she strung her brown hair through a pony tail that dangled plainly to the middle of her back.

Linda's long-time nemesis, Sara Parkins, was the leader of her pack and hailed Miller Lake's fashion princess. Wearing only designer labels, she pompously paraded around school with her entourage in tow. She thrived on her beauty and used her extraordinary green eyes and fluid blond hair to get what she wanted. When she was bored, or feeling neglected by her boyfriend, Nick Evans, she flaunted her good looks and carelessly toyed with the hopeful hearts of many naive boys, simply, for the sport of it.

Sara's two devout cohorts were Joya Davis and Debbie Harrison. Like Sara, they were blessed with exquisite features. Joya was unique, having a striking beauty all her own with glistening pools of sapphire etched beneath sable canopies of lashes and jet-black hair that twirled untamed around her porcelain face. And, Debbie, the tallest of the three, had dark, alluring eyes with almond colored hair that flowed like liquid silk down her back. Linda thought Joya was the most beautiful of the three and it greatly irked her that such gifts were wasted on the undeserving.

A cold rain pummeled the windows as Linda sat restlessly in her final class of the day awaiting the bell to rescue her. The afternoon announcements crackled from the small speaker on the wall, but she only listened with partial attention as nothing usually pertained to her. With her books securely in her arms, Linda watched the secondhand twitch on the clock, signaling only one minute until the bell would rid her of her daily dose of torment. Suddenly, she heard her own name projected over the loud speaker. Her heart slammed against her chest causing her head to throb from the sudden rush of blood and her cheeks and ears burned with embarrassment as snickers filled the room. All scrutinizing eyes were upon her, boring holes in her flesh. She cringed in her seat as the broadcast thanked her and the other volunteers for their participation regarding the dance. Far too soon, Linda's involvement with Homecoming had been revealed, giving Sara plenty of time to sabotage

Linda's dance. She chewed on her lower lip and tried to formulate a plan that would counter Sara's tricks that were, surely, forthcoming.

Linda worked amicably with her small group of volunteers, but she kept her distance, trusting no one, due to a vicious prank performed two years earlier when a handsome and seemingly nice boy handed her a party invitation on the school lawn. Considering her popularity, she politely advised him of his mistake, but he flashed a friendly grin and assured her that she was invited. As she watched the boy walk away, her heart drummed in rapid rhythm, "Joe Steele" she uttered, liking the sound of his name. Since third grade, she had maintained a secret crush on Joe. He was incredibly handsome, desired by all of the girls and proficient in any sport. Though Joe was profoundly conceited, Linda graciously pardoned his only imperfection.

Slowly, she emerged from her dreamy fog and began tearing at the blue envelope while an overwhelming state of euphoria washed over her entire body causing her to feel slightly faint from the excitement. The moment was magic, leaving her hardly aware of her trembling legs and tingling cheeks. Her eager fingers fumbled with the stubborn envelope until it was fully open, but, surprisingly, the envelope was empty. Confused, she looked to the ground to see if she had dropped the invitation and with enduring hope, she lifted her feet and twirled around, but there was nothing. Again, she looked inside the ruffled envelope but only to confirm the hoax. Suddenly, a crashing wave of laughter struck her ears and startled her. Until that moment, she was oblivious to her audience that was lurking by an oak tree. She spun around to find Sara and her puppets exulting in their impiety. Her heart folded inside her chest as grave humiliation surfaced, setting her cheeks afire. Linda couldn't laugh it off and pretend it didn't hurt as she had learned to do over the years. Anguish had already invaded her soul, leaving her void of any quick-witted response to cripple the blow of the cruel prank. She turned away from her monsters and dropped the envelope that had, only for a moment, held promise.

Rolling images of the painful incident continually infected Linda's judgment. She remained pleasant toward her volunteers, but she was unwilling to befriend any of them, even though she desperately needed a friend.

When she was younger, she had had friends, and an especially close one, Elise Barrows, but Elise moved to England near the end of seventh grade. Both girls were devastated by the move, but promised to keep in touch through email. Linda yearned for her friend to return to Miller Lake where they could venture through teenage adversities together and other social pangs of their youth, but Elise remained abroad, leaving them to become nothing more than pen pals.

Wet, gray skies continued to hover over Miller Lake while Linda and her assistants prepared floral garlands for the homecoming dance that was only a day away. Kathy Carlisle, Linda's favorite among the volunteers, was friendly and displayed many qualities of human decency, Linda had observed on several occasions, but Linda's reservations remained, leaving her reluctant to pursue any friendships.

"Are you ready to paint some more flower stems?" Linda asked, ready to drop a bundle.

"Sure." Kathy placed her paintbrush over a can of modest green paint.

"This is the last of them," Linda said cheerfully.

"I was beginning to think I'd never hear those beautiful words!" Kathy chuckled, reaching for the armload of stems. She studied Linda for a moment and mulled over an idea that had popped into her head. "Hey, do you want to go to a movie or something with me next week?"

"*Uhm*," Linda stammered, naturally surrendering to her recurring anxieties as she quickly tried to think her way out of the unexpected invitation. Her apprehension was painfully obvious, leaving them both in an awkward state. Even though Kathy seemed to be a good person, Linda still lacked trust. "Sure, I'd like that," she finally blurted, under duress. Immediately, she held her breath and awaited the inevitable joke to be played out.

"Great," Kathy nodded, revealing her benign intentions.

Guardedly, Linda looked around. There were no eager spectators, no Sara Parkins prowling in the shadows, no willing accomplices standing by; only a friendly expression glowing on Kathy's face. Relieved, Linda exhaled and allowed herself that special moment when people first become friends.

"Next week, when the dance is over, we'll make some plans," Kathy suggested, concentrating on her paintbrush.

"That sounds good," said Linda, looking forward to the event. She bent over to pick up a can of paint when she caught sight of her watch, "Oh, my gosh!" she cringed apologetically, addressing her group, "I didn't mean to keep you all so long. The good news is, you can all go home now, but the bad news is, we're going to meet here early tomorrow morning around eight to finish. Will that be all right?"

"But that's Saturday morning! That's way too early," a voice bellowed from the small group.

A few more grumbles circulated the room while Linda gasped, pretending to be shocked by her volunteers' protests. "I'll bring my mother's donuts," she bribed, behind a devious smile.

WILSON'S BAKERY was the most preferred in town and, for twenty-five years, it remained famous for its range of pastries, desserts and breads. What tickled Linda was the fact that even Sara's family was passionate about the goods created inside her parents' bakery. Faithfully, every Friday morning, Mrs. Parkins compiled a list and sent one of her housekeeping staff to purchase the family favorites.

It was midnight when Linda pulled her father's Buick into the driveway. She had sent her volunteers home earlier while she stayed a few extra hours to work on the homecoming decorations. When she pulled the keys out of the ignition, she noticed a light on in the garage. Curiously, she looked through the garage window to find her father still working on the "masterpiece" as they affectionately called their secret project.

"Daddy!" she whispered, coming through the door. "What are you still doing up? It's midnight."

Mr. Wilson was a jolly, portly man with thinning hair that held traces of gray and his blue eyes were kind, expressing his gentle nature. He smiled at her, "Is it really? I hadn't noticed. There were just a few things that needed tweaking, that's all," he said in his defense.

"But you have to be at the bakery in three hours," Linda frowned.

"Don't worry about that, I'll be just fine," he said, brandishing his exuberance as he tightened the final bolt and flicked the switch to the *on* position. Together they stood in the brisk air, sharing a moment of triumph as they marveled at their joint venture.

At *7 a.m.*, music blared from Linda's alarm, welcoming a new day, but she was already awake because her life was about to change for the better, she believed. Excitedly, she hurried into her clothes, hardly allowing an hour to pass before she was at the school with a gallon of orange juice and a box of donuts.

"Donuts!" Nathan Heddinger yelled as soon as he spied Linda with the familiar pink and white box.

Like a swarm of bees, the entire group converged on Linda and attacked the box of donuts. "I'll just set these down," her voice rolled in laughter as she escaped the hungry mob. Moments later, the mangled box lay empty on the floor next to the spent orange juice jug. Linda looked on, delighting in the rare moment as she gazed around the room. It had been far too long since she indulged in the joys of youth. It was a new day and she was among fellow students without her steady companion, *trepidation.*

"We're nearly done." Linda reached for another string of flowers and dangled precariously over a ladder inside the gymnasium.

"I thought we'd never get this far," said Kathy, admiring her work. "I just hope Sara doesn't wreck any of it."

"Given her history, I'd be surprised if she didn't."

"If you don't mind me asking, what is her problem? Why does she target you more than others?" Kathy looked up toward Linda.

Linda laughed, "That's easy. It's because my brains beat up her beauty."

"What?"

"It's a long story, but I got stuck working on a group project with her in seventh grade," Linda shook her head. "It didn't go well. Anyway, I did all of the work and the teacher realized it and called Sara out on it in front of the class."

"Gulp."

"*Uh-hum*, exactly. I couldn't lie to the teacher when she asked me which part of the project was mine. And Sara just stood there like an idiot…expecting me to cover for her."

"That sounds like Sara," Kathy nodded.

"It was really funny at the time, but she's hated me ever since."

"That's why I hate group projects."

"Me, too."

"Have you ever stood up to her?" Immediately, Kathy wished that she had posed her question more delicately so as not to sound accusatory.

"Are you kidding? Nobody stands up to Sara." Linda's eyes sprung open, "She'd pulverize me!"

Kathy resisted the urge to giggle. "Do you know what I think?"

"No. What?"

"I believe that most people are really only terrified of Sara."

"What? Are you serious?" Linda was dumbfounded.

"*Uh-hum.*"

"But she's so popular."

"That's because nobody wants to get on her bad side. They're scared to death of being in your position."

Linda let the idea settle for a moment. "I've never thought about it that way before."

"It's true," Kathy nodded and continued, "Sara may think she's queen bee, but her *reign* is limited. And, if you think about it, her superficial life is really kind of sad. She doesn't have what you and I have. Nothing is real."

"You almost have me feeling sorry for her!" Linda laughed at the irony.

"It's crazy isn't it?"

"Yes." Linda was amused by the revelation.

"Just remember, high school isn't your destiny, it's only a mere passage to the rest of your life."

"You're right," said Linda, absorbing all that Kathy had told her.

"You'll stand up to Sara when the time is right. True, she may react more aggressively for a while, but I believe the risk to be worthy."

Suddenly, Linda was deep in fantasy, putting Sara in her place.

"Don't go poking her with a sharp stick or anything!" Kathy quickly advised.

Linda burst out laughing.

"Just making sure we're both clear on that."

"Yes, we are," Linda laughed. The clock had just struck twelve when the doors thrust open. Shrouded in the sun's brilliant glare, a gleaming presence appeared in the doorway. Rays of the sun's firelight danced around the edges of the mysterious figure, promoting all the grandeur of a knight in shining armor. "Hey, it's my dad." Linda jumped off the ladder and headed toward him.

Mr. Wilson surveyed the room, looking to enlist a few boys to assist him with the cargo he had waiting in the bed of his pickup truck. He spotted Nathan and Jerry Helm, "Pardon me, fellas, will you help me bring something in from the parking lot?"

"Sure," Nathan answered for both himself and Jerry as he steadied his ladder against the wall.

Mr. Wilson revealed his fatherly pride when the students gathered around the magnificent water fountain. "Linda designed it herself," he boasted.

"Yeah, but you built it, Dad."

Small rumbles of praise filled the room as the volunteers surrounded Linda's lush creation. Green, leafy vines that were delicately woven throughout the fountain carried an abundance of colorful flowers consisting of russet, blue, gold and vermillion. Twinkle lights, intricately laced within the seasonal foliage, glowed with opulence throughout the elegant six-foot monument of contoured glass and copper-colored rods.

"During full operation, the water will flow from five levels, fusing a blend of color, light and fragrant water," Linda explained, holding up a bottle of concentrated floral fragrance. Her head tingled as all expressed their genuine approval. Happily, she looked at her father to enjoy their moment. His eyes smiled back at her and then he picked up his wrench to secure all of the bolts before leaving.

After everyone else had gone home, Kathy and Linda stayed behind to put on the finishing touches. "You're still planning on going tonight, right?" Kathy sensed that Linda had changed her mind about attending the dance.

"Yeah," Linda answered pensively, still dangling on the fringes of uncertainty. It had been only two hours since Kathy suggested going to the dance and, already, Linda's mind had flip-flopped a dozen times.

"I think you'd really regret it if you didn't go."

Linda smiled feebly, thinking. "I just hope that if Sara hasn't already made any plans of sabotage that my being there won't encourage any."

"Good point, but I say go to the dance and to heck with worry."

Decidedly, Linda nodded, yielding to Kathy's campaign, "You're right. I'll pick you up at *7:30*."

"Good. And don't worry about not having a date. I don't have one either. We'll go stag. Wait...can girls go stag?"

Linda laughed.

"You're not going to regret this, I promise!"

Chapter Two

Over the distant horizon, an orange moon offered friendly salutations as Linda stood on her front porch taking in the evening splendor. Awkwardly, she clumped toward her father's car in a pair of stiff heels she'd only worn once at her cousin's wedding. "Girl, you've got five minutes to get used to these shoes," she chided herself.

Inside the Buick, Linda smoothed out the wrinkles in the dress she had just borrowed from her mother for the impromptu affair. "Oh, what have I gotten myself into?" she fretted, staring dismally into the rear view mirror with regret as she adjusted her glasses and noticed her curls had already lost their bounce.

As soon as Kathy got into the car, Linda started feeling more optimistic about her decision to attend the dance until she pulled into the parking lot. Her wary eyes followed the colorful train of students entering the gym. "I'm not so sure I'm ready to go in there," Linda stiffened in reticence as Kathy reached for the door handle.

"Linda, don't worry. You look fantastic! I mean that."

"Thank you, but suddenly I'm petrified."

"There's no need to be petrified. Just be yourself."

Not wanting to be a downer, Linda forced herself to rally, "All right, I'm ready."

The gym had been fully transformed into a magical garden. Colorful draperies made from paper flowers disguised the marred gymnasium walls while an exciting blend of fresh flowers replaced the ever-present odor of sweaty socks. Linda looked toward her fountain and silently thanked Jerry for accomplishing his most important task. She had intended to arrive early and turn the fountain on herself, but a small fiasco with the curling iron forced her delay.

Brenda Cassivetti spotted Linda and Kathy at the door. "Linda, you've done such a great job. This is absolutely beautiful!" Her genuine enthusiasm rang in her voice.

"Thank you, I'm glad you like it," Linda beamed.

"I hope you're on the prom committee," Brenda shouted as she was pulled to the dance floor by her date.

"Wow, I didn't think Brenda knew who I was." Linda could feel her toes curling inside her shoes from the thrill.

"See what I mean? You would have missed that. Isn't this great? And now you're glad you came, aren't you?" Kathy smiled smugly.

"Yes, I am," Linda happily admitted, glowing from the idea of finally being accepted. She saw some admirers lingering beside the fountain, gazing into the shimmering light that played inside the gentle cascades. Her entire creation was a complete success, truly articulating the magic and ambience she had strived for. She hadn't felt that happy in a long time. A weight had been lifted. "Things are looking up," she nodded, smiling at her new friend.

"They sure are. I wonder what Mrs. Watson wants," said Kathy, looking at the art teacher who was waving at them.

Linda adjusted the uncomfortable shoe on her left foot and stepped forward. "Hello, Mrs. Watson," Linda and Kathy spoke in unison.

"Good evening, ladies. I must say, Linda, when I asked you to head-up this project, I wasn't expecting such an outstanding presentation. This is better than anything we've ever done before!" Mrs. Watson looked around the room in admiration and then took another bite of her cookie before continuing, "The yearbook photographer has been snapping up dozens of pictures."

"Really?" Linda's face lit up with another smile. "I've really enjoyed doing it and Kathy has been indispensable." Linda patted Kathy's shoulder affectionately.

"That's wonderful to hear because I'd like to ask the both of you to work up some more of your magic for prom. I realize it is privileged to the junior class, but I've already spoken to some of the girls and they definitely want you on their panel. So, what do you think?"

"We'd love to." Linda quickly shot a look toward Kathy, searching her face for approval.

"Absolutely," Kathy nodded with enthusiasm, "count me in."

Linda's attention wandered briefly as she flirted with new ideas for prom.

"I know I speak for all of us when I say that we eagerly anticipate your next achievement. I'm sure you're going to knock our socks off…again," said Mrs. Watson.

"I hope so," said Linda, "we'll get started on some ideas right away."

"Wonderful. Do try the punch, it's marvelous." The elderly woman licked her lips inquisitively, attempting to identify the curious flavor.

Linda and Kathy headed toward the refreshment table and filled two cups before taking a table near the fountain. Linda leaned back in her chair and looked around the room delighting in her colorful symphony. All the powers of a magic wand could never create the happiness Linda felt at that moment. Her artistic torch had set the room ablaze with all of the enchantment she desired and her head was so high in the clouds from the overall approval that she never noticed she wasn't invited to dance. All that mattered to Linda was that she had made a striking impression on all those present at the dance and her amazing accomplishments were being recorded in the yearbook. She had surpassed her goal.

Kathy accepted offers to dance with a few young men and she even gave her phone number to one of them, Bradley Meyers. She was a medium sized girl with blond, wavy hair that bounced upon her shoulders whenever she moved. Large blue eyes revealed her positive nature, twinkling zealously every time she spoke and her zest for life was contagious to those who interacted with her. "There's Nathan." Kathy waved them over to their table.

"Hello, ladies." Nathan stole a seat opposite Kathy, "Did Jerry make it here yet?"

"He's around here somewhere." Linda offered, taking a sip of her punch.

"Did you just get here?" asked Kathy, slightly distracted by Linda who was conducting a serious study on her punch.

"Yes, just now." Jerry cleared his throat, "We've arrived fashionably late," he mimicked in his best snob voice. "Theresa insisted," he added with a roll of his eyes. Nathan, a charismatic drama enthusiast was tall and quite handsome with dark hair. He had a magnetic personality that seemed to draw many admirers, Linda being one of them.

The dance was a success, offering many shining moments for Linda. Her table rattled with laughter every time Nathan delivered a joke and she was so caught up in the magic of the evening that she had completely forgotten about Sara Parkins.

Suddenly, the doors sprung open, nearly crashing into the walls. All eyes shifted, capturing the venomous figure inside the doorway. It was Sara Parkins giving way to a cheesy rendition of a grand entrance. The mere drama, evidently rehearsed, continued as Sara intentionally paused in the threshold, gracefully draping her lean body against the door frame to create an alluring impression while her entourage waited in the wings. Slowly, she surveyed the crowd and devoured their envious gazes. Like a rabid dog thirsting for water, Sara lapped up their pools of envy as she took Nick's arm and moved confidently into the room.

Linda's skin tingled with repulsion at the sight.

"Well, that was cheap," Kathy chuckled, looking on in ridicule. "I think I'm actually embarrassed for her."

"Me, too!" said Linda, surprised by her admission.

Kathy studied the interaction between Sara and her followers. "See? They fall all over her as if she is of some importance." Kathy shook her head, "They've all been sucked into her fantasy."

Linda nodded, further understanding Sara's inner workings. It was a defining moment. Sara was no longer the monster Linda had come to loathe and fear, but rather a hollow, desperate soul who constantly sought endorsement from other nobodies. Truly, she was a pathetic creature. "You know," Linda paused, "I really *am* starting to feel sorry for her."

"See what I mean?"

Linda leaned back in her chair, relishing the phenomenon. "It's amazing what a new perspective can do."

"It certainly is." Linda tasted her punch again before deciding it was terrible. She pushed the cup farther away on the table and spotted a beach ball bobbing around a field of students. A moment later, the ball slammed into the cups of punch on Linda's table and, like a torpedo, she shot out of her seat before the punch dripped on her mother's dress. Kathy grabbed a stack of napkins from a nearby table and began dabbing at the puddles.

"I didn't want that punch anyway," Linda joked, taking a handful of napkins from the pile.

"Yeah, it was kind of weird. I wonder if somebody spiked it," Kathy frowned with rising suspicion.

"Do you think so?" Linda sniffed the wet napkins. "Oh, he's coming back!"

"Who?" Kathy's eyes darted from the table and when she saw him, she immediately smiled.

"Would you like to dance again?" Bradley tried not to appear nervous.

Linda watched the blossoming couple on the dance floor before her attention locked onto Sara who was promenading around the room and thrusting her self-importance on all her peers, making certain that each had an opportunity to see her new twelve-hundred-dollar dress.

Rumbles of trite conversations billowed in Sara's wake as she expertly worked the room. Linda kept an eye on the ever-roaming Sara, wondering if some sort of dreadful scheme was underway. The dance was clearly a success and that would certainly drive Sara to swift action. Sara could never overlook an opportunity to spoil Linda's victory.

A continual glide brought Sara and her gang uncomfortably close, tripping Linda's alarm. Discreetly, she pushed her chair backward using Nathan as a barrier in hopes to dodge Sara's keen eye, but Nathan and Theresa jumped from their seats and shimmied to the dance floor, leaving Linda a lone spectacle at the table. Like a beacon, her vulnerability was exposed, immediately triggering Sara's radar. With her allies in tow, Sara steered her way to her prey.

Confined to her rampant thoughts and void of any escape from the pending doom that swiftly approached through Sara's noxious stride, Linda remained frozen. She felt Sara rapidly moving in on her, so she quickly tucked her head beneath the table as if to be picking up a dropped item on the floor. Maybe she didn't see me, Linda hoped quietly to herself below the table's surface. She could feel Sara's lingering presence. *I must look ridiculous!* Linda needed a dignified escape, but she couldn't think fast enough. Inside her head, squalls of jumbled words competed with wrangling emotions and then, suddenly, a rising storm of courage lifted Linda to her feet where she met Sara's icy stare that was already embedded with malice.

"Looks like a good place for you, *Lardo*. Why don't you just stay down there for a while and give our eyes a rest," Sara sneered.

A stream of chuckles followed the sharp remark while Linda's face reddened with blood-scorching retaliation and, with all her fierceness, she looked her rival squarely in the eye, "Sara, go somewhere else and frolic in the winds of your own wickedness. And take your toadies with you," she commanded in a brazen tone. Linda prepared for Sara's immediate retort, but neither fists nor words came forth. The audience eagerly listened and waited for Sara to devour her opponent with a string of outrageous insults, but Sara remained silent. Her mindless followers looked on at the developing situation, all expecting a swift exchange of verbal artillery.

Linda realized that she had the upper hand and knew that she had better act quickly before Sara reloaded. Daringly, Linda giggled, "Oh, Sara? You might want to locate a Kleenex. Soon!" Linda calmly turned away from Sara and made her way through the growing crowd of students, leaving Sara in a bewildering state of cowardice and humiliation.

Shrouded in darkness, an isolated corner provided retreat where Linda recovered from her encounter with Sara. Adrenaline raced throughout her veins charging her with intense waves of exhilaration. She was liberated, finally free from her monsters, realizing that she always had the key to break out of Sara's prison. Her mind stirred with all sorts of things that she wished she had said to Sara while given the opportunity, but, overall, she was grateful that her dignity never suffered and that she came away from the scene unscathed. Linda knew that there would, most likely, be a fine to pay for embarrassing Sara, so she kept her eyes on the crowd, ready for Sara to ambush her.

Linda's gaze lingered at the refreshment table where she watched Billy Elders, a solid member of Sara's elite, looking cautiously around the room as he finagled two shiny objects, presumably flasks, over the punch bowl. Nick Evans and Todd

Mathews, Sara's other prime associates, hovered suspiciously close to Billy to conceal their menacing operation. Disgusted with their actions, Linda sighed, realizing that she would have to be the one to alert a chaperone of their misdeed. She didn't need *informer* attached to her high school resume, so she had to be careful about her imposed mission.

A stampede of questions swelled inside Linda's head. *Was Sara so humiliated that she actually left the dance? Is she merely out smoking a cigarette?* Linda frowned, deep in thought while waiting for the endless song to end. "*Psst!* Over here," she gestured to Kathy and Bradley when the song faded.

"What happened? What are you doing over here?" Kathy asked, warily shifting her eyes.

"I'll explain," Linda donned a peculiar expression.

"Oh! I just wish I could have seen it," Kathy squealed, when Linda described the incident.

Bradley made himself comfortable on an empty chair as Linda continued her story.

"Where on earth did you come up with that phrase?" Kathy was seemingly amused.

"I have no idea," Linda replied, shaking her head. "It just flew out of my mouth. I know it sounds really corny, but Sara is too stupid to know the difference. Right?"

"I think it's perfect," Kathy giggled, "and the Kleenex reference…priceless."

"It's certainly not what I had planned in all my fantasies!" Linda cringed.

"It never is," Kathy laughed.

Bradley cast an approving nod toward Linda and a sense of validation came over her. She got so wrapped up in her story that she nearly forgot about the tainted punch. "I'll be right back," she told them after describing what she had seen.

"All right, we'll meet you at that table over there." Kathy pointed at an empty table.

Bradley pulled a chair out for Kathy to sit in and then he pulled his chair closer to hers. "I'm starving. Do you want me to get you anything?"

"No, thanks, I'm fine," she smiled.

"Well, the deed is done." Linda plopped down in a chair beside Kathy. "Any sign of Sara yet?"

Kathy shook her head, "No."

"Interesting," Linda's eyes wandered into the crowd.

"I'll be back in just a minute," Bradley stood up and headed for the food table.

Nervously, Kathy fiddled with the plastic table cloth in front of her.

"You like him, don't you?" Linda grinned.

Kathy's cheeks turned brighter, "Yes, I do. A lot."

"If you guys want to dance more, or just want to be alone, please don't let me get in the way."

"No, that's all right," Kathy leaned back in her chair, "we're going out next Saturday."

"That's terrific!" Linda's face lit up. "Where?"

"He wants to take me horseback riding at his grandfather's estate."

"I'm really happy for you and now I'm really glad we came here tonight," Linda's eyes sparkled with sincerity.

"Me, too," said Kathy, looking into the crowd. "I wonder where Sara is. Oh, I'll never forgive myself for missing the expression on her face when you told her off. Honestly, I'd give my left eyebrow to see it."

Linda laughed out loud. "You'd look pretty silly with one eyebrow."

"Yeah, but it would be worth it."

Little did they know, but Sara was in the midst of an insidious attack. She emerged from behind the water fountain with an ominous grin plastered across her smug face. Alarmed, Linda looked at Kathy, whose eyes were already fixed on Sara. Something was, indeed, amiss.

The dance had grown wild from the effects of the tainted punch. Joe Steele and his friends were sloppy drunk and falling all over their dates. "They're not even in the same clique," Linda huffed, watching Joe take a direct swig from Todd's small flask.

"Well, stupid bears no prejudice," Kathy shook her head.

Linda's eyes were on Joe. "I'm worried about him. He's getting pretty crazy over there." Her face wrinkled in concern.

"I don't know why they think they have to drink in order to have fun. They're acting like asses."

Linda agreed and then caught a glimpse of Sara taking a seat beside Joya at a nearby table. Instantly, Sara's groupies surrounded her like a football huddle.

"Sara, where have you been?" Joya demanded. "We've been looking all over for you."

"Well," she started, with eyes enameled in spite, "there has been a slight change in our plans tonight." She shot a glance toward the water fountain, "A better idea presented itself to me."

Sara could feel Linda's steady gaze upon her, shrouding her. Their eyes locked for a moment before Sara turned away.

"Tell us, what did you do?" Debbie asked excitedly.

"Not here," said Sara, with a menacing smile. "I'll tell you later."

Linda watched Sara and her twisted clan, wishing she could hear their conversation.

Bradley returned with a napkin full of cookies and sat down next to Kathy. "Who wants a cookie?" He waved the small bundle over the table.

"I do," Kathy reached out her hand.

"I figured you might," Bradley smiled and then offered the bundle to Linda.

"No, thank you." Linda smiled at him and then turned her attention back to Joe who had grown increasingly drunk. Her nerves rattled inside her skin as Joe stumbled around the fountain. He swayed back and forth in his state of drunkenness, splashing water on encouraging spectators.

"Things are really getting out of control," said Kathy, looking around for a chaperone.

"We'd better get someone over here." Linda stood up and then disappeared. A moment later, she and Mr. Updike returned in time to see Joe climbing up the fountain. "No!" she shouted. Suddenly, Joe was on the floor buried in wet debris.

Screams from the horrified crowd broke the music when all eyes caught sight of the jagged shard of glass lodged in Joe's throat. "Call *911!*" Linda yelled as Mr. Updike rushed to Joe's aid. Soggy decorations, in puddles of scented water, surrounded Joe on the cold tiles and blood-stained water pooled at Linda's knees when she knelt down beside him. Minutes passed, making her more frantic. She looked toward the doors hoping to see the paramedics, but none had arrived. A sound of desperation escaped her tense throat when she looked toward Joe and then back toward the empty doorway. Again, when she looked at the entrance her eyes grazed Sara Parkins in the crowd. Immediately, her eyes fell back on her. Something was wrong with Sara. She was trembling and her face had turned ghostly white. Linda gasped, realizing that Sara's unforgettable expression was a silent confession. *Sara rigged the fountain!* Linda glared at Sara, mouthing the words, "You did this." Her accusing eyes were condemning, reigning over Sara's entire existence. Quickly, Sara turned away to deny Linda's critical discovery.

The multitude of stunned witnesses remained motionless in eerie silence. Mr. Updike worked quickly to administer first aid as precious minutes ticked away on the clock. Helplessly, Joe looked up toward Linda as he tried to speak. Only blood gurgling from his throat could be heard. Linda prayed out loud as she remained beside Joe's quivering body.

Mr. Updike continued his attempts to save Joe while Linda held Joe's weakening hand. "You're going to be all right, Joe. Just hold on. You're going to get through this. Just relax and we'll wait for help together." She brushed the damp hair away from his eyes as she spoke tenderly to him.

Kathy and Bradley waited outside for the paramedics. Her body shivered in shock as the scene replayed in her mind. Instinctively, Bradley removed his jacket, wrapped it around her shoulders, and briskly rubbed her arms to soothe her.

"Bradley," her teeth chattered, "do you think he is going to be all right?" she dared to ask.

"I don't know." Solemnly, his eyes shifted downward, "it looked pretty bad."

The smell of Joe's blood caught in Linda's throat. Anxiously, she looked to Mr. Updike for good news, but he had done all that he could to sustain Joe. A surge of hope shot through her body as she heard the approaching sirens. "Joe, they're coming! Hold on!" She looked into his handsome face, willing him to live, when she saw life fade from his beautiful blue eyes. Mr. Updike tried immediately to resuscitate Joe. Again and again, he tried.

"Joe, don't go! Come back! Fight, Joe! Open your eyes!" Linda's mournful pleas echoed throughout the gym, but he was gone.

After a meager investigation by local police, it was determined that the fountain was simply unstable, thus leading to Joe's unfortunate demise. Although a wrench was found near the scene, it went ignored along with pertinent testimony offered by Kathy and the other volunteers describing a sturdy fountain. The police simply disregarded any claims of foul play and firmly stated that it was only a horrific accident and nothing more, but Linda knew different. Evil had played its hand that terrible night.

Joe Steele was a local icon, loved by all, and had a promising football career ahead of him. No more newspaper articles would be written describing Joe's latest achievements and the many universities who had offered him full scholarships would have to seek another football hero. The whole town was outraged over Joe's death and needed to subdue their pain with blame, albeit, misplaced blame.

Town members and the school administration refused to hear Linda's claims of sabotage involving Sara. They scorned and reprimanded her for "sinking as low as to blame an innocent person." And Mr. Parkins threatened Linda's family with a slander suit if the "unfounded allegations" continued, leaving Linda and her family forever silenced.

Initially, the Steele family considered launching a wrongful death suit against Linda's family and the school, but after speaking to their attorney, they promptly dropped their case, citing that they didn't want their son's memory eclipsed by his state of drunkenness at the time of the accident.

Beside his gravesite, she knelt down and left a single white rose on the new blanket of sod that had covered his grave four days earlier. "I'm so sorry, Joe," Linda whispered, as tears spilled onto the white petals.

Chapter Three

Due to the community's reaction over Joe's death, the school administration could not guarantee a peaceful learning environment for Linda, so they encouraged her to complete her education online or attend another school. Linda opted for home study and would receive her diploma via mail, sadly, without ceremony.

The weeks following Joe's death were dark and painful as Linda and her family tried to recover from the homecoming nightmare. Endless calls of harassment began the following morning after Joe's death, prompting Mr. Wilson to request an immediate change of phone number. Business at the bakery had slowed down considerably, but Mr. Wilson maintained confidence that things would improve after the townspeople had time to heal and allow reason to return.

One morning while getting the newspaper from the front porch, Linda was horrified to find the word, KILLER, painted across her garage. Within moments of the dreadful discovery, Mr. Wilson was on a ladder covering the malicious rendering with a fresh coat of dark green paint.

Ben Pyke, their good neighbor, walked across the street with two paintbrushes and a sobering grimace, "This town has gone crazy." Bitterly, he assessed the vandal's work.

"I don't know what to do," Mr. Wilson confided, stepping off his ladder. "I don't know how much longer this is going to continue." With downcast eyes, Mr. Wilson shook his head hopelessly and then he smiled, in spite of his internal torment. "I sure appreciate you coming over here and helping me out," his eyes watered with sentiment.

"That's what friends are for and I'm happy to help." Ben smiled and smoothed his paint-soaked brush over the cruel scribble.

Six weeks after Joe's death, Mrs. Wilson sat at her kitchen table making a list of groceries for the upcoming Thanksgiving dinner. "Linda, is there anything else you want me to add to the list?" she called out from the kitchen, hoping to lighten Linda's spirits with preparations of a holiday. Mrs. Wilson's round cheeks hinted to her Scandinavian heritage and wispy blond hair, seeded with gray strands, sprung from her bun as she spoke.

Linda surveyed the list and patted her mother's shoulder. "No, it all looks good to me," she smiled, recognizing her mother's heartfelt efforts.

Linda followed her mother into the living room where Mr. Wilson sat reading the newspaper in his favorite chair. "Can you get some more of that low-fat ice cream?" He tilted down the pages as she approached.

"You got it." Cheerfully, she leaned over to kiss her husband goodbye.

Linda had been reading her book on the sofa for nearly an hour when Mr. Wilson tumbled from his chair and crashed to the floor.

"Daddy, what's the matter?" Linda shrieked as she scrambled to her feet, throwing her book sideways.

He clenched his arm, gasping for air.

"Daddy, I'm calling for help, hold on," Linda yelled from the kitchen.

When she returned with the phone in her hand, her father was lying quietly on the floor. A mysterious calm had swept over him. He had reserved his final breath for her. "Tell Mom I love her and I love you, Linda," his strained words faded, leaving her in dead silence.

Linda stretched out over her father, rocking him in a tight embrace, "Please, Daddy, come back! Don't leave us. We love you!" she wailed.

"Linda!" The *911* correspondent shouted through the phone.

"I'm here," Linda sobbed, "tell me what to do!"

As the *911* operator instructed Linda in the proper CPR procedures, the sirens drew close, igniting hope. She jumped to her feet, swung the door open, and waved on the paramedics. "Please, hurry!" she shouted and returned to her father's side.

Urgently, a paramedic worked on her father in a desperate attempt to revive him as Linda watched intently, waiting for signs of life. Several moments passed and still there was nothing to suggest a return from death. Finally, the paramedic raised his head slowly, meeting Linda's pleading eyes and he shook his head apologetically, indicating that her father had passed.

"No, please keep trying! He's real strong. Please, do it again!" Desperately, Linda hurried over to the floor and grabbed the paddles, shoving them into the paramedic's hands.

Her haunting eyes, bathed in tears, begged him to try again and so he did. Some time had passed when he finally raised his head and uttered, "I'm so sorry."

Linda sobbed inconsolably while a police officer approached, attempting to comfort her. Immediately, she recoiled and began scolding the officer, "It's your fault! If you had done your job six weeks ago my dad wouldn't be dead." Linda jumped back and screamed hysterically. The officers tried to tame the beast, but Linda continued thrashing around the room, ranting, "My dad is dead because you didn't investigate Joe's death! Sara Parkins killed Joe and you stood idly by not doing your job and now my dad is dead because the stress killed him!" Linda fell to the floor beside her father and crouched over him as if to protect him.

The kindly paramedic, who had come to rescue Joe that fateful night, had also answered the call to Linda's house. Immediately, he recognized her. "Linda," he coaxed, "please calm down, you're going to hurt yourself. I'm so sorry about your father. We did all that could be done for him. Your dad was a good man. I knew him well. Come sit down with me on the sofa."

Linda glared at the two police officers standing opposite her beside the stone fireplace. The paramedic motioned to the officers to step outside as they were clearly adding to her distress. "Tell me how we can reach your mother?"

Still hyperventilating, Linda sat down on the sofa and tried to answer his question through her stampeding sobs. "She's at the store," she finally managed.

A hard lump settled in his throat as he reached for the phone that was beside the still figure on the floor.

Torrential grief consumed Linda, ravaging her tender soul, and born from the ashes of her father's dead body, came a ripening vengeance that promised misery and turmoil for Sara Parkins and her menacing friends.

Linda's mother sold the bakery and retired after the death of her husband because it was apparent to her that Linda needed her at home. For a very short time, she observed Linda's emotional decline and decided to have Linda hospitalized, realizing that she was riddled with grief and exhaustion.

While in the hospital, Linda learned to better conceal her feelings and confine her pending vendetta to the secure corners of her mind, far out of the reach of her mother and meddling doctors who would surely foil her plans. Surprisingly, they didn't support her plan to avenge the tragic deaths. "Linda, you need to move on with your life," they kept telling her, which irritated her further. Maybe she could resume her life after taking her revenge, she thought.

When Linda was discharged from the hospital, Mrs. Wilson strongly encouraged continuing therapy, but Linda cleverly assured her mother that she was healthy again and coping well. Meanwhile, Linda's short-lived friendship with Kathy dwindled as Linda's spirit was devoured by anguish and burdened with heavy plans of revenge. She was untouchable and impervious to any well-meaning efforts from Kathy who strived to bring her friend out of the depths of despair. Kathy was clueless to the magnitude of Linda's misery, not realizing that Linda's grim plans of revenge already owned her soul and after a few awkward visits, Kathy eventually moved on and never returned.

On a cold, rainy night, Linda sat in her father's favorite chair, pondering Sara's fate. She had been toying with the idea of murder by way of *accident. Fire? Poison? A hideous car crash?* Every idea delighted her as she fantasized about reading newspaper articles describing Sara's horrible and untimely demise. Finally, she put the ideas of a tragic death to rest because she didn't want the town taking pity on Sara nor her family. In time, a better plan would surface, she trusted, staring into the flames inside the fireplace. Somehow she would dismantle Sara's life. "Soon," Linda promised.

Lost and drowning in hatred, Linda's private obsession had become a dreadful sickness. Slowly, her existence had given way to anguish and from this cruel affliction, a new creature was born—Lola. Realizing how important it was for

29

her daughter, Mrs. Wilson found significant purpose in using her daughter's new name, recognizing Linda's need to reinvent herself.

Lola did not pursue her college dream after receiving her diploma, instead, she had answered an intriguing ad in the newspaper. If given the job, she would serve as a crewmember aboard a large yacht based out of San Diego, which carried prominent passengers worldwide. Training was included.

After two brief telephone interviews, Lola was approved as a trial crewmember. With only a short time to prepare her body for the strenuous tasks ahead of her, she immersed herself in a self-devised program to strengthen her body. Every morning before dawn, she dressed up in her jogging suit and took to the quiet streets of Miller Lake to increase her endurance. When she could run six miles with little effort, she visited the gym four times a week to concentrate on her upper body strength. On other days, Lola could be found in the town library with her nose buried in a book studying maritime navigation, weather patterns and geography. She looked forward to her new life on the seas where she could perfect her schemes against her enemies and escape the hateful climate of Miller Lake.

A new autumn brought cooler air and a bouquet of colors that meandered through the picturesque valley, but Lola could hardly appreciate nature's gifts as the anniversary of Joe's death was approaching. She was relieved to be leaving her town before the dreaded date, knowing that the local paper would post some kind of emotional tribute to him, reminding all of that tragic night.

On the evening before her flight to San Diego, Lola and her mother sat on the porch swing reminiscing older and happier times. The swing swayed back and forth with a gentle creek, lulling Lola's mind into a peaceful place where she lingered in an unwrinkled memory. She was thinking of the day when her father hung the swing for her. The cherished memory had become an enduring gift presented by him many years before her life was ravaged by Sara's evil designs.

The two silhouettes moved gently under a crescent moon when Lola looked up toward the darkened sky, "Do you remember when Daddy used to tell me that those were my stars and nobody else's?"

Mrs. Wilson nodded, sensing that Lola was still deeply troubled by the tragedies, "They're still yours, if only you'd take them."

Her mother was right, Lola knew, and she did yearn to be free of her burden, but hatred possessed her conflicted heart, steadily pumping vengeance throughout her entire being. She was trapped inside her emotions where a fierce storm was brewing and, when the time was right, she would strike and claim retribution.

"I'll miss you so much, Mom," said Lola, hugging her mother in the airport the next day. "Please don't worry. I could face the devil tomorrow and beat him at his own game."

Mrs. Wilson shook her head, attempting to erase the unsettling remark.

"Seriously, Mom, the worst has already happened."

And like a flame to oil, Lola's words ignited fear, startling Mrs. Wilson. She threw her hands up over her ears as if to negate Lola's alarming proclamation. "Don't say that! You're tempting fate!"

"I'll be fine...really. Things are going to be all right." Tenderly, she looked into her mother's eyes and grinned, "I promise I won't let anything happen to your favorite child."

Mrs. Wilson smiled, "I know," she forced herself to say, still certain that something terrible was going to happen.

Lola looked at her watch, "I had better be on my way."

Mrs. Wilson nodded and hugged her daughter goodbye. "Stay safe and enjoy this new adventure. I'm happy for you, Lola. I mean that."

"Thank you, that means a lot to me," Lola smiled and blew her mother a kiss before stepping through the metal detector, "I love you."

A tear slid down Mrs. Wilson's cheek as she stood silent for a moment watching her only child fade into the distance. "She's going to be all right," she said, believing.

After arriving in San Diego, Lola's taxi sped along the California freeways, capturing many of the city's treasures she had read about in the Miller Lake Library or had seen online. The dewy oceanic breeze caressed her skin leaving a salty

31

taste upon her lips while friendly palm trees whisked past her window. Between the many hills and buildings, Lola caught only small glimpses of the seaside and then the ocean invited her eyes to explore its majesty. "It's beautiful." The sun had already begun its glorious descent and was touching the horizon, spilling orange and white diamonds onto the shifting waters of the mighty Pacific Ocean. "What a glorious city," she said, yawning and wishing that she had slept better the night before her trip.

"Yeah, it's what keeps me here." The driver made a right turn and accelerated.

"I can see why," she said drowsily.

The city had grown dark when the driver grumbled in irritation. Quietly, he cursed the traffic, which had come to a dead-stop. "This could take a while," he sighed.

"How long, do you think?"

"From the looks of that mess, I'm thinking...*a while*." There's an accident ahead and no other routes available from this position. We'll just have to wait it out."

"All right," she said, making herself more comfortable. Heavy fatigue tempted her to close her stinging eyes. Despite her many attempts to stay awake, she faded off to sleep and dreamt while the cab slowly made its way toward her destination. Suddenly, the force of the braking taxi launched her limp body forward, hurling her to the floor. She scrambled back into her seat, hoping he hadn't noticed the mishap. Humiliated, she swiftly counted out her bills and leapt out of the vehicle when a startling image of the motel grabbed her attention. Aghast, her voice cracked, "Excuse me, sir," she said, forgetting her embarrassment.

"Yes, ma'am?" He opened the trunk to gather her baggage.

"I think we're at the wrong place."

"I assure you, this is the place you told me you wanted. See that sign over there?"

Lola turned her head, blinking a few times to focus her eyes on a sign that was planted at the edge of the rugged parking lot. Crooked lamp posts were dotted throughout the dismal terrain offering a scarce glow, but not so scarce that she couldn't read the name of her new home. The dilapidated motel, surprisingly open for business, boasted a larger WELCOME sign as if to mock her. After the driver's fare and tip were in his eager hand, he sped off leaving Lola alone in a deserted parking lot to ponder her predicament. With great hesitation, she picked up her bags from the crumbling pavement and looked around like a lost child does when seeking his mother. "What have I done?" She nearly cried, feeling foolish and scared.

Rapid footsteps approached, interrupting her anxious thoughts. "Lola? Are you Lola?"

She spun around to face the stranger. Her eyes landed on a stocky, medium-sized fellow who was swiftly coming toward her.

"Yes, I'm Lola." She stood pathetically looking at the sad ruins of what was once considered human civilization.

"Pleased to meet you!" The stranger extended his willing arm to shake her hand.

Lola dropped her bags and grasped his calloused hand firmly, remembering to give a solid handshake as first impressions can never be recreated.

"I'm Mike Hunter, the captain's first mate," he stated proudly with an engaging smile.

"Hello," she shook his hand again. "Well, you already know who I am," she chuckled nervously.

"I was afraid if I wasn't out here to meet you that you might just climb back into the taxi and head home," he laughed. "Can't say that I'd blame you."

"Yeah, about that," she cleared her throat, "am I really at the right place?" She had surrendered more of an opinion than intended. Lola half expected to see a beautiful hotel grow out of the ground at any second.

"Unfortunately, yes." His words confirmed her nightmare.

"Oh," was all she could say as she struggled to accept her fate.

"We'll be here for several weeks before we move on."

Her somber gaze surveyed the remains while she considered hasty plans of retreat.

"No worries, love," he smiled kindly at her. His tone was disarming, providing comfort she so desperately needed. "You'll love the boat. She is a beauty…just like a floating palace. You'll see. These accommodations are only temporary," he reminded her, hoping to relieve her apparent anxieties.

She was charmed by his friendly Australian accent and wondered if it was his handsome face or his peculiar pronunciation of words that put her at ease and made her want to pursue the mysterious venture. As they stood beneath the light post, she could see he had wide blue eyes with faint freckles across his nose and sun-bleached curls that bordered the inner rim of his baseball cap. It was in that moment that Lola realized only remnants of Linda remained. This new revelation promised that she could handle anything and a slagheap motel wouldn't send her running. Linda was gone, never to be revived, but Lola could handle anything.

"You'll meet Captain Andre tomorrow." He picked up her luggage and steered their direction with a jerk of his head.

"Thank you," she said, nodding at her bags.

"You're welcome."

"I'm looking forward to meeting the captain."

"You'll like him. Everyone does." Mike pushed through the motel door, "That is Pascal Maison," he said, pointing to a tall, dark-haired man across the room.

"Pleased to meet you, Lola. I trust you had a good trip?"

"Yes, it was my first time on a plane and I really liked it," she answered, trying not to be bashful.

"That's good," he nodded, looking around the room. "So, what do you think of Shangri-La so far?" he asked with an air of sarcasm.

"Well, it's definitely making an impression on me." She attempted to mimic his humor.

"Just keep in mind, this is only short-term." Pascal yawned and rolled into his bed.

"I'll just consider it one of my many adventures," she told him.

"That's the spirit," Mike smiled approvingly. "Captain Andre is really going to like you."

"I hope so." Thank God they recognize this awful place for what it is, Lola thought, feeling more relieved.

"We'll visit more in the morning," Pascal nodded politely before pulling a blanket over his shoulder.

"I look forward to it."

"That slug already sleeping is Eddie Turner," Mike explained, pointing to a large heap under a blanket.

Eddie raised his hand slightly, a mild attempt at a greeting. "Nice to meet you," he garbled in a semi conscious state, drowsily opening one eye and then pulling the blanket around his neck.

Trying not to laugh from the strangeness of it all, Lola spoke to the lump beneath the blanket, "I'm glad to meet you, too." She turned to Mike with a peculiar grin. Suddenly, a loud vibration rattled the picture against the decaying plaster on the wall beside her. She jumped from the surprise.

"That would be our beloved Sheila Collins in the shower. The pipes complain from time to time, but you'll get used to them."

"Oh, no problem." She tried to appear unruffled.

"You and Sheila will be bunking together in that big bed over there and I will be here on the floor."

"Oh, I see. Don't you sleep on a bed or at least a cot?"

"I usually use an air mattress, but I popped it this morning on my way out."

"I'm sorry," she said, seemingly concerned. "Will you be all right down there...on that floor?"

"One night on the floor won't kill me...I hope," he said playfully.

Truthfully, Mike would have enjoyed the luxurious comfort of a real mattress, but he was the youngest among the crew and he felt it was his duty to offer up the better sleeping arrangements to the others. "Well, get your duds organized and if you're hungry there's a little refrigerator in the kitchenette over there with some meat and cheese in it and maybe an apple, too."

"All right, thank you."

Mike pulled off his shirt and stripped down to his blue boxers before taking to the floor. Her eyes shot toward the ceiling, allowing him privacy and to conceal her own awkwardness over his near nakedness. She smiled to herself, remembering the part of the captain's contract where he had explained adverse and uncommon living arrangements for his

35

employees. You can't get any more unusual than this, she thought.

"G'night, Lola," Mike offered before turning to his side.

"Goodnight," she whispered, daring another glance at him. Fluttery sensations swirled inside her stomach as she pondered the friendly stranger on the floor. The subtle scent of his soap still lingered in the air, stirring her further.

In the shadows of the large, rundown room, Lola studied her new surroundings, enduring all of its *charm*, when Captain Andre's clever strategy presented itself to her. His arrangement of the most inferior accommodations, that clearly defied all civilized and, perhaps, legal practices, were to cultivate a sturdy crew. She was wise to her eccentric leader's tactics and acing his first test was not going to be a problem, she thought, grinning inside her shrewdness.

Again, the sound of the rattling pipes gripped her attention and with returning trepidation, her heart pounded rapidly because on the other side of the bathroom door was Sheila, the one person she was most nervous about meeting. Lola hoped and prayed that they would hit it off, but she still worried the woman wouldn't like her. The moment she most feared arrived with an irritating pitch as the door opened with a creak, jerking Lola from a quick prayer.

"You must be Lola," Sheila smiled warmly and reached for her hand.

"Yes, and you're Sheila," she answered, bumping up her enthusiasm. "I'm very pleased to meet you."

"You don't know how happy I am to see you." A welcoming grin lit up her face. "I've been counting the days until your arrival. In fact, I worried that you wouldn't come at all!"

"Really?" Lola was surprised. "I've been looking forward to this for so long," she revealed, allowing herself to breathe a little easier.

"These rogues are all right, but they can be a little much at times." Sheila glanced over their sleeping bodies. "It'll be nice having another woman around."

Lola felt her tension collapse inside Sheila's genuine smile.

"Being that you're still here and didn't already call for a taxi tells me plenty about you. I think you're going to do just fine." Sheila blotted her long strands of red hair with a towel.

"Thank you," Lola smiled humbly.

"You're probably wanting to get into the bathroom. Let me just get my things out of your way and it's all yours. Don't worry about the noisy pipes, you won't wake those guys. They can sleep through anything, I assure you."

"All right, thanks. I'll be out in just a minute."

After stepping inside the bathroom, Lola's eyes shifted from corner to corner, inspecting the dreary motif. Rippled tiles, hinting to the color of white, covered the walls of the tiny bathroom while a small light dangled above her head. Delicately, she hung her gray suit on the flimsy towel rack and admitted to herself that she had seriously overdressed for the occasion. The twenty-five-watt light bulb flickered overhead, threatening to leave her in utter darkness. "Don't you dare," she warned, glaring at the meager light source. She stood in her camisole, facing the mirror and was very grateful for having lost forty-five pounds before leaving Miller Lake. She hardly resembled the lonely girl from back home.

Sheila was sitting up in bed with a novel when Lola emerged from the bathroom wearing a pair of blue sweat pants and a t-shirt.

"Feel better?" Sheila looked up from her book.

"Yes, a shower is like good medicine, isn't it?"

"*Uh-hum*," Sheila agreed, closing her book. "Why don't you hit that light and we'll get caught up in the morning," she suggested, smothering a deep yawn. "Forgive me, but we've been up since three this morning."

"Oh, my! Three? I'm sure you are exhausted." Lola fluffed a lumpy pillow.

"Yes, it's been a long day."

"I couldn't sleep at all last night. I guess I was a little nervous," Lola whispered.

"You've got nothing to be nervous about. You'll see," Sheila said kindly and slid beneath the blankets before closing her eyes. "Goodnight."

"Goodnight." With a flick of the switch, darkness filled the room leaving Lola temporarily blind. She blinked several times to adjust her eyes as she felt for the edge of the bed. Carefully, she crawled under the covers so as not to disturb the stranger beside her. Quietly, she lay in bed assessing her situation and focusing on the oddity of her present circumstances. Only a few minutes had passed since their brief introductions and there she was, simply trusting that they wouldn't kill her in her sleep and use her corpse for some satanic ritual, or sell her into slavery in some foreign country that nobody has ever heard of. It had never occurred to Lola that they could be pirates or drug-runners or human traffickers! She was so desperate to leave Miller Lake that she'd never even considered investigating them!

For several moments, wild ideas invaded her peace and then those unpleasant thoughts were interrupted by more unpleasant thoughts. Tickling sensations began trailing up and down her legs. She lay still in the shadows, reminding herself that it was only her intrusive imagination disturbing her and not small bugs having their way with her limbs.

Everyone was fast asleep except for Lola. A gentle chorus of snores and blankets rustling from the sleeping strangers circulated the room while she resisted the urge to wiggle away the tickling twitches that were still bothering her.

Curiously, her eyes wandered to the floor where she could see the top of Mike's head as he slept beneath a white blanket. His silhouette was motionless. Innocent. Shafts of light from traveling cars glided slowly across the wall inside the motel room and for a long time, her eyes followed the subtle beams until she fell into a deep sleep.

Chapter Four

Captain Andre Spencer was tall and muscular with handsomely sculpted features that embellished all of the right places, Lola quickly observed, favoring his deep ocean-blue eyes that sparkled against his sea-bronzed complexion. His black shoulder-length hair battled the wind as he addressed his crew just after dawn. Lola stood on the dock gleaming in his presence. He was simply magnificent, embodying a powerful mystique that commanded her utmost respect. His sturdy hand reached out, grasping hers in a sincere handshake before he guided her up the ramp to board his yacht. She had expected to meet a grimy little man missing either an eye or a limb and, possibly, some teeth. Obviously, her idea of a sea captain had been tainted by classic novels' depictions of such and, perhaps, the shoddy motel played host to her presumption as well. She was pleasantly surprised. Relieved.

The yacht was enormous, resembling a palace just as Mike had promised. The sixty-three-foot vessel housed six bedrooms: The captain's quarters, three luxurious guest suites and two rooms for crewmembers. The salon was larger than her living room at home and the galley was most impressive, complete with all of the modern appliances. Imported fabrics, wood and marble embellished the floating masterpiece. Lola had never expected such grandeur.

As originally promised, the days were long. Every morning began with scrubbing and polishing the immaculate yacht to remove harmful elements left behind by the sun and sea. Lola didn't mind the arduous tasks as it was all a part of seafaring success and it served as a great workout program for her to keep in shape.

"When you're done there, Lola, the captain wants me to teach you how to tie knots." Mike smiled as he approached her with a bundle of rope. Unbeknownst to her, he had eagerly volunteered for the duty as it provided a valid excuse to be alone with her.

"All right," she smiled, tossing a brush into a bucket of murky water. "Perfect timing, I'm done now." She wiped her forehead with the back of her hand and bent over the bucket.

"I'll take that," Mike reached for the bucket.

"Thank you, but I had better do it myself. I don't want anyone thinking I'm pawning my chores off on you guys," she said lightheartedly.

"Understood," he smiled back, respectfully. "Meet me at the stern when you're ready.

"You got it."

Lola watched carefully as his nimble fingers expertly worked the cord, sprouting loops and rings from simple strands of rope into strong knots. He has fine-looking hands, she thought to herself as she tried to manipulate the first piece of rope he had given her. His charm was very distracting, she learned early on in the lesson. "Oh, no! What have I done?" Her smile disappeared as she held up a mass of tangled rope. "What was I working on? The bowline or the half-hitch? No, wait…it's the bowline. Right?"

Gently, he reached for the clump of rope, "Yes, we're working on the bowline." His alluring grin further jumbled her thoughts.

Why does he have to be so damn handsome?

"Learning knots takes some time," he said, still smiling.

He did it again! Don't look at his face…only look at his hands! Oh, but he does have nice hands. Don't look at his hands…don't look at his hands!

"You just have to be patient," he continued, tugging at the rope. His hand brushed against hers causing a pleasant tickle inside her stomach. "See, Lola? You've almost got it. All we have to do is just unwind this a little bit and back this end out and there you go. Let's do it again, but we're going to try something a little different this time." He stood behind her and extended his arms around her waist where she could plainly see his hands working the knots in front of her. "If I tie it this way, you'll see it as if you're tying it yourself. Personally, I think this is the easiest way to learn."

"That makes sense to me." She hid the mischievous grin that crept across her face when his arms came around her again.

Back at the motel, Lola slumped on the bed and inspected her finger tips that were worn tender from her knot training. She smiled guiltily, admitting to herself that, perhaps, she might have prolonged the session a little bit because his company was simply wonderful. Warm waves of embarrassment flooded her cheeks as she wondered if Mike was wise to her girlish antics and then it occurred to her that he might think her to be daft, instead! *What was I thinking?*

At that moment, Mike looked away from the TV and smiled at her, almost as if he had heard her thoughts. She returned a quick smile and darted her eyes toward Sheila for escape.

With a new day, came a new lesson, which was sail hoisting. Repeatedly, the sails were hurled at the captain's command until proficiency was a regular occurrence on Lola's part. She became more excited as she became more adept and productive. The entire crew worked very well together, like a finely oiled machine, just as the captain had hoped. He was pleased.

When Lola had first arrived in San Diego, Captain Andre had given her several books to read, many of which, she was already familiar with due to several visits at the Miller Lake Library. Early on, he marveled at her intelligence and thirst for more. She simply devoured his free knowledge. Her dedication and thriving interests prompted him to further tempt her nautical appetite and, oftentimes, he would create problematic scenarios involving navigation and weather, challenging her to solve them. She always did very well, which encouraged her further. On her free time, she could be found poring over sight reduction tables and charts to enhance her new-found abilities. Using a sextant along with charts and celestial fixes such as the sun, moon and planets, Lola began to fully grasp the fundamentals of maritime navigation.

Finally, the captain introduced her to the yacht's engine, his baby. Eagerly, she absorbed all he had to offer as she was determined to earn a stable position under his command. She loved her new life and hoped she would be accepted as a permanent member.

Initially, when Lola replied to Captain Andre's ad in the newspaper, she thought she would be competing with other rookies for the position, but on her first day working with the captain and crew, she realized that she was the only recruit. Intense pressure gnawed at her as she felt that all eyes were steadily fixed on her. And she was right. The entire crew genuinely liked her and all were interested in her progress.

By late November, Captain Andre had already made his decision. He was pleased with Lola and on the sly, he arranged to officially induct her as his newest member if she wanted the position. It was the anniversary of her father's death, he knew, though he kept his furtive information to himself. "Everybody, listen up," he announced, motioning all to gather around him. Shielding his eyes from the sun's glare, he stood regally on deck, donning an earnest smile. "In celebration of Lola becoming an official member, we're all going on a short trip to Catalina Island."

Everyone on board cheered and began chanting Lola's name. Her face burned from embarrassment and her knees began to quiver from all of the attention. Never before had she experienced such rapture. In her sneakers, she stood frozen, trying to decipher the captain's announcement and when she realized what he had said, she thrust her arm out to shake his hand in acceptance of the grand appointment. "I'm very honored, Captain. I accept!"

"Thank you, Lola," he nodded.

"And I won't let you and the crew or your passengers down. I promise." Little did they know, but Lola had spoken with an air of prophecy.

Captain Andre squeezed her hand, "It's been a privilege teaching you and I know I speak for all of us when I say we look forward to many journeys together." He had tender eyes, like her father's, she noticed.

Pop! Came a sound from behind Lola's left ear. Quickly, she spun around to find Sheila brandishing a new bottle of chilled champagne and a wild grin painted across her face. "We've been saving this bottle just for you. We couldn't wait for this day," Sheila blurted, letting her excitement shine.

Lola laughed, "You guys are the best. Thank you all for your patience and endless support," she emphasized, "this is the best thing that has ever happened to me—" And right in the middle of Lola's heartfelt speech, the entire crew, including Captain Andre, formed a circle around her. Her eyes shifted as she carefully studied the peculiar grins mounting on each of their faces. Suspiciously, she asked, "What's going on?"

Sheila reached up and poured cold champagne over Lola's head. The group broke out in a chorus of whistles and celebratory howls and Lola squealed in laughter as the cold bubbles washed over her head and shoulders.

"Forgive me," Sheila laughed, "but it's tradition." She placed the bottle into Lola's damp hands. "And now we all drink from this bottle until it's empty. You go first."

Lola, happy to oblige, lifted the ceremonial bottle to her lips and swallowed her first taste of champagne. She turned to pass the bottle back to Sheila when Mike cunningly intercepted the bottle. His smoldering eyes locked onto Lola's as he took the bottle from her hand and tipped it up to his mouth. Immediately, she felt herself blush and hoped the crew hadn't noticed.

When the bottle was emptied, Captain Andre placed it onto a table. "For this short venture, I will be your guest and your passenger," he raised his left brow and directed his attention toward Mike. "I will, however, supply lobster and wine for the occasion. For those of you who are interested in traditional holiday fare, talk to Sheila about a turkey, I'm sure she could remedy that situation." He winked at Sheila and then turned back to Mike. "I've appointed you Captain for the trip."

Mike puffed with pride. Becoming captain was his life-long desire. "You can count on me," his eyes twinkled as he faced the captain, accepting the offer. He enjoyed serving as first mate, but he dreamed of sailing his own vessel where he would take passengers all over the world, just as the captain had done, except Mike would someday take a wife to share in his ocean journeys, unlike the captain whose only bride was the sea.

Mike was born of the sea, a legacy spanning three generations of skilled seamen preceded him. Salt water flowed through his veins and he knew no other life, nor would he want to. Already, he had saved thousands of dollars and when the time was right, he would purchase his boat.

The captain was not an impulsive man, so his offer served as significant reward, confirming his solid confidence in Mike's proficient nautical abilities. He loved Mike like a son and relied heavily upon his infinite capabilities. He knew that one day Mike would realize his own dream and move on and when he did, the captain wouldn't stand in his way nor would he take advantage of Mike's devotion. As much as it pained the captain, it was nearly time to cut the sails loose and let Mike go.

Mike was thrilled by the implications of the captain's decision and at the same time, he recognized an opportunity to impress Lola. However, romance was a foreign phenomenon to her, leaving her oblivious to Mike's increasing affection for her. Besides that, Captain Andre's stern lecture regarding any onboard romances constantly resonated inside her head…"I don't want any of my crew distracted by emotional clutter and anyone engaging in any romantic affairs will be replaced promptly." Though Lola thought Mike to be the most handsome creature in the world, she kept the captain's words sacred and abandoned any inclination to explore the wonderful mysteries that dwelled within Mike.

Nightfall crept over the city ending an exciting day aboard the yacht. Reflecting on her new life, Lola stood inside the motel shower as warm water gently rinsed her tired, sun-colored flesh. She looked forward to the overnight journey where she would spend her first night upon the peaceful ocean waters and share a Thanksgiving dinner with her new friends, whether it was lobster or turkey, it didn't matter. She had grown fond of the crew and reveled in the fact that she finally had a place of belonging. Indeed, she was among true friends.

The morning after her initiation, Sheila and Lola rose with the sun and set out to purchase the supplies for the Thanksgiving cruise. Captain Andre, Pascal, Eddie and Mike performed their daily maintenance procedures on the boat and had plans of visiting their favorite pool hall later in the day.

At the front of the pier, Lola unfastened her seatbelt and pulled four bags of groceries from the bed of the Dodge pickup.

"I'll bring the other bags after I park the truck," said Sheila.

"All right, see you on board."

"I'll take those." Mike lifted the bags from Lola's hands as she approached the yacht.

"Thanks, I'll let you," she laughed. Her sweet smile clutched his heart.

"The captain's down in the engine room. He wants to see you and Sheila when you have a minute," Mike told her as they made their way to the galley.

"All right. I'll just put these things away while I wait for Sheila. Do you know what he wants?"

"Not sure, but he's in a good mood." Mike hoisted the bags onto the counter next to the sink.

"Good. For a minute I thought I had done something wrong." She sounded relieved.

Mike reached into a shopping bag and pulled out a bottle of wine, "You could do no wrong," he said, placing the bottle in her hand.

"Well, I'm glad to see that I have you fooled," she joked.

Gently, he cupped her shoulders and resisted the urge to kiss her. His eyes searched hers for an invitation and while they stood face to face, a thousand unspoken words were exchanged, merging their souls, but only for a second. She dove inside the refrigerator with the wine and a sack of potatoes to escape his mesmerizing charm. *Don't look at him!* The cold vapors swirled around her face, bringing her back. "Thanks for your vote of confidence," she managed, risking his glance and wondering if he, too had just experienced the same extraordinary event.

"You're welcome." He grabbed a stray apple from the bag and bit into it.

He made her nervous, yet she thrived in his company, tempting her to further explore the enigma. "Where did you say the captain was?" Casually, she wiped her hands on a towel and led Mike out of the galley when she heard Sheila approaching.

"He's down with the engine fiddling with the oil."

"Mike!" Eddie's voice blasted from behind them, "Come here, I want you to take a look at something."

"Be right there." He turned back toward Lola, "Well, duty calls." His reluctance to leave her was apparent. "Tell the captain we're ready to leave when he is."

"I will," she stated mildly, trying to deny her increasing interest in him.

"Captain?" Lola's voice called out.

"Yes, in here."

"Mike said that you wanted to speak to us?"

"Yes, we're going down to O'Doole's to shoot some pool and I thought you and Sheila would like to spend the rest of the day doing what women like to do." He stood up from his crouched position and wiped the grease from his hands.

Lola flashed a grin toward Sheila. "I know just what I want to do. Thank you, Captain. If you need nothing else, we'll be on our way."

"Nothing more today," he said, picking up his wrench.

"Sheila, you once suggested that I do something different with my hair, so I'm seizing the opportunity," Lola declared, leading Sheila back to the Dodge truck. "Besides occasional trim jobs and the *great bubblegum fiasco* in first grade, I've never cut my hair."

"Seriously?" Sheila looked closely at Lola's hair.

"Yep. So, I'm ready for something new."

"Well, it's about time," Sheila said, committed to the task.

Inside the salon, Lola and Sheila thumbed through several pages of hairstyle magazines before Lola agreed on something that Sheila insisted was perfect.

"With this style, you can keep your length, but the layers will add more fullness and frame your face better. And let's do highlights, too. All right?" Sheila pointed to a page inside the magazine.

"Whatever you say," Lola willingly conceded and followed Sheila to the desk.

Within moments of making her decision, Lola sat in the styling chair, draped and wet-headed, awaiting the stylist to begin his work. He came beside her and raised his sheers. *Swik, swik*, the swift blade of his scissors echoed inside her ears as she watched remnants of her youth tumble to the floor.

"So, you want some highlights, you say?" The charismatic stylist caressed her hair. "Well," he paused, "let's go with an ash blond color, but just a few subtle accents. I don't want to demean your genuine beauty."

Lola was surprised by the unexpected compliment. "Go ahead and do what you think. You're the expert." She repositioned herself inside the chair and shot a trusting grin.

When his work was complete, Lola eyed the mysterious stranger inside the mirror. Before leaving Miller Lake, she replaced her glasses with contact lenses and, now, with her new hairstyle and recent weight loss, she hardly recognized herself.

The stylist was thrilled with Lola's transformation, all possible by his artistic hands and expertise. He offered extra pointers on hair care and showed her examples from the book on how to fix her hair for casual and formal occasions. Touched by his personal interest and dedication, Lola tipped him with a fifty-dollar bill before leaving.

"To go along with this new hair-do, we've got to get some makeup to complete this masterpiece," Sheila suggested, stepping out onto the sidewalk in front of the salon. "And let's get you some new clothes to outline that figure you've been hiding beneath these sweat pants. These just won't do," Sheila crinkled her brows, scrutinizing Lola's comfortable apparel. "Want to go to SAKS?"

"I'd love to."

Upon her father's death, Lola received a hundred-thousand dollars from a life insurance policy that he had purchased exclusively for his only child. Until this point, she'd only used a small portion of it on her airfare to San Diego, contact lenses, a laptop computer and a very modest wardrobe. The rest of the money, she had vowed, would go toward avenging the deaths of her father and Joe.

Expertly, Sheila worked the fine store like a familiar puzzle, gathering items for Lola's new wardrobe. The fitting room was stuffed, looking more like one's closet. Lola shook her head, "I can't imagine a need for all of these things." She gazed at the colorful assortment, "But I want all of it!"

"Trust me, Lola, there's a need." Sheila tossed a shrewd smile.

"Even with what I already have? I don't want to be the *Mr. and Mrs. Howell* of the cruise."

Sheila laughed and then said, with added poise, "A lady must always be prepared."

"Can't argue with that." Lola tucked her head inside another dress and wiggled into it. "So, tell me again why we're not shopping for you."

"Like I said before, we can shop for me another time. Today we're concentrating on you." Sheila zipped up the black cocktail dress at Lola's back.

"Yeah, but it would be so much more fun if you got some new things, too," Lola tried to entice her further.

"This *is* fun," Sheila smiled back.

"You sure have a lot of self control."

Sheila snorted in amusement, "Yeah, well it came at a stiff price."

"Oh, I see." Lola didn't press the matter further, deciding to leave Sheila's personal choices alone.

"There now, I think this one is going to be my favorite." Sheila assessed the beauty standing before her.

"You've said that about all of them," Lola commented, smirking in Sheila's reflection.

"Yeah, well that's your fault. Everything looks so nice on you."

Lola smiled, fidgeting inside the dress.

"Here, turn around," Shelia commanded.

Lola twirled on her toes, "Well?"

"It's magnificent," Sheila's eyes flickered with approval.

"Good, then we'll add it to the keep pile. Now, are we done?"

"Yes, but—"

Lola interrupted with a slap to her own forehead, already interpreting Sheila's response. "Let me guess, you want me to try on just *one* more. Right?"

"Well, yes. Now that I look at you in this dress, I also want you to try on another one that has been screaming your name. I ignored it earlier because it's a bit pricey. But it's worth trying on...just for fun. So, humor me this last time and then I promise we're done."

"Are you sure?" Lola teased, looking at her watch. "I'm just kidding. Actually I'm having a lot of fun. You've managed to get me into clothes that are way beyond my norm and I like it." Lola admired the elegant details in the dress that she was still wearing. "Shopping has just never been my thing...but keep an eye on me, I could get used to this."

Sheila chuckled.

"I guess this means that you're going to retire my sweats and t-shirts?"

"Retire them? *Ha-ha-ha!* I was thinking more on the lines of a bon fire!"

"*Agh!*" Lola gasped in shock.

"I'll be right back." Sheila winked at her and slipped through the door.

Lola turned again toward the mirror. Etched inside the delicate black dress that hung just below her knees, Lola's shapely figure surfaced and she realized that she had a body worth appreciating. With an approving smile, she reached for the clasp at the back of her neck and quickly discovered that she was trapped. Several times she fiddled with the hook, but it wouldn't release. "Sheila," Lola called out softly, hoping Sheila was still nearby. "Are you out there?" With no answer, Lola peered through the door and spotted Sheila holding up a royal blue dress in front of a mirror. "Oh, that's gorgeous. Why didn't I think of this sooner?" she conspired with herself.

"It's me," Sheila returned a few minutes later with a tap on the door.

Lola opened the door and took another dress from Sheila, hardly looking at it before hanging it on a crowded hook inside the fitting room. "Hey, Sheila, would you go find some purses that will match all of these?"

"You're really getting into this, aren't you?"

Lola grinned inside her scheme.

"I'll be right back. Now, try on that dress and let me see it."

"Yes ma'am. Wait! Don't go yet. Get me out of this dress first," Lola squirmed inside the dress. "I can't seem to get this darn hook to work."

"Oh, this is a stubborn one." Sheila tried to manipulate the clasp. "There we go."

"I was scared I'd have to be buried in it."

"Lola, you're a treasure," Sheila laughed and left the tiny room.

Through the door, Lola watched Sheila disappear *en route* to the large gallery of small purses and other fine hand bags. Quickly, she slipped on the new dress that Sheila had brought to her. She would have to look at it later, she thought, as she prepared for her mission. Luckily, Sheila was on the other side of the store, so Lola made her move, bolting toward the targeted sections to gather a few items that she had seen Sheila admire earlier. And, at warp speed, she finished off her spree with the royal blue dress, three sundresses, and a few pairs of slacks with matching tops.

Using clever serpentine maneuvers, Lola made her way to the clerk's register, narrowly escaping Sheila's roaming eye. "Please, let's keep this purchase a secret from my friend over there," Lola puffed, hoisting the merchandise up onto the counter. "It's a surprise," she added, looking over her shoulder.

"Certainly," the clerk smiled back at her as she immediately began scanning the tags.

"Would you be able to deliver these things today to this address?" Lola quickly wrote down the motel's address on the back of a perfume sample card that was sitting near the cash register.

"Absolutely, that won't be a problem."

Lola studied the clerk's face as she read the address, hoping the clerk wasn't familiar with the old motel.

"What do you think of these?" Sheila entered the fitting room with eight purses dangling on her arms as if she was a store display.

"They're perfect."

Sheila held a green clutch against the dress that Lola was wearing. "It is a perfect match, just as I—Lola! Are you all right? Is it that hot in here?" she asked, noticing Lola's red face. "You look like you've been running a marathon." Instinctively, she fanned Lola with the purse.

"Yes, it is pretty warm in here," Lola straightened her grin, guarding her secret.

Sheila's eyes darted toward the black dress with subtle green accents that looked so lovely on Lola. "I do love this dress." Turn around and let me see the whole thing. I'm sorry, Lola, but you have to take this one as well. It is absolutely stunning and I would never forgive myself if I let you leave this place without it."

"Good, I like it, too." They both laughed as they surveyed the huge assortment that covered the walls. "I think I'll wear this salmon top with these jeans for the rest of the day." Lola pulled the blouse and jeans off their hangers.

"Well, I guess we've done enough damage here. It's on to the makeup counter next. Right?"

"Yeah. I've never even tried on makeup before. Well, only mascara a couple of times," Lola admitted.

Sheila turned around, arms loaded with half of Lola's new wardrobe, "Seriously?"

"*Uh-hum.*"

Half an hour later, Sheila stood beside Lola, completely overcome by Lola's beautiful emergence. "You're gorgeous!"

"Thank you." Lola suddenly felt awkward.

"Why on earth have you been hiding all of this?" Sheila asked tenderly.

"I don't know," Lola smiled humbly. Throughout her young life, she had always been convinced that she was very plain and hopeless as far as her looks were concerned.

"You're just like a beautiful butterfly who has finally decided to leave the cocoon." Sheila was thrilled to have lent a hand in Lola's incredible transformation.

"A butterfly. I like that."

Where mediocrity once banned Lola from existing among a privileged guild, she had suddenly become an elite member. Her beauty was her passport to this once forbidden territory. Contentedly, she examined the new woman inside her reflection, but subtle waves of regret began to toy with her as she wondered what her life would have been like if she had sooner made the changes regarding her appearance. Maybe she would have been spared all the cruel events throughout her life.

On her way to the parking lot, smudges of Sara Parkins' image popped in and out of Lola's head, painfully stirring her emotions. Though the anniversary of her father's death lingered, nurturing her silent suffering, Lola had successfully handled her state of melancholy, but threads of her distress were threatening to unravel. Oh, what would Sara Parkins think now? She wondered, tasting enduring bitterness from her unforgettable past. Lola's eyes grew narrow, intense with hatred for Sara as she shoved all of her new packages and bags behind the passenger seat of the truck. Her childhood was a mess with all of the wasted years fearing Sara and her idiot friends. She was lonely all through school and was treated as the class freak, all because of Sara Parkins. Lola could eventually forget all that and move on, but Sara had made a grave mistake that terrible night and for that, Sara must surely pay. Again, Lola's mind was occupied, conjuring new ideas for Sara's pending doom.

"It's kind of funny," said Sheila, fastening her seat belt.

"What's funny?" Lola asked, aiming for recovery.

"You just spent over fifteen-hundred dollars on clothes and makeup in that store and then we're going back to sleep at that place they consider fit for humans." Sheila giggled and stuffed a piece of gum into her mouth.

Lola appreciated the humor, but was still shaken by Sara's harsh invasion.

"Are you all right?" Sheila put the truck into reverse. "It's buyers' remorse isn't it?" Before Lola could answer, Sheila rambled on, "Lola, I'm so sorry. I just got so carried away in there. I encouraged you to spend more than you had expected to. Didn't I?" Sheila's forehead crinkled in shame.

"No, I had a great time today," Lola nodded. "When it comes to things of this nature, I'm definitely in need of a coach and with what the captain provides us, I've hardly spent a dime since first arriving here." She patted Sheila's shoulder and grinned, "Really, I'm just tired. But it's a good tired," she added, while her heart wrestled with the awakening beast.

From a simple thought, Lola's quiet vengeance had re-ignited with a fury, but for Sheila's sake, she coaxed herself into a better frame of mind. Lola would take her vengeance when she was ready, she decided, but until that day, she would live and live well, free from the effects of Sara's perpetual poison. Sara would remain in the tiny corners of her mind until Lola was ready to make her move. No more surprise attacks, she assured herself.

Chapter Five

"I'm starving," Sheila groaned, pushing through the motel door and heading directly toward the kitchen after a long day of shopping. She pulled out a whole chicken and took it to the sink to wash it and with a few remaining spices left on the shelf, she created a wonderful concoction filling the room with aromatic reward.

While Sheila finished dinner preparations with a green salad and rolled biscuits, Lola placed her new clothes inside plastic bins for the long ocean journey. Several times, she peered through the window awaiting the special delivery from SAKS. Finally, a small white van pulled up in front of the motel. Lola giggled as she watched the driver check the address twice before pulling the goods from his van. *I know just how you feel, mister.* Lola swung the door open, "Hello! You can just put those on the bed over there." She pointed at the bed she shared with Sheila.

"All right," the driver nodded, stealing curious glances around the room.

"Thank you very much." Lola slipped him a nice tip on his way out the door. "He probably thinks we're hookers," Lola mused as she locked the door behind him.

"Hookers? Who was that?" Sheila appeared from the kitchen with a fresh dusting of flour across her forehead.

Lola laughed again.

"What is all this?" Sheila's eyes surveyed the bags and boxes sitting on the bed. Did we forget some things at the store?" She looked utterly confused.

"No, these are just a few things that I wanted you to have." Eagerly, Lola pushed the packages forward. "Go ahead, open them."

Sheila sat down on the bed, wiping her hands on the towel tucked inside her belt loop. "Lola, what have you done?" Her eyes glistened with gratitude as she looked tenderly toward the many gifts awaiting her.

"I just picked up a few things that I thought you would like."

"A few things?" Sheila scanned the bags and boxes and shook her head in disbelief.

"I wanted to express my appreciation for everything you've done for me."

Sheila's eyes rounded in sincerity.

Lola picked up a box, "Here, this one looks interesting. Open this first." Excitedly, she hurled a box toward Sheila.

"Oh, my goodness, I loved this dress!" Sheila held the stunning blue dress against her chest. "But how did you know that?" She looked puzzled.

"I saw you admiring a few things today. And while you were on that purse caper, I snuck out of the fitting room and grabbed a few things."

Sheila thought for a moment, "That explains why you looked as if you had been running a marathon today."

Lola laughed, "I was and I didn't want you interfering with my plans."

"I'll forever cherish these things and the person who gave them to me." She wiped a wandering tear. After she opened the final package, she got up from the bed and hugged Lola tightly. "Thank you," she sniffed.

Warm, friendly feelings, like those inspired from a favorite aunt's hug penetrated Lola's heart as Sheila wrapped her arms securely around her shoulders. It had been too long since Lola felt the comfortable embrace of a loved-one. She missed her parents terribly and the grandparents who had died too soon in her young life. Lola knew then that she had another true friend, and this one, she wouldn't abandon like she had done with Kathy.

The afternoon faded into twilight as Lola and Sheila shared stories about their lives over a few beers.

"Mike told me you were married once." Lola lifted her bottle and swallowed.

"Yes, I was," Sheila situated herself in the old recliner.

"Are you comfortable talking about it?"

"Oh, sure. It's seems like a million years ago now." Sheila paused for a moment in reflection. "We'd met in college and fell in love right away. Charles was such a prince in the beginning, but it didn't last."

"What happened?"

"Our first year of marriage was great. After college he landed a great job at a pharmaceutical company and everything was going well. We even bought a house. Then one day I discovered that I was pregnant."

Immediately, Lola's thoughts wandered to the whereabouts of Sheila's child.

"I knew Charles would be thrilled, so I decided to surprise him at work. Nobody was around, including him, so I slipped into his private office where I could wait for him. I sat on his couch for several minutes, helped myself to a bowl of M&M's and then decided to hide in the closet to add to the surprise." Sheila groaned, "Well, the surprise was on me." She placed her hands over her face as if she was reliving the incident. "The anticipation was killing me and then finally his office door swung open and just as I was about to spring into action with my fantastic news, I saw his secretary following closely behind him to his desk. Instantly, I felt really stupid and it all seemed so corny. I didn't know what to do and I was completely embarrassed, so I just decided to hide inside the closet until she left. I prayed that they wouldn't catch me in there. I suddenly felt like I was a criminal or something."

"Yeah, that would be kind of awkward."

Sheila nodded. "I saw Charles unlock his desk and then he pulled out a small vial and mirror from the drawer."

"Oh, no!"

"I'd only seen that done in movies, but I quickly recognized what they were doing. I watched cocaine spill from the vial onto the mirror." Sheila's eyes softened in sadness. "I stayed still inside what had become my dungeon. I was terrified that I would sneeze or cough or something. It was hell watching them carry out their secret." She hesitated, "I know this sounds crazy, but I was jealous, too," she confessed. "My husband was breaking the law and engaging in perilous activity and I was jealous," she rolled her eyes, disgusted with herself. "But they had a secret together, though a potentially deadly secret; they shared it."

"It was intimate," Lola said perceptively.

"Yes," Sheila sighed, relieved by Lola's understanding. "Images of our time together paraded through my mind, but nothing ever suggested drug use."

"What did you do then?"

"I just waited in the closet until they left and then I went home and waited for him. I didn't know how to handle it. I was devastated by an overwhelming sense of betrayal and disappointment. I calmed myself down and made us a nice dinner with candles and everything, hoping to set a peaceful mood where I could broach the subject and discuss it with him calmly. I even stopped at a clinic on my way home and picked up some brochures on addiction and recovery."

"It sounds like you were very committed to helping him." Lola sensed a tragic ending as Sheila had never before mentioned a child.

"Yes, I was willing to do anything for him, but totally unprepared for his reaction. He immediately started screaming at me and accusing me of spying on him. I yelled back and told him that he had to stop his drug use immediately and fire that secretary right away. He exploded with a fury that I've never seen before, so I ran upstairs to our bedroom to gather some clothes because he obviously needed some time to calm down. It was terrible. We stood at the top of the stairs yelling at each other and then his anger suddenly turned so violent. He really scared me, so I ran to my car and he chased me into the garage. I threw the car into reverse and he yanked me out of the seat and in the struggle I landed under the car."

"Oh, no!"

"I never even had the chance to tell him about the baby until the doctor informed me later that I had lost it."

Lola's shoulders sunk as she searched her heart for consoling words.

"I didn't give him a second chance," Sheila said stiffly.

Lola blinked several times to evaporate the tears before they filled her eyes. Silence hung over them for a moment before she spoke. "Losing a baby has got to be the most horrible thing in the world on top of a husband's betrayal."

Sheila nodded quietly.

"What happened to Charles?" Lola attempted to override the rampant emotions triggered by Sheila's devastating story.

"He tried for months to make it up to me, but nobody could fix that. He eventually quit calling."

Lola reached for a tissue, wishing she could say something profound at that moment.

"A few weeks later, I left the hospital and cleaned out our savings account. I sold our good stuff to our neighbors and worked a few odd jobs here and there and that's when I met Captain Andre," Sheila smiled and shifted her words to a cheerful tone.

"How did you meet the captain?"

"I was waiting tables at a seafood restaurant when I first came to San Diego. I had served him and his crew several times and listened in on their conversations because they were always so interesting." Sheila flashed a guilty grin. "It sounded like fun and one day I got up the nerve and asked the captain if he needed extra help. And there ya go, I've been with him for six years now and I'm very happy." She nodded contentedly.

Lola smiled, inspired by Sheila's solid recovery and will to persevere. She tossed her empty bottle into the trashcan beside the bed and leaned back against the headboard.

Sheila reached into the ice chest and pulled out two more bottles. "Last two. Want one?"

"Why not?" Lola attempted to stifle an untimely belch.

"How old are you again?"

"Nineteen."

"You seem so much older."

"I hear that a lot," Lola smiled, "I'm an old soul."

Sheila agreed. "Well, don't tell your mother I let you have a beer. Our secret, all right? This is just a special and rare occasion," Sheila emphasized with a stern nod.

Lola grinned, "All right."

"Speaking of secrets, do you want to know a big secret?"

"I love secrets. I've got a few of my own that I'll let loose on you some day." Lola folded her hands across her belly, eager to hear Sheila's secret.

"This motel isn't really where we live when we're not at sea. Captain Andre just rents this place when he's training new crewmembers."

"Finally! Everyone keeps telling me that this place is only temporary, but nobody has been willing to divulge anything else regarding a permanent situation...despite all of my attempts to elicit such information from you guys," Lola smirked.

"Sorry about that," Sheila smiled sheepishly. "Orders, you know."

"I understand," Lola said forgivingly.

"Just so you know, I have felt guilty for not telling you anything, but now I believe it's time you know. You've certainly earned it."

"True," Lola agreed.

"Anyway, when we're training a new member, we stay here at this *lovely abode*. It's the captain's way of testing the crew, you know, to see how we all handle less than desirable situations together."

"I figured that out my first night here." Smugly, Lola took another swig of her beer. "I knew there had to be some kind of strategy behind it. Well, I hoped there was, at least," she giggled.

"Yes. Captain Andre is just putting you through rigorous training and he's testing your motives."

"Testing my motives?"

"Yeah, but I'll get to that in a minute."

"Has anyone ever failed this…training?" Lola interrupted and rearranged a pillow behind her.

"Sure, there's been a few. Some don't even stay their first night here. They see this dump and run as fast as they can from this place." Both Sheila and Lola erupted in laughter.

"Too bad for them. Who am I replacing?"

"Morgan. He was a nice fellow, kind of quiet, but he had to leave suddenly because his father became ill and his mother needed him at home to help run the family company, or something like that. We haven't heard from him since he left," she said, dismissing him with a shrug of her shoulders.

"So, I take it he won't be returning?"

"Don't think so, but you needn't worry about that at all," Sheila assured with a firm nod. "The captain is keeping you for as long as you will stay. You've already proven to be a better worker than Morgan ever was."

"Really?"

"Absolutely."

Lola was relieved to hear that.

"Captain owns a huge house here in San Diego. Not far from here."

"He does?"

"Lola, it's huge," Sheila demonstrated enormity with her hands as beer sloshed from her bottle.

Many times, since arriving in San Diego, Lola had tried to imagine the captain in his own home, but the concept of huge never entered her mind. She envisioned him in a seaside bungalow or something similar.

"He comes from a lot of money. But his love isn't for money, it's the sea."

Lola sat quiet for a moment, wondering which of her many questions she should ask next while Sheila was still in the mood to share. "Does he have family nearby?"

"His parents are deceased, but he has a brother who lives in Europe somewhere. They call each other from time to time, but I've never met him. The captain considers us more of his family and has opened his homes to all of us."

"What do you mean?" Lola dared to envision civilized accommodations awaiting her.

"When we're not on the boat, we all live at one of his estates. That is, if we want to," Sheila added. "Renting a place of our own just isn't economically sensible because we're always traveling for extended periods of time all over the world. So, that's why the captain shares his homes with us."

"That's very generous of him. But doesn't he grow tired from having his crew on the boat *and* in his homes all of the time?"

Sheila chuckled, "His houses are so big that when you need your own space, it's not a problem. I can spend days there and never bump into anyone else. His house here has a staff of seven, five patios, eleven bedrooms, tennis courts, riding stables, two pools and—"

"Two pools?" Lola interrupted.

"Yes, and you get your own bathroom," she was delighted to say.

"My own bathroom?" Lola's eyes fogged over.

Sheila giggled, "I figured you've suffered plenty and it's time I acquaint you with some of the permanent plans."

Lola smiled, "I would have stayed, regardless, but it's just nice to know there is something beyond this." She looked around the room.

"I remember my time in training. I was just so desperate to escape my old, dreary life that I was willing to do anything."

"I know exactly what you mean." Lola was thinking of her past.

"His home in New Zealand is astounding. You are in for a grand adventure." Sheila pulled her hair into a rubber band and leaned back into the chair.

"I can't wait to hit the open waters," Lola groaned, longing for the day they sailed into the feral blue seas.

"I do love staying in his homes, but one day I hope to have a home of my own," Sheila smiled dreamily.

"It won't be long before you have a family and home of your own," Lola said, believing.

"I want to have a house full of kids, but I had better hurry and get on with it as I'm already thirty-four." Sheila's smile crinkled, "But, first, I need a husband."

They both giggled.

"I've got someone in mind," Sheila revealed with a gleam in her eye.

"Do I know him?" Lola raised a brow, already certain it was Eddie.

"I can't say anymore as I don't want to jinx it." Sheila smiled impishly.

"I understand...I guess."

"I know that sounds stupid, but I'm cursed with a ridiculous superstitious nature." Sheila waved her hands as if to rid herself of the condition. "Anyway, the reason the captain didn't want you knowing about our regular living arrangements is because he first tests his recruits by their willingness to see a bad situation through and how well they operate under harsh conditions. Through all that, he believes he gains a better understanding of their true character. If potential members knew that they would have a pretty lavish lifestyle while traveling the world with him, then they'd be here for all the wrong reasons. The captain seeks out people who have a genuine desire to enrich themselves without great emphasis on material reward."

"He is very clever." Lola thought for a moment, "I can laugh now, but when I first saw this motel, I quickly developed some pretty scary ideas about this whole situation and I seriously questioned my future with this enterprise. I imagined the boat being in terrible disrepair with leaking ports, missing parts, rust, mold...you name it. I was truly expecting the worst. And if you only knew how I pictured the captain before meeting him," Lola interrupted herself with a burst of laughter. "Needless to say, I was quite relieved to see the *Clarisse* in all her splendor...*and* the captain," she admitted with a telling grin.

"Yeah, he's certainly not hard on the eyes." Sheila placed her bottle down on the television, smiling. "You must have been terrified when you first arrived here."

"That would be an understatement."

"The captain's tactics are a bit eccentric, but the results are worthy."

Lola nodded, understanding the depth of opportunity the captain had laid out for her.

"This has been an amazing adventure for me," Sheila took another drink. "I didn't think I could stand slinging plates of crab to hungry mobs of finicky people much longer. After Charles, I never pursued my teaching career. I don't know why. But I'm thoroughly happy now," Sheila's eyes brightened as she spoke. "I love this crew and preparing fancy meals for our passengers. They are so caught up in the adventure that anything I make pleases them. Heck, I could serve them tuna casserole and they'd think it was ambrosia."

"That's because you're a marvelous chef."

"Well, thank you. I once considered going to culinary school, but I love my life the way it is right now."

Lola nodded, "It is a good life," and together they laughed, toasting each other with a steep raise of their bottles.

"My favorite passengers are Bill and Nora Wells." Sheila repositioned herself in the recliner. "Every year, usually during the first week of December, we take them to New Zealand. In fact, they are going to be your first passengers."

"Lola was happy to hear that her first passengers were well-liked.

61

"The Wells are old friends of the captain's." Sheila paused briefly, "they were to be his parents-in-law."

"Really?" Lola was always very curious about the captain's personal life and this new information increased her interest.

"Sadly, the captain and his fiancée, Clarisse, never had a chance to make it down the aisle."

"What happened?" Lola sat upright from her reclined position.

"Clarisse died suddenly from a heart condition one month before their wedding. Nobody knew that she was ill until she collapsed in the bridal boutique."

"Oh, that's terrible!"

"Yeah, it was," Sheila nodded. "She was exquisite inside and out. Do you want to see a picture of her?" Before Lola could answer, Sheila had jumped from her chair and pulled a small photo book from her purse.

In her hands, Lola held a small vestige that offered a precious glimpse into Captain Andre's life. Her eyes were fixed on the haunting photo that revealed a part of his story. Suddenly, she felt as though she were trespassing.

"That picture was taken when we were in Hawaii, just a couple of months before she died."

Lola's shoulders wilted with that reality. "So, that's how he came to name his boat."

"Yes, he bought it a year after we buried her."

Again, Lola looked at the photo to better acquaint herself with the wonderful person who had loved her captain so much. Her long black hair poured over his shoulder as she leaned lovingly against him in the shot. "They look very happy here," she said, embracing the picture with her eyes and wrestling the lump that was developing in her throat from hearing another heart-wrenching story.

"They were good to each other."

Tears threatened as Lola's heart grew heavier with the realization of the captain's great loss. "That's so sad and yet he remains so kind." She swallowed hard hoping to relax the stubborn lump that seemed to have swelled to the size of a walnut. When that didn't work, she swilled some more beer and cleared her throat. "So, tell me more about Mr. and Mrs.

Wells," she suggested, seeking a happy diversion.

The conversation rolled on as the aroma from the searing chicken taunted Lola's appetite, forcing her to swipe the last two cookies from the cupboard and tossing one to Sheila.

"I'm just as excited for your first journey as I was for myself." Sheila's smiling eyes followed Lola back to her bed. "I can't wait for it to begin for you."

Lola sighed and closed her eyes, imagining.

"Don't tell anyone that I've told you all this. I've just rambled on and on," she scolded herself. "Whatever you do, don't tell me any of the secrets that you may have pent up inside you. I can't be trusted."

Lola laughed, "I'll remember that," she feigned caution with a stern brow. "Seriously though, I appreciate your confidence."

"You earned it," she nodded. "Did you know that you are the third recruit I've helped train since I started working with the captain."

"I am?"

"*Uh-hum*." Sheila took another drink of beer. "And hopefully the last?" Her inquiry came with an encouraging smile.

"I assure you, I have no plans on going anywhere. I'm very happy here."

"I'm glad to hear that. Did you know that the captain hires a private investigator to perform extensive background checks on all of his potential crewmembers?"

"No, I didn't," Lola answered, slightly startled.

"At first, I thought that was a little creepy, but then I realized how important it was. I mean, you don't want to be out in the middle of the ocean stuck on a boat with a dangerous maniac."

"Yes, that's true." Instantly, Lola's mind conjured images of Captain Andre reading newspaper articles that were heavily laced with bias regarding Joe's death. And more unsettling to her was his knowledge of her brief stint in the psych ward at the hospital. Lola bit her lip and squirmed at the alarming revelation. "He knows everything," she mumbled and wondered why he still chose her.

"What did you say?" Sheila asked, getting up from the chair. "You look washed out, kid, are you feeling all right?"

"Oh, I'm fine, just hungry. When is that chicken going to be done?" Lola hoped to shake the uncomfortable feelings brought on by the captain's complete knowledge of her past.

"Well, it's done now, I was just holding off a bit while waiting for the guys to return, but we can go ahead and eat now if you'd like."

"No, I'm fine. Really," Lola insisted.

The sound of jiggling keys turned their attention toward the door. "They're back," Sheila announced, dutifully heading toward the kitchen while Lola made her way to the bathroom.

Pascal pushed through the door and behind him came a clattering Mike and Eddie with a bag of ice and a case of beer.

"Tell me again, who's the best pool shooter among us?" Pascal teased, as he paraded around the room wielding three, twenties.

"Oh, great one," Mike bowed at Pascal's feet, "you are."

"And don't you forget it," Pascal joked, folding his twenties neatly and tucking them inside of his wallet.

"It was only luck," Eddie stated with a firm pat to Pascal's shoulder.

"Yeah, just wait. I'll show you up again." Pascal's mild retort came with wave of his wallet, reminding all in the room of his winnings.

"Anyone hungry?" Sheila placed the biscuits into the oven.

"Smells good. What are we having?" Mike sniffed the air and headed directly toward the small oven to take a peek. "Oh, Sheila, you know how to put me in a good mood." Mike rubbed his hands vigorously together. "We thought we'd start our holiday a little early with a bit of the amber fluid." He passed bottles to Eddie and Sheila.

"How long till dinner?" Eddie reached for his small notebook next to the television.

"In just a few minutes," Sheila replied.

"All right, thanks." Eddie took his beer to the old recliner chair that no longer reclined and flipped on the television to catch up on the daily stock report. Immediately, he began writing figures on the small pages inside the book, mumbling quietly to himself.

While Eddie carried out his daily ritual, Lola joined the others at the table. Mike tried not to stare, but he was taken in by her beauty. For a moment, he floundered in a stupor, trying to maintain his cool demeanor. He sat down beside her and took a swig of his beer and hoped to appear casual in front of the others.

He was so near Lola that she could feel his body heat mingling with her own. She wondered what it would feel like to touch him. Perhaps an accidental brush against his arm would satisfy her curiosity, she thought. Her idea was so clever that she dared herself to act on it and just as she was about to, she lost her nerve and pretended to be adjusting her sandal instead. Thoughts of what she almost did made her laugh, leaving an idiot grin planted on her face.

"What's going on with you, Lola?" Mike asked, clearly amused.

"I don't know," she laughed even harder.

Mike's peculiar expression queried the others at the table.

"*Uhh*," was all Sheila could muster for the moment as she was quickly calculating the number of beers she had given Lola.

"I think it's the beer. It must be going straight to my head," Lola confessed, still grinning fiendishly.

"Oh, I see you're drinking beer these days, are ya?" Mike tried not to let his eyes linger.

"No...I mean yes! Actually, I was just conducting a bit of research today," she grinned.

"Oh, is *that* what we're calling it?" Mike chuckled.

"*Uh-huh*," Lola giggled again and looked to Sheila for an explanation as to her odd behavior.

Sheila burst out laughing and looked away from the table while she tried to compose herself.

"You ladies sure have the giggles tonight." Pascal noted the small amount of beer remaining in Lola's bottle. "Sheila, how much beer?" He shifted his eyes toward Lola.

"I've only had two...I think. Right, Sheila?" Suddenly, Lola wasn't so sure.

Again, Sheila was at a loss, "*Uh*, I think so."

"Well, in that case, you better have another," Mike twisted off a bottle cap. "For the cause," he added, clanking his bottle to Lola's while stealing a long look at her.

"Cheers!"

"You look really nice tonight, Lola," he dared to say in front of everyone. "I mean, not that you don't ever look nice, but tonight especially, you...I mean—"

Lola smiled and jumped in to rescue Mike from himself. "Thank you. I got a makeover today."

"I think she looks wonderful, too." Sheila stroked Lola's hair.

"Yes, the new hairdo and stuff are nice," Pascal tossed in with a nod.

"We got the works done." Lola's brilliant smile lit up the room.

Saying nothing, Mike's expression indicated that he approved.

"Sheila was my personal consultant." Lola looked at the flour on Sheila's face that she meant to tend to earlier. "Let me just take care of that right now." Lola leaned over the table with a dish towel and blotted the flour on Sheila's face.

"Biscuit flour?" Sheila asked, hardly troubled.

"*Uh-huh*," Lola smiled sweetly.

Throughout the meal, Mike was drawn to Lola and he could no longer hide it as he had done for the past several weeks. Several times, she could feel his warm gaze upon her, inviting her to look at him and when their eyes met briefly, each quickly turned away as if to deny the attraction.

Lola had never summoned that kind of attention from anyone before and she was becoming increasingly self-conscious. Every word she spoke sounded stupid to her ears and she was certain that her laugh equaled the annoying pitch of a hyena. Butterflies tickled inside her stomach causing an alternating imbalance of discomfort and euphoria, but after another beer, mysteriously, her anxieties began to lighten.

When the meal was over, Sheila reached across the table and started collecting dishes, but Lola intervened. "Sheila, tonight the kitchen is my domain."

"No, we always do it together. I can't let you do that."

"Sheila," Lola continued, but was interrupted by a hiccup, "just relax and enjoy yourself for a change," she schemed, aware that Eddie was preparing for his evening walk and without dishes to stop her, Sheila could join him.

"I'll help," Mike offered, leaping from his rickety chair.

"There...see? I have help. No excuses now." Lola grabbed a fresh beer and handed it to Sheila, "Give this to Eddie," she said shrewdly.

"Yes, ma'am." Sheila dashed out the door.

Over a sink of dishes, Mike and Lola found their ground. They laughed through a menagerie of jokes and humorous tales illustrating their youth. He was intelligent and funny and strong and capable, all of the things she needed. She desperately wanted him, yet he had no idea how she felt. Briefly, she allowed her mind to conjure a future with him, but her fantasies quickly faded as unwelcome thoughts crept inside her head. The captain's firm lecture regarding the perils of onboard romance returned with a stiff warning and then, on top of that, she started to question Mike's flirtatious behavior. Was it merely his nature or perhaps the influence of beer? Was she simply misinterpreting him? Her intrusive questions could have spoiled her fun, but she surrendered to the effects of the bubbly spirits and allowed them to overrule her nagging reservations. "Tonight, we live!" she laughed, popping a cap off of another beer.

"Take it easy there, love," Mike took her bottle and put it on the table.

"And no more worries!" she went on, wagging her finger. "And to heck with rules!" *Hiccup.*

Chapter Six

Morning came like a club to the head when Lola first opened her eyes. A mysterious malady had arrived sometime in the middle of the night, consuming her. Motionless, she remained in bed afraid to move so much as an eyelash. The epicenter of this new affliction was situated inside her throbbing head, leaving her weak and wilted. She wished she could sleep the day away and escape her self-induced trauma, but dawn had arrived and enlisted her. Gently, she sat up and dangled her legs over the edge of the mattress while waves of nausea rose up to greet her. Curiously, the lamps inside the motel room had taken on an unfriendly demeanor, she thought, squinting past them on shaky legs.

"Tell me, Lola, how is your research coming along?" Mike grinned cunningly, observing her condition.

Slowly, she turned to face him, "*Hmm,*" she moaned softly, forcing a smile that ricocheted inside her skull, "I've come to an important conclusion."

"And what is that?" he asked, somewhat amused.

"Drinking beer is really stupid."

He shook his head and laughed before casting a summoning grin toward Pascal. "Are you thinking what I am, mate?"

"Lola, we've got just the remedy for that," Pascal chimed in from across the room, darting toward the small kitchen with his coffee cup sloshing all the way.

"Hold on a minute, Lola, we'll have you fixed up in no time." Eagerly, Mike joined Pascal in the rescue operation where he pulled out a jug of orange juice and several other items from the refrigerator.

Lola returned to the foot of her bed to observe the swift and calculated maneuvers occurring inside the kitchen. She marveled at their synchronization.

"It's almost done, Lola," Mike projected in a loud whisper.

Pascal cracked an egg against the glass.

"*Eww!* Was that an egg? Is that safe?" Lola asked when the raw egg plopped into the murky potion.

"Of course it's safe," Pascal snorted, giving it a good stir. "And it will grow hair on your chest, too."

"What?" her frail voice sounded in alarm.

"That's what my dad used to tell me." Pascal admired his concoction before handing it to Mike.

"I assure you, Lola, it won't grow hair on your chest," Mike kindly intervened, "but it *will* make you feel better." He came toward her and placed the strange brew in her hand. "It's a very special tonic we invented. Or rather, improved," he corrected. "It's an old recipe from Pascal's pap, but we made it better."

Pascal nodded in pride.

"You can trust us," Mike urged, as he watched Lola carefully examine the questionable ingredients inside the glass.

Trustingly, she looked at her eager attendants and dismissed further discretion. "Here we go," her voice quivered. She squeezed her eyes closed and swallowed. "*Agh! That's terrible!*" A colorful medley of incoherent words filled the room, surprising Mike and Pascal.

"It may be nasty, but it works," Mike rested his hand on her shoulder to comfort her.

"You've got to finish it all though," Pascal advised caringly.

"Are you kidding?" Lola studied the elixir once more, deliberating behind a twisted scowl.

"Just drink it up real fast and get it over with," Mike coaxed.

She took in a deep breath and then swilled the rest of the cure-all in three gulps. Another round of gags led to a rushing stream of tears that drizzled down her cheeks. "*Yuck!*" she wailed, immediately wiping her tongue with the sleeve of her sweatshirt.

"Now, just drink this and the remedy is set." Mike handed her a fresh bottle of water.

"Gladly," she gurgled, grabbing the bottle.

"Oh, no! They didn't!" Sheila gasped, as she came out of the bathroom with a towel wrapped around her head.

"Oh, no, what?" Lola's eyes bulged.

"Believe me, honey, it's better if you don't know." Sheila quickly shot a penetrating look toward Mike and Pascal, scolding them with her sharp green eyes. She tried to stay mad, but she quickly felt herself yielding to the humor of it all.

"Was it safe?" The victim dared to ask as she peered inside the tainted glass.

"I guess it's safe, but a simple ADVIL and a glass of juice would have cured you just the same." Sheila struggled not to laugh.

Lola looked accusingly at the two culprits standing beside her.

"True, but this works a whole lot faster," Mike defended.

"Lola, sweetie," Sheila was still trying to hold back, "you've got to watch out for these two." She started to giggle, but quickly recovered. "Next time you get into trouble, come to me first," she managed.

"Trust me, I will," said Lola, glaring at the perpetrators.

Within the hour, Mike expertly guided the magnificent vessel out into the open waters toward Catalina Island. With the exception of waking up to her first and last hangover, it was Thanksgiving morning and a beautiful morning at that, Lola thought with promise, taking a deep cleansing breath as she watched the harbor fade slowly into the distance. She turned and caught another glimpse of Mike, her new captain, standing at the controls doing what he did best. He looked so handsome, she could almost forgive him, she thought, forcing her eyes away before he caught her staring at him again. She wandered to the galley and poured herself a cup of coffee and refilled Sheila's mug while she was at it. "So, how can I help?"

"Thanks, but I've got this covered," Sheila smiled, dropping a freshly peeled potato into an oven dish. "You can read your book, fish, relax...do anything you would like to do today."

In other words, get out of your kitchen, right?" Lola laughed.

"Exactly," Sheila ground more pepper over the potatoes.

"Well, holler if you need me." Lola flashed a wild grin as she stole a raw potato from the dish. She strolled through the salon and picked up her book when she heard Mike and the others shouting. She hurried to the deck to see what was causing the commotion.

"Lola, look!" Mike was pointing vigorously at something in the ocean. "It's a blue whale!"

Lola ran to the bow and stared intently where Mike was pointing. "Please come back," she whispered, hoping to coax the docile beast back to the surface. Her eyes were fixed on the sea and then the water broke, allowing her a brief introduction. "There it is!" she yelled, hardly able to control her excitement. "It's magnificent! And so huge!" Her eager eyes scanned the waters, waiting for another glimpse of the enormous creature.

"I'd say it was eighty to ninety feet!" Eddie shouted, hoping for an *encore*.

"At least," Pascal interjected, preparing his camera.

Just in time, Sheila joined the spectators on deck to catch the final appearance of the mighty whale before it disappeared.

Lola turned to Pascal, "Did you get it?"

"I sure did." He looked into his camera and shared his catch.

When the evening sun touched the horizon, Sheila lovingly set an elegant table in the dining room. Heaping bowls of broccoli, green salad, roasted potatoes, fruit kabobs and wheat rolls surrounded a large tray of fresh lobsters upon the table. "Dinner is ready," she called out for her guests as she lit the candles.

"Place cards? Fancy," Lola commented, circling the festive table with her eyes. "Move over, Martha," she added.

"I thought it would be fun," Sheila smiled, admiring her efforts.

Lola took her place beside Mike, concealing her excitement to be close to him.

"You really outdid yourself, Sheila." Eddie looked over the table.

"Well, I just wanted Lola to know that we *can* be civilized." Sheila placed a bottle of wine onto the table. "Well, some of us at least," she sighed and frowned at Pascal who was stabbing at the bowl of potatoes with his own fork.

Lola giggled, "May I ask the blessing?"

"Oh, sorry," Pascal mumbled, looking slightly embarrassed as he quickly returned his fork to his plate.

After the meal, everyone gathered in the salon for a game of poker while Lola settled into a nearby chair preparing to read a novel.

"Are you sure you don't want to play, Lola?" Sheila asked again.

"Yes, I'm sure. I really don't know how to play, but I promise that I'll give you the opportunity to teach me soon," she assured, peeking over her book.

"No time like the present, I always say," Mike declared, clearing a space for her at the table.

A chorus of pleas broke out, encouraging Lola to join them.

"*Hmm*, fresh blood," Pascal sneered playfully, rubbing his hands together.

Captain Andre was amused by Pascal's *naïveté*. Lola was very sharp and the captain knew that she would stand up very well to the seasoned poker players at his table, including himself.

"All right, if you are all sure you don't mind taking time to teach me, I'll try." She placed her book on the chair. "But I warn you, I've never played cards before, so I may be a hindrance to your game."

"Here, Lola, come sit by me," Mike insisted, tapping the chair to his right.

"*Hmpf*, I'm not so sure I should trust you."

Everyone at the table laughed.

"You can trust me," Mike smiled innocently and picked up the cards. "All right, since I'm the best player here, I'll explain the game to her."

"Perhaps the cards will tell another story," Eddie teased.

"Care to wager on the side?" Mike suggested with a stiff grin.

"I wouldn't want to take advantage," Eddie returned with a smirk.

The captain shook his head, "Just deal the cards."

Mike shuffled the cards and dealt each player their first hand. "Lola, we're going to start with regular five-card draw. Everyone, this time around isn't for money, we're going to walk Lola through all the different kinds of hands and let her have a go at it before we drop down any chips."

Mike leaned in closer to Lola to look at her cards. Her breath became shallow at his closeness. He was intoxicating, leaving it nearly impossible to concentrate on the rules. She felt her face grow warm as her complexion burned red. Was it obvious to the captain or the others? She worried in silence. Her mind was whirling with straights and trips and royal something-or-others when she finally realized that she had to get a firm handle on her emotions. *Ignore him!*

After several rounds, Lola picked up the game quite well, in spite of his distracting charm. At the end of the evening, Mike had been confirmed the winner.

"Told ya I was the best," Mike boasted, collecting the final pot.

"Yes, I know," Lola acknowledged, "I guess I'll have to practice that bluffing thing you do."

"Who me? Bluff?" Mike smiled devilishly as he gathered the cards.

"Pascal," Eddie called out, "wake up, dude."

Pascal didn't budge.

"He's going to regret sleeping in that chair like that," Eddie shook his head and stepped away from the table.

A strange expression mounted on Mike's face as he stood hovering over Pascal's flaccid body. "Should I just nudge him, or go for the more subtle approach and tickle him? Oh, this is too tempting." He deliberated his next move and then looked to Lola to summon her input.

"Don't look at me," she laughed.

"Pascal knows he shouldn't leave himself wide open like this. He hates to be tickled, but as I see it, it's an invitation." Mike then uncurled his fingers, flexed them expertly and reached for Pascal's vulnerable ribs.

"I wouldn't do that if I were you," Pascal warned, opening his eyes.

"*Agh!*" Mike jumped back, "I thought you were sleeping, mate!"

"No, merely inspecting the inside of my eyelids," he groaned, as he stood up, rubbing his overstuffed belly.

Lola laughed at Mike playfulness.

"Sheila, that was a wonderful feast. Thank you," said the captain as he and Pascal headed toward their rooms.

"Yes, thank you, Sheila," Pascal moaned, pointing at his swollen stomach.

Sheila giggled, "You're welcome and goodnight."

Mike's fun-loving nature lured Lola into another fantasy.

"What are you looking at?" Mike asked, capturing Lola's gaze.

"Oh, nothing. Just making an observation."

"Well, I hope that's a good thing."

"You needn't worry," she smiled.

Mike's smoldering eyes landed on Lola, melting her.

"Sheila, I'll help you clean up," Lola offered, hoping to seek diversion from Mike's luscious glances, but her voice went unheard as Sheila and Eddie were already heavy in discussion debating politics and the fate of the country. Each was passionate about their beliefs and each tried desperately to convert the other. With arms full of dishes, Eddie and Sheila's conversation carried them away into the galley, leaving Mike and Lola alone.

"I guess they have it covered," Mike shrugged his shoulders.

"I think so," she smiled, zipping up her jacket. "Care to join me on deck?"

"Yes, I'll be out in a minute."

The raven sky, dotted with countless diamonds surrounded Lola, sweeping her up into its brilliance. She wrapped a blanket around her shoulders and waited for him.

"Here," Mike returned with a cup of coffee.

"Thank you." She took the warm cup from his hand and tried to think of something interesting to say. The words frayed inside her head from the awkwardness of being alone with him in such a romantic setting.

"Those two are an interesting pair, aren't they?" Mike commented, flipping a chair around to face Lola.

"Yes, they are." She was relieved that he had launched the conversation.

"So, do you think Eddie and Sheila would make a good couple?" He took a sip of his coffee.

"I think they're perfect for each other." Lola was thrilled to answer that question, but was surprised by his asking.

Mike nodded and said nothing.

"I know that Sheila's interested." Lola waited, hoping Mike would fill her in on Eddie's position.

"Well, they're certainly feisty enough to handle each other," he joked.

Lola agreed and didn't beat around the bush, "So, is Eddie interested?"

"Eddie's pretty reserved about his personal affairs."

Lola dismissed the vagueness of his answer. "I think it would be wonderful if they were a couple." She straightened the blanket across her legs. "Of course, the captain wouldn't approve," she said in a cautious tone. Suddenly, she remembered her escapades from the night before, where she deliberately sent Sheila off to be alone with Eddie. A rush of guilt swept over her as she realized that she had blatantly disregarded the captain's rules by playing matchmaker.

"Oh, don't worry about the captain," Mike smiled, "he already knows there's some kind of intrigue between the two of them."

"Really? And he's all right with that?" she asked, feeling hopeful and possibly forgiven for her roguish antics.

He nodded and smiled back at her with his twinkling eyes.

For a moment, she thought about what he had said.

"And you needn't worry about your scheming of last night," he said, grinning.

"I see that you were on to me," Lola cleared her throat, attempting to subdue her embarrassment.

He chuckled, "Yeah, it wasn't too hard."

Lola placed her hands over her face and groaned. "I feel like such a fool. But, in my defense, I really wasn't myself last night," she explained, looking up at him with her innocent eyes.

"Lola, I think you were more yourself last night than ever. I really enjoyed our time together and getting to know you."

"Really?"

"*Uh-hum.*"

75

"I enjoyed it, too," she dared to admit out loud. And for a moment, she considered her complicated situation with him, realizing that she wanted him more than ever, but her domineering senses returned with a firm warning. *Don't read too much into it, the captain's rules still apply to you.*

Mike looked out into the darkened sea, "I never get tired of this."

Contentedly, she followed his gaze to the smudges of moonlight that floated on the water. "I've been looking forward to this night for so long…my first night spent on the ocean."

"You'll never forget it," he said with meaning as he looked into her eyes. "I feel sorry for people who can't live this life."

"Me, too." She turned away to escape his beguiling blue eyes, realizing that she could get lost in him forever if she surrendered. Like velvet, his voice stroked her ears, enticing her further, but beads of caution swirled inside her head leading her back to sanity. *Ignore him. This could be disastrous!* Despite her obedience, his compelling essence encouraged her lingering fantasies.

His sultry gaze sent a surge of heat throughout her body, leaving her dazed for a moment. He looked deep into her eyes and then kissed her on the forehead. "It's time to say goodnight."

Her thoughts stumbled, scrambling her words and then he was gone before she could assemble anything intelligible. *I'm probably the most boring person in the world. What else could he do but run?* She sulked. His rather curious departure confused her while the many other questions paraded around her mind, forcing her to re-examine the events of the evening and their recent conversation. What the heck just happened? She wondered as her mind shifted back and forth from pleasant thoughts to self-doubt. She pondered the matter until her head began to throb. "I don't care," she declared, "it was just plain wonderful…I think." Lola closed her tired eyes and let the gentle waves lull her into a deep sleep.

Chapter Seven

It had been just over six months since Sara shared a lavish graduation party with Joya and Debbie at the Parkins' mansion. It was a large, catered affair where half the town attended along with the traveling friends and family of the three graduates. When the prodigious event was over and all of the out-of-town guests returned to their homes, Sara spent the rest of June shopping and tanning with Debbie and Joya before jetting off to the south of France for nearly three months. It was Mr. and Mrs. Parkins' graduation gift to Sara, not that she really earned it, her father protested in silence.

Some unpleasant changes had arrived with autumn, Sara quickly realized upon returning home from her European vacation. Both Debbie and Joya had moved away to pursue their own paths, free from Sara's dominion.

Addelbrooke College, nearly an hour's drive from Miller Lake, was home to Joya where she studied for a career in journalism. Awakening ambition nurtured her talents, yielding many high marks and respect among her educators and peers.

Debbie ventured to New York City where she took a receptionist position at an international advertising agency. To pave her way toward executive status within the firm, she attended classes three nights a week at a small college near her tiny apartment that she shared with her cat.

Mr. and Mrs. Parkins naturally assumed that Sara would begin prospecting a career or furthering her education, too. Her friends had already left Miller Lake and were well on their way, but Sara wasn't doing anything at all. Initially, they kept their thoughts to themselves, waiting for Sara to make her move and when she didn't, they finally revealed their concerns on the matter, but Sara wasn't very receptive. She had plans of marrying Nick who was already working for her father's large electronics company. "So, why worry about it?" she often argued. "College would only be a waste of money," she screamed once in a very heated debate. Sara hated school and believed that she could bypass a formal education and simply succeed on her good looks and feminine attributes "when the right opportunity came along."

Sara's attitude frustrated Mr. Parkins deeply, initiating a nasty quarrel between his wife and him. "She's too far gone. You've spoiled her rotten!" Sara heard him holler, but oddly enough, she wasn't offended. She knew that she was spoiled, but she also knew that her parents would continue to indulge her every whim and they certainly wouldn't toss her out into the streets. Not their only child.

SHAHARA, a high-end fashion boutique that was situated in the hub of Miller Lake's elite, was just the opening Sara had been waiting for. She was invited to model a portion of the spring line for their catalogue and various magazines ads. The opportunity thrilled her and filled her head with fantasies.

Zelda, the boutique's owner, was a very shrewd businesswoman who maintained exclusive contracts with prestigious designers worldwide. Her boutique wasn't large, but it didn't need to be as it held the steady interest of many celebrities and wealthy politicians throughout the country.

Sara had assumed that her first modeling stint would launch her into instant stardom. Success would simply come to her, she believed. On a few occasions, she had sent out headshots to modeling agencies to satisfy her parents, but she preferred waiting until the spring ads were published because she was certain that through SHAHARA'S exposure, she would, without a doubt, be discovered.

The owner of a local department store, and also a friend of the Parkins', offered Sara a retail position in her store, but Sara wouldn't have anything to do with serving the public. The public was there for her, she believed. Visions of grandeur continued to fill her head. She would be both a super model and the lovely wife of a flourishing businessman, though Nick was not really up to the task her father worried in secret. Nick's position at the company was not to his own merit, but merely by creative design on Mr. Parkins' part to keep a close eye on Nick.

When Christmastime approached, Sara still hadn't taken a job. She lived comfortably off her parent's wealth while waiting for Nick's marriage proposal. If he didn't propose by New Year's Eve, then she would orchestrate a scheme that would guarantee a swift one. A smile slithered across her face as she sat plotting at the breakfast table.

"What do you find so amusing, Sara?" Her father looked over his newspaper.

"Oh, I was just thinking about something."

"Perhaps employment?" He raised his eyebrows with an air of hope.

"Oh, Father," she snapped, taking a sip of her orange juice.

"When your mother gets in here, we'd like to talk to you about something." His smile was calculating.

"All right," she answered with downcast eyes, knowing that the morning's breakfast conversation was going to be over her employment or lack thereof. She tore off bites of her cinnamon roll and waited for the onslaught to begin.

"Sara," her mother began, taking a seat beside her, "your father and I would like you to spend some time with Joya and Debbie in New York City."

Completely flabbergasted, Sara blinked several times with alternating glances between her parents. "Are you kidding?" She was baffled by the unexpected offer.

"No, we're quite serious," Mr. Parkins interjected.

"Your father and I agreed that this would be good for you and we've already worked out the arrangements with the girls." Sara's mother beamed with pride over her clever plan.

"Really?" Sara leaned back in her chair, taking it all in. "And they agreed?" She was surprised by the sudden change in her friends who had recently drifted from her realm. It had bothered her, but it was clear now that they had come to their senses and wanted Sara back in their lives. Sara's smug face lit up with the idea of her friends crawling back to her.

"They are both looking forward to it, too," her mother added, taking a sip of her coffee. "And don't worry, you'll be home in time for Christmas."

Sara's parents believed that if Sara spent some time with her friends that they might inspire her and get her thinking about a career and, perhaps, college. A little healthy competition among friends just might be the tool needed to motivate their daughter.

"Your plane leaves on Monday," her father announced, somewhat coldly.

Mrs. Parkins cast him a sharp look before continuing, "We just figured it would do you some good to spend some quality time with your friends."

"It *will* do me some good," Sara nodded. Her mood had dramatically improved. "Mother," she said, waiting for Shaundra Parkins to set her cup down, "may I get a few things to wear in New York?"

Mr. Parkins grumbled into his coffee cup, "I knew that was coming."

"Well…only a few things, dear." Guardedly, Mrs. Parkins waited for her husband to retreat inside his newspaper when she winked at Sara.

Delighted, Sara grinned back at her mother.

Having discovered better friends in college, Joya realized what a dull person Sara really was. She wasn't overly thrilled about spending any time with Sara, but Mr. and Mrs. Parkins were funding her trip, so she accepted the offer and looked forward to visiting Debbie in New York City.

After arriving in New York, Sara treated her friends to expensive meals and gifts hoping to fully lure them back into her sphere. She was quite confident that through her generosity she would succeed. And having no ethics, Debbie and Joya greedily accepted Sara's bounty for as long as she was fool enough to give it.

The days of doting on Sara were over, Sara quickly discovered after landing in the grand city. Joya and Debbie had, indeed, removed themselves from her reign and no longer were they comfortable merely existing in her shadow. Each was free to appreciate her own worth without Sara's influence. Sara's empire had crumbled and no longer was she the significant figure that Joya and Debbie strived to mirror throughout their adolescence.

During an evening meal at a pricey restaurant nestled in the heart of Manhattan, Sara was subjected to endure endless chatter between Joya and Debbie as they galvanized their friendship, forcing Sara to acknowledge her scant existence between the two. It was obvious that her clout was worthless and all of her favors were useless. Had they used her all those many years? She wondered as she cast a scathing glare across the table.

Several times, Sara became upset with Debbie for intentionally bringing to light the fact that she hadn't done anything with her life thus far. "You don't even have a plan," Debbie told Sara, shaking her head. "It's really too bad you're still floundering around and not exactly sure what to do with your life…you poor thing." Her tone was patronizing.

Sara recognized Debbie's false concern, but she remained composed and avoided the urge to lash out. A brief moment of uncomfortable silence crept across the table following Debbie's latest remark.

Though Joya was surprised by Debbie's veiled insults, it thrilled her, prompting her to take her own poke at Sara. "And Nick will probably propose…eventually," Joya said, without believing. "I mean, it's not a career, but it's something." She forced a smile and refolded her napkin neatly on her lap.

The added jab was nearly too much for Sara. She felt like slapping Debbie and Joya. How dare they? After all I've done for them, she huffed with blazing thoughts.

The evening promised to be a long one as they had tickets to a Broadway show after dinner. Sara knew she would blow a fuse if she had to listen much longer to the non-stop exchange between Joya and Debbie. It seemed they did nothing else but flaunt their personal triumphs. While pretending to be amused, Sara was deep in plot. She excused herself from the table, implying a restroom visit. She met the *maitre d'* at his platform, slipped him a twenty-dollar bill along with her cell phone number, and instructed him to call the number in five minutes. The scheming vixen had reprised her role and, in proud stride, returned to the table where Joya and Debbie continued prattling about their full lives, hardly aware of Sara's return.

Finally, Sara was spared her misery when her cell phone rang. "Oh that's mine," she chimed, dripping with pleasure as she reached for the small phone. "Hi, Mom. What's that? That's wonderful. Really? Just a second, let me grab a pen." Sara's hand rustled inside her purse as she searched for her pen and some paper, adding to the ruse. "All right, what is that number? I've got it. Thanks, Mom. I'll probably fly home after I meet with them. Talk to you then. Bye-bye." Sara tossed her phone inside her purse along with the pen and small notebook. Expectantly, she waited for her companions' inquiries regarding the intriguing phone call.

The staged phone call went ignored, leaving Sara to offer her own tale. "That was my mom," she offered, hiding her irritation, "she told me that a modeling agency just called and would like to meet with me right away. Isn't that great?"

Immediately, the unwelcome news spawned resentment at the table. "That's terrific," Joya answered weakly. For the past few months, Joya enjoyed the fact that Sara had spent her time idly, while she and Debbie worked hard at establishing solid careers. Now, Sara will simply land a modeling job and make her way to the top without any effort, Joya thought bitterly to herself.

"So, give us the details," Debbie said shallowly. She's never had to pay her dues, she complained inside her head.

"My mom said that the agent was very impressed with my headshots and is eager to meet with me." Sara's gleaming eyes shifted back and forth at the table.

"Really? When is your appointment?" Joya pretended to be interested.

"Tomorrow morning. Here, in New York City. I'll never get a wink of sleep tonight," Sara sighed in delight.

Joya shot a swift glance at Debbie, revealing her view on the matter and Debbie responded with a roll of the eyes. Sara observed the familiar communication between the two, realizing that she had successfully struck the intended chords.

The server came by and placed the meal tab in the center of the table. Expectantly, Joya and Debbie looked to Sara to pick it up.

"Shall we go, ladies?" Sara reached for the check and then dropped a bomb when she used the calculator on her cell phone to separate the dinner costs.

Debbie and Joya looked on curiously. Surely, she's not going to make us pay, Joya worried in silence.

"All right, Debbie, your portion of the meal comes to forty-nine and, Joya, yours was fifty-three. And we should each include at least a twenty-dollar tip." Smoothly, Sara dropped some twenties onto the table and looked to Debbie and Joya for their share.

Sara was humored by their dumbfounded expressions. Each was brutally stunned, not exactly sure how to handle Sara's unexpected whim. With some hesitation, Debbie reached for her purse while Joya slowly unfolded her wallet with the same reluctance.

The following morning, Joya slept beneath a black satin comforter inside the luxurious hotel suite while Sara quietly made her exit. On her way in to the hotel coffee shop, she purchased a newspaper and then ordered a hot cappuccino. "There has to be something in here," she mumbled, flipping through the classifieds. Her purple fingernails ran swiftly up and down the printed pages, stopping every few seconds to circle another potential contact. Finally, she stopped on one particular ad, which caught her full attention. She lifted the paper closer to her face. WANTED: IMMEDIATE OPENING FOR ATTRACTIVE MODEL/ACTRESS FOR UPCOMING MOVIE. NO EXPERIENCE NECESSARY. MUST BE 18 OR OVER WITH VALID I.D.

A wide grin, like that of the Grinch, skidded across her face. "That's it," she said under her breath, knowing that with her beauty she was a shoe-in. At this point, Sara didn't care how small the role was, she just had to get her name and face to film and, by doing so, she would put Joya and Debbie in their deserved places.

Sara took another sip of her warm cappuccino before dialing the phone number that was listed in the ad. "Hello? I am responding to your ad that you have listed in the *Times*."

"Which one?" came a raspy voice on the other end of the line.

"*Uhm*, the ad that is seeking an attractive model slash actress. Is that position still available?"

"Yes, it is. Do you want to schedule an appointment to be seen?"

"Yes, I would." Sara muffled her surprise at how easy it was. "When is your first available slot for a screen test?"

"Well, we don't do screen tests, but Bill is shooting down at the warehouse today. You can meet with him there."

"Oh, I see."

"Do you currently have an agent?"

"No. Do I need one?" Sara frowned, dreading the answer.

"No, not at all. Agents just get in the way."

"Oh, good."

"Do you have a pen? I'll give you the address."

"Yes, I do." Sara quickly picked up her pen and scribbled the address in her small planner.

The stranger's voice on the phone was gritty like that of a heavy smoker or one who had spent many years enjoying too much whiskey.

"He might want to take some quick shots of you today, so be prepared," the voice on the other end advised.

"Thank you, I'll be ready." After confirming the warehouse address, Sara returned to her hotel room without ever once considering the nature of the film company.

Hardly enthused, Joya asked, "Did you already meet with that agent?"

"No, not yet. I didn't want to disturb you earlier this morning, so I went down to the coffee shop and called him. He wants to meet with me in just a bit," she smiled and pulled the doors open to the wardrobe. "He told me that I definitely have a future and wondered why I wasn't already working Milan. Can you believe that? Milan!" Her eyes flared as she added more to the con. "Now, I've just got to figure out what to wear."

Joya's eyes followed Sara around the room until she became dizzy. Finally, she sat up and pulled the comforter around her waist.

"How's this?" Sara held up her black Diesel suit with a pair of Giuseppe Zanotti boots. "Will it do the trick?" Her acid thoughts brought a smile to her face as she detected Joya's swelling envy.

The sting from the events at dinner the night before still lingered, leaving Joya bitterly annoyed and listening to Sara's obnoxious chatter wasn't helping matters. Casually, Joya looked Sara up and down, "You look fine," was all she chose to say. In actuality, Sara looked exquisite, but Joya wasn't in the mood to cast compliments. Before going to sleep the night before, she had wished that Sara would awaken to a lumpy rash that sprawled across her entire face, but that didn't happen. "Good luck," she forced herself to say as she flopped back into her pillow and pulled the comforter over her head.

"Thanks. I better go freshen up my make-up before I leave." Sara headed toward the bathroom. "I'm not sure when I'll be back. If you and Debbie want to make some plans, go ahead and I'll catch up with you later."

Chapter Eight

A pot of green tea steeped on the stove in the galley while Lola and Sheila recovered from the morning stampede of last-minute preparations. "This morning is like a blur to me." Lola was still numb from the predawn excitement.

Sheila poked her head around the pantry door, "It's always like this right before we cast off."

Lola leaned against the sink and watched Mike and Eddie prepare for launch. Excitedly, she turned to Sheila, "I thought this day would never come."

"Me, too!" said Sheila, feeling giddy.

Lola's eyes held a gleam like that of a child on Christmas morning. She could hardly contain her excitement and briefly occupied herself by pouring two cups of tea and scrubbing the teapot.

Sheila twirled her hair in her fingers. She was thinking hard about something. "Lola, are you sure you have everything you need?"

"Yes, I'm sure. I've checked and re-checked. But thanks for asking…again," she giggled.

"I'm sorry, I get a little crazy right before we leave on these long trips," Sheila admitted.

Lola raised a brow, "*A little?*"

Sheila laughed, "Yes, a little. I'm always afraid I'm going to forget something important."

Lola took a seat, "I've seen your list…we're ready."

"You're right," Sheila nodded and picked up her cup.

"Well, I guess that ramshackle motel will just have to go on without us." Lola tried to resist a spark of sentiment she held for the old place.

Sheila laughed over her cup and then heard voices outside. "I think I hear Bill and Nora."

"Lola rose to her feet and listened to the unfamiliar voices on deck. "Let's go."

"This is, Lola, our latest recruit." Captain Andre beamed at the opportunity to introduce Lola to his friends.

"I'm very pleased to meet you." Lola reached out her hand.

"It's a pleasure to meet you, too." Bill Wells said, taking her hand. "Lola, you say? That's a darn pretty name, young lady."

"Thank you, Mr. Wells," she smiled back. His round cheeks and a round belly revealed his warm character. Bushy eyebrows sprung from the rim of his glasses while the few remaining gray hairs on top of his head bristled in the breeze.

Nora Wells stepped forward, moving out of the sun's glare. "Lola, I hear you are from New Hampshire."

"Yes, I am."

"I grew up in Vermont. We're practically neighbors."

"Yes, we are," Lola smiled.

"It's a beautiful part of the country, don't you think?"

"Yes, I do. And I'd miss it dreadfully if it weren't for these wonderful folks here." Lola looked fondly toward her crew. "They keep me pretty busy, so the home-sickness hasn't set in at all."

"That's good. Now, you just call us Bill and Nora and none of that formal stuff around us," said the tiny woman with short brown hair.

Lola agreed with a heartfelt pat to the back of Nora's hand. A fondness for them instantly sprouted inside her heart where she claimed them as her honorary grandparents. She showed them to their suite and helped Nora unpack their bags.

A balmy breeze gently grazed Lola's tanned shoulders as she reclined in a chaise the fourth day into the voyage. Sun-bleached tendrils danced around her face while she took her morning break in the sunshine. She thrived on the ocean, no longer resembling the lonely, troubled girl from Miller Lake. With contentment, came a withering vengeance where joy resumed its role and trampled her need for revenge.

There was always plenty of time to cast a line, Lola discovered early on in the expedition. Her taste for fish had ripened along with an appetite for the sport. Eddie and Sheila rarely joined the fishing party, but Pascal, Bill and Mike were always willing to set a pole beside Lola. Pascal had appointed himself as teacher when it came to showing her the proper ways of fishing. Though Mike would have enjoyed the privilege, he stepped aside, allowing Pascal to share his expertise. And it was over a tackle box that Pascal and Lola, two very diverse strangers, formed a friendship, which solidly bonded the entire crew.

For a while, Captain Andre had quietly observed Mike and Lola's budding friendship and, on one particular afternoon, while he sat nearby reading a book, it occurred to him that they could be a matched pair. For the seven years he had known Mike, he strongly disapproved of his roguish ways with women in the many harbors they had frequented. But, since Lola's arrival, Mike was showing signs of a significant transformation. The captain believed that Mike was finally becoming the fine man he was destined to be and it seemed that Lola was his vessel. When their laughter broke his concentration once more, he peered over his book and smiled favorably.

Lola enjoyed spending time with Bill and Nora. They were hearty people with wisdom to share from their many years. Most days, after the mid-day meal, Bill would retire to their room for a nap and Nora would gather her knitting needles and join Lola in either the laundry room or galley while Lola completed her tasks.

Beautiful handmade garments of colorful yarn grew from Nora's nimble fingers while the two chatted happily. Lola enjoyed listening to Nora's views on politics and current events, realizing that Nora was a well-informed woman who did not carelessly cast her opinions. She was very intelligent and Lola highly respected her. Nearly fifty years spanned the two, yet they had formed a meaningful friendship where age put no gaps. Lola missed her mother and, in her absence, Nora supplied a mother's heart.

"We'll be in Hawaii tomorrow. I bet you can't wait to step on God's good earth again," said Nora, looking up from her yarn.

"Oh, you know it! I love this boat and everything, but I'm looking forward to solid ground again. And Hawaii!" Lola exclaimed, bursting with a wave of enthusiasm. "I just can't believe that I am actually going to be there tomorrow."

"It's a fascinating place. I know you'll love it."

Impatiently, Lola planted her hands on her hips, "I swear time has completely stopped just because I'm excited about something!"

Nora chuckled and straightened her yarn. "Pardon my candor, dear, but at my age there's just no time to be delicate."

"All right," Lola's attention sharpened.

"I believe Mike is rather fond of you. What do you think about that?" She studied Lola's face.

The direct question left Lola surprised and void of an immediate answer. She hesitated for a moment and decided to see where Nora was taking the conversation. "Do you really think so, or do you think just because we're all stuck here on this boat and I'm the only seemingly available—"

"Listen here, young lady," Nora interrupted, "I may be old, but I'm not blind. That young man has it bad for you and you've hardly given him the time of day…and fishing doesn't count. Now, I already know that you're in love with him, so don't bother refuting that with me."

Lola felt exposed when her colorful cheeks revealed her secret. Nora was right.

"What is stopping you?" Nora sat back against the cushions and waited.

Making sure that nobody could overhear them, Lola guardedly looked over her shoulders, "Oh, he's definitely got my attention. It's just that the captain has these rules about—"

"Oh, rules *shmools*," Nora interrupted again, "Andre has a tender heart when it comes to matters of love. Believe me, I know what I'm talking about. He just doesn't want any cheap and recreational affairs on board," she said, waving her knitting needle.

"I agree. I think that's a proper rule," Lola nodded.

"Well, certainly it is!" Nora's eyebrows sprung with emphasis. "But this is something completely different." She followed her statement up with an earnest smile.

A sense of hope stirred in Lola. She liked what Nora was telling her.

"When it's genuine love, you need to do something about it, not ignore it!" Nora's wide eyes landed on Lola, "Life is too short and you never know when true love will come your way again. Now don't worry about Andre. He already suspects that there's something between the two of you, anyway."

"What?" Lola nearly fell off her sandals.

"There's nothing to worry about," she smiled, assuredly.

Lola considered Nora's critical statement for a moment and decided to force her concerns aside, giving way to trust Nora and the special relationship she shared with the captain. "I've never even had a boyfriend before and I really don't know what to do. I guess I'm kind of scared," Lola admitted.

"Dear, you think too much and you're too darn careful. Just relax and you'll figure it all out. I'm going to go take a nap. You'll know what to do. Just put a little trust in yourself." She collected her yarn and needles and prepared to leave the room.

"I'm going to think about what you told me," Lola smiled. "Enjoy your nap."

After the evening meal was over and the dishes were put away, Lola joined the poker game. Her hand had improved dramatically, forcing all those who played with her to sharpen their own skills. "Let's make it, twenty," Lola's eyes sparkled as she challenged Mike in another round of Texas Hold'em.

Mike rubbed his jaw and attempted to read her face. "I call," he said, dropping his cards.

Bill chuckled, watching them square off at the table. "I'm glad I folded."

Eddie dealt the turn card, "Four." Lola didn't flinch. Her high card was a king, no pairs and Mike already had a pair of queens. Eddie then flipped the river card, "We have a king!" He laughed hard and slapped Mike's shoulder, "You've taught her well, my friend."

"I did...didn't I?" Proudly, Mike shot a spirited grin toward Lola and pushed her winnings toward her. "How did you know a king was coming?"

His twinkling eyes were nearly blinding, she thought, before casually answering him, "I just went with my gut like you told me."

Impressed, he shook his head and grinned.

Lola was crazy in love with him and in spite of his dizzying smile, she remained steady while her thoughts wandered, alternating between him and the game. With each stolen glance at him, her heart skipped a beat and when he spoke, her breath caught in her chest where she would cease breathing for several seconds at a time. Nora's words still echoed in Lola's head, prompting hidden strands of courage to emerge from the banks of her heart. Lola was determined to take that risk with Mike and nothing would stop her.

"*Hmm*, your eyes flicker with such mystery. I wonder, what does the lady ponder?" Mike's piercing eyes locked on to Lola's as he placed the stack of cards in front of her.

Gently, she drew in a deep breath and expertly shuffled the cards before returning an alluring smile. It was dangerous, yet exciting, she thought, pleasuring in the delicate pains that swirled inside her stomach.

Recurring regret had gnawed at her every time she thought about the Thanksgiving trip when she first suspected he was interested in her. The pending doom from not adhering to the captain's rules, combined with her own inadequacies, had kept Mike from knowing how she really felt about him. But she would remedy that shortly, she plotted.

After dealing the cards, Lola tossed a red chip into the pot, which caused the others to fold immediately. "Tomorrow after we land, I'll take everyone out for dinner with these winnings," she offered, trying to thwart a tinge of guilt that arrived when she raked in another pot.

"I'm going to hold you to that," Mike laughed.

"As well you should! Some of this money is yours," she teased, pointing at her cache.

Eddie burst out laughing, "She's got ya there, mate."

Mike chuckled, "Yes, that she does." And his heart, too, he knew.

Sheila observed the subtle exchanges darting back and forth between Mike and Lola during the game. She loved playing witness to the blossoming relationship but kept her thoughts to herself. "By this time tomorrow, we'll be in Hawaii."

"I can't believe it!" Lola dropped a white chip into the pile. "I probably won't be able to sleep tonight."

Sheila smiled, matching the bet.

Lola loved playing cards with her friends, but she wanted the game to end soon so she could spend time alone with Mike. To speed things up, she devised a plan. Casually, she gave her cards another glance and shrewdly dropped five blue chips into the pot.

"There she goes again!" Pascal grumbled, tossing his cards down onto the table, "I fold."

"Oh, Pascal, you'll win your money back…eventually," Lola giggled. "And, if not tonight, at least you'll have a feast waiting for you tomorrow."

"Sounds good," Pascal nodded, casting a friendly wave as he headed to bed. "Night, all."

Yes, it worked! Lola held her breath, secretly hoping that everyone, excluding Mike, would retire for the evening. Various scenarios played out inside her head as she planned her next move. Rumbling chairs, scraping across the floor, interrupted her tender designs. All were leaving, including Mike! Her heart sank as she watched him walk away, offering only a cheerful *goodnight.*

Dejectedly, Lola wandered out on deck and situated herself in a lounge chair with her favorite blanket. Normally, the night air soothed her tired body as the moon's shimmering light nurtured her soul, but this night brought a sense of disconcertedness and she couldn't find the will to summon her familiar solace. All day she had hoped to spend some time alone with him and capture his heart before anything else interfered. Perhaps Nora was wrong, she considered. Maybe Mike wasn't interested at all. The moon slid behind the clouds, leaving her in near darkness. She closed her eyes and hoped sleep would arrive soon.

An evening breeze moved in and swirled around the ship, tossing her hair upon her cheeks when a gentle stroke smoothed away the wandering strands from her face. She opened her eyes and saw Mike standing beside her. Without a word, he reached out for her hand and pulled her up against him. Tenderly, he cupped her face and kissed her with intensity. She melted inside his warmth. His passion was overwhelming, making her drunk inside his rapture. She felt as though she could completely give herself to him as she loved him so much and Mike would have allowed her if he didn't love her. Lola was special and with all of his willpower, he slowly pulled away, leaving desire still warm upon her lips.

The moon returned and spilled its light on them. "I've been waiting for you," she heard herself say.

"And I have been waiting for an invitation."

She smiled up at him.

"I've wanted to do that for so long," he confessed, looking into her eyes. He plugged his iPod into the nearby port and took her hands, guiding her to dance with him.

He led her in a gentle sway as she leaned comfortably against him. She felt lightheaded and wondered if he was holding her up or if she was dancing on air. She couldn't feel her feet at all.

Nearly an hour had passed when he told her that he had to go before Eddie returned.

Still under the influence of his intoxicating charm, she nodded, hardly aware of the rest of the world.

"For now, let's keep us a secret."

"All right," she whispered, finally coming around. The precious words, "keep us a secret" resounded in her head, bringing an endless smile to her face. She leaned in for a final kiss goodnight and then soft-footed to her quarters before Eddie discovered their secret.

Quietly, she climbed the ladder to her bunk and slid beneath a red comforter. Her heart was full, exploding with promise of love and happiness as she tried to fall asleep, though slumber did not come easily. The boat rocked lightly and she wondered if Mike, too, was awake and thinking of her or if he had simply fallen asleep, immune to such excitement. Ripples of doubt began to trickle in, but then Nora's words returned to guide her. Nora was right; she thought to herself, I do overanalyze everything.

Next morning, Lola jumped out of bed earlier than usual and hurried through all of her morning tasks as she couldn't wait to see him at the breakfast table. When the laundry was finished, she joined Sheila in the galley and helped her prepare the morning meal.

"Lola, you look so different today. What's going on with you?" Sheila asked, hoping to hear the real reason behind Lola's sparkling mood.

"I'm just excited that we're landing in Hawaii today! Can you believe it? Of course, you've already been there, so this is no big deal to you." She followed Sheila out on deck with the silverware and, spotting the binoculars on the table, she positioned them over her eyes to catch first glimpse of the magical island awaiting her in the distance.

Sheila grinned and decided to play along with Lola's charade for a little longer, for she knew exactly what was behind Lola's glow. "I still get caught up in the thrill every time we enter port. I'm so happy I get to share in this experience with you."

Lola smiled, "I am, too." She lowered the binoculars to her side when she felt his eyes on her. Her heart pounded as a revealing grin crept across her face. At that moment, she didn't dare look at him, knowing that her simple glance would surrender their secret to all those nearby.

"*G'Day*. How are the ladies doing this fine morning?" he asked from the station above them.

Lola swallowed hard and tried her best to compose herself. Casually, she raised her hand to block the sun and looked up toward him where he stood handsomely at the helm, "We're fine and how are you?"

"I couldn't be better," he shot a tell-all grin.

"Now, I am certain as to what is going on with you," Sheila's eyes flickered with merriment as she turned to look at Mike. "Well, it's about time." She kept her tone low for only Lola to hear.

Feeling like she'd just been caught with her hand in the cookie jar, Lola's eyes enlarged with panic.

"Don't worry, your secret is safe with me," Sheila assured.

Flustered, Lola's smile crumpled across her face. She didn't know how to respond to Sheila's discovery.

"Glad to see he's finally made his move," Sheila mumbled while hustling platters of food out to the table. She called everyone to breakfast, allowing Lola a quick and comfortable exit from their conversation. "We'll talk later," she winked.

Everyone shared their fondest Hawaiian memories over plates of bacon, scrambled eggs and toast when Pascal brought up dinner plans. "Hey, Lola, don't forget that you promised us all dinner tonight," he reminded.

"How could I forget something like that? I'm looking forward to it. In fact, I'm going to let you decide where we go."

Nora laughed hard over her eggs.

"No way, don't let him do that! He'll pick one of his favorite dives." Eddie's plea sounded in desperation.

"All right," Lola said hesitantly, seeking input from the others while smiling apologetically past Pascal.

Pascal returned her smile with a grunt of irritation, causing Lola to laugh.

"I know of a place," Mike's voice emerged from the table.

Lola looked at him and, for a brief moment, the rest of the world vanished and only they existed. She forced herself from his binding charm, "What is it?"

"It's a great place," Mike continued, "Sheila, you know the place I'm thinking about. It's that one situated on a cliff and you can overlook the ocean from your table? I can't remember the name of it right now, but I know where it is."

"Yes, I know what you're talking about. That's a great place for Lola on her first night. Good idea. It's called THE ORCHID."

"Yes, that's the one." Mike looked pleased.

"My sincere thanks to you both," Eddie punctuated his relief with a sigh.

Pascal reached over and smacked Eddie on the head with his cap. "I don't have bad taste. Some of the best places are off the tourist scene. That's where you find the real food and you're not dropping a month's salary to eat." Pascal's dark eyes searched the table for support. Finding none, he put his red cap back over his curly brown hair and shook his head.

"Pascal, this is special. It's Lola's first night," Sheila gently explained. "And besides, she's paying, so what are you worried about?"

"Thank you, Pascal, for your concern regarding my financial interests, however, I assure you that I can handle dinner for the whole lot of you as you've all been so generous with your recent poker contributions," she joked.

Captain Andre laughed along with the others.

"I just wanted to do something nice for all of you," Lola added.

Satisfied, Pascal smiled, "Then I'm looking forward to it."

After breakfast, Lola studied Mike, thinking over what Sheila had told her about his childhood. A drunk had killed his father when Mike was young. His father was a successful fisherman and his legacy lived on through Mike's vast knowledge of boats and of the sea. When Mike was old enough, he had spent most of his days at the docks offering to work for the sailors that had known his father. Quite often, those sailors would take Mike out on short fishing trips and entertain him with stories of the many adventures they had shared with his father. Captain Andre was so inspired by the young man's enthusiasm and willingness to learn that he hired Mike on his sixteenth birthday, shortly after he earned his degree in general education.

When Captain Andre guided the vessel into the harbor, Lola watched Mike prepare for the landing. She forced her eyes from his solid muscles and looked toward the Big Island, which welcomed her with all of its grandeur of tropical elements and lush green hills, valleys and mountainous peaks. Dotted along the coastline were some intrusive buildings, but Lola looked beyond them and enjoyed the island splendor.

Suddenly, she felt Mike's gentle approach, "It's one of the most beautiful places you'll ever see. I can't wait to take you sightseeing," he said, pointing out a few landmarks.

Chapter Nine

A black limousine brought Lola and the others to a hotel that was owned by Captain Andre, one of his many side ventures. Eagerly, her eyes roamed the majestic white structure with its exquisite grounds and stunning architecture. Rambling palms surrounded the impressive estate while several kukui trees sprawled the meticulously manicured lawns.

"It's beautiful." Lola looked on, hardly believing what she was seeing as she stepped out of the limo.

"Yeah, it makes living in that old motel worth every minute it, doesn't it?" Sheila chuckled. "Now, you know why we didn't mind that old place so much."

"I never expected anything so...grand!" Lola was stunned by the comparison.

Everyone headed for the lobby but Mike and Lola. She wanted to spend a few more minutes exploring the grounds. Brilliant floral borders bursting with carnations, hibiscus, orchids and other flowers, which Lola couldn't identify, traced the walkways while bulging baskets of other flowers swung over her head. Fragrances from the friendly blooms offered up their greetings, but they soon overpowered her, making time travel possible. Suddenly, she was a prisoner to her memories and was instantly hurled back in time where Joe was fighting death in a puddle of perfumed water, only to die in her arms. Lola struggled to free herself, but feared she was quickly falling victim to the cursed memories.

The others had already taken the elevator to their rooms while Mike and Lola wandered into the lobby. He placed her room key in her hand, noticing her odd expression, "Everything all right?"

"Yes, I'm fine. I'm just getting my land legs back," she smiled.

He nodded, believing her as they made their way to the bank of elevators. "Perhaps you should lie down for a while and get something to eat. Break into that basket of fruit that's in your room."

"I will," she said, adding more cheer. Together they stepped into the elevator.

"If you feel like it, we can squeeze in a little sightseeing before dinner."

"I'd really like that."

"Just call me when you're ready. I'm in room *1007*, just below yours."

"All right, just give me a few minutes and I'll be good as new." She smiled convincingly and pressed the button to the eleventh floor. A moment later, she walked the long corridor toward her room trying to rid herself of the excruciating memories that were staging a revolt inside her head. "*1104, 1105, 1106*," she uttered as her eyes shifted back and forth down the vacant hallway. "Don't bring it here," she begged herself, shoving the keycard into the electronic port. A green light flickered for an instant and with a twist of the knob, she entered an immaculate suite.

A sweeping presence of fine wood and fixtures filled the room while a subtle blend of green, blue and mauve textures flowed throughout the elegant setting. Centered in the room, on a beautiful round mahogany table, was a basket stuffed with a tempting assortment of fresh fruit, crackers, cheese and bottled water. And beyond that, a large crystal vase boasted a dazzling array of tropical flowers on top of a credenza. The impressive display of flowers was certainly pleasing to the eye, however, when she caught a whiff, she quickly placed the bouquet out into the corridor to escape the unwelcome reminders that promised to steal her happiness.

While exploring the magnificent suite, she dropped her purse on the sofa and discovered a beautiful bed chamber beyond a set of double doors. Between two windows was a four-poster bed layered in jade-colored fabrics and matching pillows. She brushed her hand over the soft spread and sat down, bobbing up and down to measure the level of comfort. Beside her, on a bedside table, was a candlestick lamp and next to that was a hand carved wooden box. Curiously, she lifted the lid and found inside a TV remote along with a pen, stationary and Bible. She pulled the Bible out of the box and placed it on the night table.

Across from the bed was a massive mahogany armoire that was inlayed with intricate floral designs. Gently, she stroked the hand-carved details when a comfortable breeze moved through the room, drawing her to the balcony. Sheer curtains swirled inside the gentle wind as she passed through the French doors to the terrace. She leaned over the railing and watched the surging waves rush forward until they died along the beach below her.

As the tumbling waves dissolved along the shore, it occurred to her that the striving waters symbolized life, with each wave serving its own unique lifetime. Some misguided waves crashed chaotically against other waves only to disappear inside the watery mass, sadly, never reaching their potential. Other waves followed along with the mightiest of waves only to make their way to the end of an unchallenged life with little effort and little reward. Finally, the prevailing waves sprawled fearlessly, deep into the shore reaching a triumphant end. Lola studied the waves a while longer and then she knew exactly what she had to do. In determined stride, she opened the door to the corridor and affectionately retrieved the beautiful bouquet of flowers that she had earlier rejected. Tenderly, she adjusted the blossoms and smelled their pleasant perfume, deciding to appreciate their sweet gifts without the taste of sorrow.

After her luggage arrived, Lola ate some cheese and bread from the basket and then changed her clothes before testing out the luxurious bed that had been tempting her. She felt her eyes grow heavy as soon as the green satin touched her skin, "I'll just rest here for a few minutes."

A strong breeze whipped through the room, abruptly waking her from a deep sleep. Her stomach tickled with anticipation as she hurried for the phone and pressed the numbers to his room, but, to her dismay, his phone rang without an answer. Disappointed, she replaced the phone inside the cradle and sighed, glaring at the clock beside her. "Oh, Lola, you're an idiot," she groaned, throwing herself back against the bed, ready to dump tears. "He couldn't wait forever!" Suddenly, the door to her suite vibrated with a rapid knock, rescuing her from the depths of self-pity. She crossed her fingers and hurried to the door, hoping it was Mike.

"I'm glad to see that you're feeling better," he said, wielding a grin worthy of a trademark.

"Mike! Please, come in. I was merely trying out the bed and, well, I apparently went to sleep. I didn't mean to keep you waiting so long."

"No worries. You must have needed it." He took a full assessment of her with his welcoming eyes.

"I guess I did. Anyway, I feel fantastic now."

"I can see that," he said with a shameless grin. He closed the door behind him and then looked at her as if he'd never seen her before, "You're so beautiful."

"Thank you." She felt herself blush and wished she could stop doing it. "Hey, you're not wearing your cap." Curiously, she reached up and touched his hair, exploring his soft curls with her finger tips. "I like it," she purred.

For the moment, he was paralyzed; a helpless captive in her magnificence. Suddenly, he lunged for her, seeking her soul when his mouth seized her lips. His willing prisoner was trapped inside his fire until he slowly pulled away. "Kisses like that carry heavy consequences," he cautioned in a strained voice. She ignored his warning and met his passion with another kiss. He had to interrupt her spell...soon. Reluctantly, he backed out of the most powerful embrace he had ever experienced. "We've got an hour before our dinner reservation," he managed, aiming for recovery. Part of him wanted to yield to his desire and keep her there, but he knew what he had to do. No other woman had affected him like Lola. In only a short time, this beguiling young woman had fully captured his roving heart. "I thought we'd take the limo around town for a bit," he suggested, countering temptation.

"I'd love to. Let me grab my purse."

He spotted a bottle of water in the fruit basket, "Do you mind?"

"Not at all."

"It's really warm in here," he commented, loosening his blue shirt.

"I hadn't noticed," she giggled, opening the door to the corridor.

Her eyes were fixed on the windows inside the limousine as it traveled through town. "It's more beautiful than I ever dreamed."

"Yes, and it only gets better," he squeezed her hand.

For the next hour, they revealed only small fragments of their lives, unburdened with the real drama that had left scars on each of their hearts.

"*Excusa! We go git de others now, sir?*" The limo driver interrupted, using his best English.

Mike looked at his watch, "Yes, please. Wow, we burned that hour fast."

"It's amazing how you can get lost in—" Lola stopped herself, faltering with her thoughts, "It's just amazing how fast time flies here," she corrected.

Deliberately he smiled, interpreting her original thought.

He's reading my mind! Immediately, she raised her glass to her mouth, wondering if he really knew what she was thinking.

The limousine pulled up in front of the hotel where the rest of the crew waited beneath the elegant awning. Lola felt her cheeks redden when she realized how obvious it was to the others that more was going on between her and Mike than just mutual interests in sightseeing and fishing. Like a child facing the school principal for an infraction, Lola's nerves jumped inside her skin as Captain Andre approached the car.

When they arrived at the restaurant, Lola told everyone about her tour through town, highlighting specific landmarks in hopes to shed focus from the fact that she and Mike had made the tour together. "I wish Nora and Bill could have joined us tonight," she added, realizing how much she missed them.

"It usually takes them a day to rest up. They'll catch up to us tomorrow," Eddie explained.

"I understand," Lola nodded, looking forward to seeing them the next day.

The sun was beginning to set upon the ocean, casting brilliant hues of pink and amber upon the linen tablecloths. Dozens of white candles flickered inside crystal sconces throughout the restaurant adding more to the romantic setting. Soft conversations filled the room while Lola's mind traveled to a distant paradise with Mike. She wished she could package the night up in a box and keep it safely with her forever. He was growing more handsome by the moment and when he spoke, his voice played her heart like a finely tuned instrument. She had fallen hard for him and realized she could never let him go. Lola was deep in fantasy when a stranger's voice lured her out of a love-induced trance. "I'm sorry, sir, I didn't hear you?" she stammered.

The waiter returned a smile and asked again, "Are you finished with your plate?"

"Yes, I am. I'm sorry, I guess I was just on another planet." Nervously, she laughed.

Eddie knew where Lola's thoughts had taken her. He'd seen that same look in his sister's eyes when she had fallen in love. He kept his observations to himself and signaled to the waiter that he, too, was finished with his plate. "What a feast," he groaned, leaning back in his chair. "I can't believe I did this to myself...I pulled a Pascal!"

The group laughed in unison at Eddie's painful gluttony.

Pitifully, he rubbed his swollen gut.

"I tried to warn you," Sheila reminded him, lightly poking his belly.

Lola studied Eddie's features for a moment. He had thick, blond hair that complimented his green eyes and situated between his Roman nose and mouth was a blond mustache that carried faint red highlights. A few rugged lines defined his handsome face and indicated a few years at sea.

"What do you all plan on doing for the rest of the evening?" Captain Andre placed his empty glass down onto the table.

Lola waited for the others to respond because she wasn't exactly sure how to answer the captain's question. She didn't want to presume anything, so she stalled by counting out her cash for the meal tab.

"I'm meeting a friend later, but feel free to use the limo," the captain offered.

Sheila turned to Eddie, "What do you think?"

"I'm worthless right now. I'm going to chill in my room in front of the television while I recover. Care to join me?"

Mike looked around the table, "I'd like to continue showing Lola around town. Would anyone else care to join us?" he asked, hoping all but Lola would decline.

"I think I'll hang out with Eddie and make sure he doesn't die," Sheila laughed.

"That's probably a good idea," Mike smirked at Eddie.

"I'll pass, too. I've seen enough of this beautiful island and, besides, I've got a date with a TV, my own room and a six-pack. That's all I need. Well, unless you can produce a lovely companion to keep *me* company," Pascal grinned.

"Sorry, man, you're on your own." Eddie rose to his feet.

"*Ah*, it's just as well. Women are only trouble, anyway," Pascal grinned.

"I beg your pardon," Sheila raised a stiff brow.

"Present company excluded," Pascal swiftly corrected, smiling politely in amends.

Sheila laughed at him and patted him on the shoulder before pushing her chair under the table. "Come to the restroom with me, Lola."

"Sure."

"We'll meet you all at the car in a minute," Sheila told the group.

Lola placed her napkin down on the table and followed Sheila toward the back of the restaurant.

The door was hardly shut before Sheila exploded in excitement, "Lola, you have to tell me everything about you and Mike!" Lola attempted a response, but Sheila went on and on, not giving her the chance. "Mike is a keeper…a genuine person. I know he's had a few *admirers*," Sheila said with a slight shrug of her shoulders, "but something has been going on in him since you arrived and it's something that I've never seen before. He's in love with you, Lola, truly!" Sheila had to catch her breath, "I have wanted to say this for so long."

Lola laughed at Sheila's animation. She was touched by her sincere enthusiasm and she wanted to tell Sheila everything.

"Do you realize that since you came to San Diego, Mike has undergone a complete change? He hardly drinks or cusses…and he even uses the word, *please*." Sheila shook her head, "You've put quite a spell on him."

"I didn't mean to," Lola defended.

Sheila smiled at Lola's innocence.

"I've never felt this way before in my life," Lola admitted. "I mean, I've had crushes on guys before, but this is different. I'm crazy about him."

Sheila's eyes glistened with sentiment, "I'm glad."

"Mike suggested that we keep us secret for a while. So, keep this between us. All right?"

Sheila laughed again. "I will," she agreed, instilling trust. "But just so you know, everyone already knows."

"What?" Lola gasped.

"The chemistry between the two of you is as obvious as a candle in the dark."

"Seriously?" Lola was shocked and suddenly felt betrayed by her own self. "I thought I was being so careful."

"The week you arrived, Eddie told me that Mike was smitten with you."

"Really?"

"Yes, and he says that Mike talks about you all of the time."

"He does?" Lola couldn't stop smiling.

"*Uh-hum.*"

"As long as we're on this subject, what is the deal with you and Eddie? Is he the one you were telling me about at the motel?"

Sheila's eyes brightened as she deliberated her answer.

"I just confessed, now it's your turn."

"Yes." Sheila grinned like a schoolgirl. "But it's all a bit complicated. He is an odd one."

"What do you mean?"

"I know he's interested, but he and I are playing it safe. Perhaps too safe."

"We think you two are the perfect pair."

"You and Mike have been speculating?"

"Well, of course!" Lola giggled, "I'm very fond of Eddie and I think he's just right for you."

A wrinkle formed across Sheila's forehead, "I know I love him, but he spends a lot of time alone with his journals." Her frown increased, "It's kind of disturbing. I mean, journals are great and all, but he's so dedicated...more like obsessed.

He can't get through a single day without spending time in isolation with his journals." She studied Lola's face, soliciting her opinion.

"Oh, don't let that bother you. Maybe that's how he sorts out his problems," Lola offered, hoping to encourage Sheila. "A lot of people do that sort of thing."

"Well, I hope it's not an indication of a lot of problems."

They both laughed.

"I'm just so curious about what he writes in them. And he's so protective of them. He doesn't accidentally leave them sitting around so it's impossible to *accidentally* find one and *accidentally* read one," Sheila said, unashamed.

"Sheila!" Lola giggled.

"I know. I'm bad, right?" Sheila laughed at herself.

"Maybe he's really writing a novel!" Lola's eyes sprung open with the notion.

"Who? Eddie?" Sheila quickly scoffed at the idea.

"You never know," Lola shrugged her shoulders.

Sheila looked up from the sink and stared at Lola through the mirror. "Wouldn't that be something...if he really was writing a novel?"

"I'm sure you'll find out someday." Lola reached for a towel and handed it to Sheila.

"Maybe. Anyway, you and Mike go have fun tonight and call me in the morning." Sheila grabbed the handle and opened the door.

Mike and Lola returned to the limo and continued their tour alone. He filled two glasses with club soda, dropped some lime into each glass and leaned against her. She looked up through the glass roof to see the night sky. "The stars seem to be following us."

"You like the stars, don't you?"

"Yes, I do. In fact, they are all *my* stars and nobody else's," Lola laughed at herself. "That is what my father used to tell me."

"Your pap was a good man, I can tell."

Lola nodded reflectively, "Yes, he was."

"I've got an idea." Mike picked up the phone and gave the chauffeur a new set of instructions.

In mere moments, Lola found herself on top of a darkened cliff above the ocean. Below her, she could hear the water breaking fiercely against the jagged rocks. Mike unfolded an old woolen blanket that he had pulled from the trunk of the limo and then guided her down beside him. "This is the best place to see the stars."

"It's magnificent," she exclaimed, burrowing her shoulder into his chest. "I'm happy to know such places exist outside of my imagination."

Mike looked up and spotted a star sliding across the sky, "Quick! Make a wish!"

Lola stared into the sky and made her wish.

"Well? What did you wish for?"

"I'm not telling," she smiled playfully.

Mike leaned in and kissed her and a moment later, she sighed, "It just came true."

He felt her smiling against his cheek, "I wonder what would happen if I made a wish."

She looked at him in the scant moonlight, "Judging by that grin on your face, it's best if you didn't make any wishes at all."

He laughed and pulled her closer to him.

His kisses were still on her mind when Lola awoke the next morning. The memory of the night before lingered as she snuggled his jacket, whispering, "I love you." Suddenly, the phone rang sharply, startling her. Clumsily, she picked it up, "Hello?"

"Good morning, love," his jolly voice broke the morning silence. "I have arranged for a picnic and was hoping you would join me."

"A picnic? I love picnics." She left out the part that she'd never been on a real picnic before, except for lunch in the park with her parents.

"Great. Can you be ready in an hour?"

"I can." Lola covered the mouthpiece and squealed in delight, not realizing Mike could hear her.

"I'll be in Pascal's room."

"All right." She quickly hung up the phone and hurried to the dresser noticing a photo of her mother that she had placed there when she unpacked her bags. Staring at the person inside the frame, she realized that she had been so wrapped up in Mike that she'd forgotten to phone her mother when they first arrived on the island. She picked up the phone, dialed the familiar number, and was saddened to leave only a message.

After a shower, Lola dressed in another new sundress, one Sheila had insisted was fabulous. She was now aware of Sheila's strategic motives that day in SAKS. *A lady must always be prepared.* She smiled to herself, warmed by her dear friend's intentions.

With fifteen minutes to spare before meeting Mike, she ran to the hotel gift shop and purchased specially selected treasures and a post card to send to her mother, as Christmas was only three days away. On the post card, she jotted down a tender message and detailed some of the events regarding her first night in Hawaii. Intentionally, she had excluded her involvement with Mike thinking that if she spoke too soon, she would jinx her happiness. It then occurred to her, as she affixed the stamp to the card that a little bit of Sheila had rubbed off on her. "Excuse me, ma'am," Lola leaned on the counter, "is it still possible to have these items delivered by Christmas?"

"Yes, we can overnight them. We can even gift wrap them here, if you would like," the friendly cashier suggested.

"Yes, I'd like that. The address is here on the post card." Lola handed over her debit card along with the post card. She was happy to be able to send some things to her mother in time for Christmas.

"All right, I'll take care of this right away." She returned Lola's bank card.

"Thank you very much and have a Merry Christmas!"

"You, too."

When Lola knocked on Pascal's door, Mike drew her in with his hands around her waist, kissing her all the way through the threshold. She was surprised by his public display of affection, but she couldn't resist him. "Oh, I missed you," he said, kissing her again.

Lola smiled awkwardly at Pascal.

"No worries. I just tried to tell him everything, but he was already on to us."

"Well, it wasn't hard," Pascal chuckled, sipping his coffee. "I trust you will behave yourself today?" He looked sternly at Mike through the rising steam over his cup.

Mike rolled his eyes and groaned, "Oh, here it comes."

"Lola, keep him in line. Mike can be a rascal at times," Pascal teased.

"Thank you, Pascal," Lola giggled, "I will."

"We'll be leaving now," Mike grumbled, taking Lola's hand. "Catch you later, mate."

"Take care of our girl."

Chapter Ten

"I've rented a Jeep, so that I can show you some great places here, far from the over-rated tourist scene. You've got to experience real Hawaii," Mike explained, as they waited for the elevator.

Lola secured herself inside the Jeep with the seatbelt and took notice of the huge basket sitting on the back seat that Mike had specially prepared for their picnic. She was moved by his personal efforts.

"Ready?" he asked excitedly.

"Yes," she answered in her usual exuberance.

Isolated, winding roads laced with lush greenery and scattered flowers led them to a place where they could picnic overlooking the ocean. "This is beautiful. How in the world did you ever find such a place?"

Mike only responded with a grin and that was good enough for Lola. He reached inside the basket and pulled out a smorgasbord he had packed at seven that morning. A bottle of sparkling cider accompanied by cheese, fruit, crusty bread, European chocolate and Hawaiian jerky sprawled across a beautiful red blanket. The creases of the new blanket were still stiff, making her smile as she imagined him standing in the store deliberating the theme of their picnic.

"When did you do all of this?"

"This morning," he seemed pleased with himself. "I hope you're hungry."

"Are you kidding? I'm starving."

"It's so refreshing to hear a lady admit that she's hungry. So many women are trying to be perfect that they think it's a personal flaw to be hungry." He shook his head.

"*Hmpf*, not me," she said, reaching for the jerky.

The hours passed away like minutes as they sat atop the grassy hill. "So, what do you want to do with your life," she asked, popping a chunk of pineapple into her mouth.

"I want to own my own boat some day and sail people all over the world. I love working for the captain, but my dream is to use all that he's taught me and do something with it...just as he expects me to."

"It sounds like a wonderful life." Her eyes squinted with another bite of the tart pineapple.

"I'm glad you think so." His happy eyes smiled back at her. He twisted and propped himself up on one elbow with his legs stretched out onto the grass behind him. "You know, I've saved a lot of money and I'm nearly ready to buy her. She's just waiting for me to finish a few more tours and then she's all mine."

"Tell me about her."

"She's magnificent, but she needs a little tender loving care. I'll take you to see her when we get to New Zealand."

"I can't wait. I bet she's a beautiful boat."

Mike nodded, "Aye, she is and she has a soul, too."

Lola was touched by his passion.

"My favorite passengers are those who have never sailed before or haven't wandered too far from their own backyards. It's fun to share in their first-time adventures. I'm not the lonely sailor type. I enjoy people…lot's of them. I even want to have a bunch of ankle biters someday. At least five."

"Oh, my! Five?" Lola's eyes rounded with delight and then she laughed hard.

"What?" Mike sat up, looking nearly insulted.

"Oh, I just got an image of you with five children dangling from your hips and elbows. It's a nice picture though."

Mike leaned back and studied her face, anticipating her opinion on the matter of children. "What about you? Do you like kids?"

"I adore children. I want plenty of them, too. I never had any brothers or sisters because my parents had me kind of late in life. They had tried for years and when they gave up trying…*Bam!* There I was. I was their miracle, as they had put it."

"Indeed, you are."

"Thank you," she smiled and stretched out on the blanket beneath the hovering clouds. The corners of the picnic blanket waved in the subtle breeze and clusters of trees rustled in the background. Lola inhaled nature's sweet aroma and sighed happily. "Never would I have imagined spending Christmas week on a beautiful hillside in sandals and a sundress." She sat up and sipped her cider, gazing at her pleasant surroundings. "Where I grew up, Christmas always came with snow, frosted trees and carolers bundled up in some kind of woolen garb." She stalled for a moment, lost in time. "It's magical," she said, highlighting her memories with a whisper.

"Do you miss it?"

"Not like I thought I would. I am having the time of my life."

"You know, not many people realize this, but in Australia, Christmas comes during our summer. I always pictured Father Christmas in a pair of sunglasses and swim trunks." Mike laughed at his childhood memory.

She smiled as she envisioned Mike as a small boy. "Have you ever experienced a white Christmas?"

"No, I haven't. Well, sort of," he corrected. "About five years ago I was held over on a plane in Denver and that's about as close as I've come." He hesitated for a moment, "Perhaps you could arrange a white Christmas for me?"

"I'd love to." She wiggled her toes, delighted by the idea. She had grown quite comfortable with Mike and ended up sharing with him her entire history. It was something she hadn't planned on doing quite so early in their relationship, fearing it would spoil things.

"When I first met you, I saw the sadness in your eyes, behind your smile. I'm really sorry for you, Lola. I know it was awful for you. When I was eleven, a drunk took my pap away from me. It was really hard on my mom and brother and me, but she did a fine job taking care of us, in spite of our loss. My dad was a good man. Everyone liked him." His voice became soft.

"I'm sure he was a great man. The apple doesn't fall far from the tree, you know. You honor him well."

"Thank you," he nodded. "I've made a few mistakes and have done some things that my pap wouldn't have liked," he confessed, grimacing playfully.

Lola chuckled and then her thoughts wandered. "A young boy shouldn't be without his father."

"Yeah, there are certain things a boy shouldn't learn from his mother, either!" He donned an expression of fright.

Lola laughed hard and smoothed the wayward hairs from his face. "What ever happened to the drunk?"

"Oh, he got two years in jail." Mike shook his head.

Lola gasped, "That's all? That's merely a slap on the wrist." Immediately, she searched his eyes, hoping she hadn't ignited an old hurt by her reaction.

Mike nodded, but was more interested in her story. "So, getting back to Sara, she's gotten away with being a monster her entire life because she's rich and pretty and then gets away with killing a guy and you're to blame?" He rubbed his jaw, mulling over all that Lola had told him.

"Essentially, yes. It was my fountain. That's all that everybody cared about. I know Sara didn't intend to kill anyone by rigging it. Her objective was to publicly humiliate me, but people died as a result of her menacing hands." Lola paused a moment and continued. "The town was so enamored by her beauty and her family's influence that the authorities never looked into my claims of sabotage. While Sara went on with her life, without conscience, her family threatened to drop a slander suit on us for my naming her the saboteur. She is so evil." Lola straightened and looked into his face. "Remember when we arrived at the hotel yesterday and suddenly I became ill?"

"Yes."

"Well, when I smelled all of those flowers, it just took me straight back to the awful night Joe died. I'm still working on erasing that part of my life. I guess it will just take some more time," she nodded, believing.

"Lola, I don't know if you'll ever be able to erase those horrific events of your life, but I do know, personally, that the pain will ease over time. First, allow yourself to forgive and then heal. That's important." He took her hand and squeezed it. "You're lucky that you remained so kind after living through all of that."

"Oh, but I wasn't for a long time. I vowed revenge to the fullest extent—next to murder," she confessed solemnly. Since her hospital stay, she'd never uttered a word of her plans to anyone. "And," she hesitated, "I was still planning to exact my revenge when I accepted this position. With help from a private investigator, I've been able to keep tabs on Sara and her friends no matter where I am. He's been emailing me updates every week."

"Really?"

"Yes." Lola bit her lip, waiting for his reaction to her shocking admission.

"You were pretty serious."

"Yes, I was. But it seems my need for vengeance has vanished." She felt completely restored by her new life.

"It's hard to imagine you so bitter." Mike's eyes rounded in empathy as he spoke. "There was a time where I wanted to annihilate the savage drunk that killed my pap," he admitted ashamedly and looked off into the distance.

"You did?" She was consoled by his unexpected confession.

"Yes," he looked into her eyes, "but then that beast would have taken two innocent lives; my father's and then ultimately my own. My pap wouldn't have wanted that and it would have been a cruel thing to do to my mother."

"Yes, you're right," she agreed strongly. She thought for a moment and was compelled to purge everything. "Sometimes I had attacks where my anger would ignite without warning and I immediately wanted to lash out and make her pay for all that she had done, regardless of the consequences." Lola sighed, "It's an incredible burden to harbor such hatred, as you well know."

"Yes, and an unnecessary burden," he emphasized.

Lola nodded in understanding. "I guess somewhere on this journey, I've finally figured out that Sara isn't worth it. Just like the drunk who killed your father."

"That's right. Sara isn't worth it," Mike stated firmly, knowing Lola still had a lot of healing to do. "Sara has nothing but venom hidden beneath her pretty exterior and if you allow it, she'll continue persuading you to swallow her poison, even now, when you're thousands of miles away."

"How did you get so smart?"

"Life has taught me a lot and I paid attention," he said soberly. "Sara lives in a miserable world and she carries with her a dreadful secret that will plague her throughout her life. She may pretend to be innocent, but she knows what happened. She'll never experience real peace or real joy that you will. That's all the revenge you need, Lola." Mike leaned back on the blanket and pulled her close to him and they both drifted off to sleep.

Suddenly, giant swords of lightning collided with a round of deafening thunder above the two sleeping bodies. "*Agh!*" Lola shrieked as she awakened to a violent storm.

Quickly, they scrambled to their feet and with one smooth stroke, she yanked the picnic basket and blanket from the ground and together they ran for the Jeep, laughing all the way.

"I love the rain," Lola squealed as she fastened the Jeep's tarp over the passenger side of the vehicle.

"Yeah! Me, too!" he shouted over the rumbling storm. "But I would have welcomed a wee bit of a warning."

"You got your warning with that first crash of thunder."

Mike blinked through the pelting rain to catch another glimpse of her. She was captivating.

"My side is on," she announced, jumping into the Jeep.

"I couldn't be more wet if I were in the shower," he commented, sliding into his Jeep seat.

Waves of goose bumps sprawled over her arms causing her to shiver.

He turned on the heater and shared his idea, "The hotel is at least an hour away, but there's a village just down the road where we can get some dry clothes. It's time you got yourself some real Hawaiian wear."

"Sounds good," she replied, not allowing her teeth to chatter. "Just make sure I don't look like a tourist trying to look like a native."

Swiftly, he gripped the handle and thrust the Jeep into gear. Moments later, a road brought them to the small village nestled among the trees. An elderly shopkeeper greeted them at the door with a warm smile as they stepped inside the small boutique. "Welcome. How may I help you?" she asked with a hint of her island tongue.

"We're in dire need of some dry clothes." Mike peeled his damp shirt away from his skin.

"I see that," the friendly shopkeeper replied, noting their situation.

"Lola, she'll take good care of you. I'll just grab something from over here."

"Come with me," the shopkeeper instructed. Her hair was handsomely woven in a long braid down her back. Lola admired the elegant tress as she followed her to a rack of dresses.

On the other side of the small boutique, Mike poked around a few racks and made a hasty selection before making his way to the fitting room.

With a confident smile, the shopkeeper held up a navy blue form-fitted dress, embellished with tiny white flowers. "You like this?"

"That one is very nice. I'll take it." Lola reached for the dress and a few minutes later, she emerged from the fitting room. She was striking, leaving Mike speechless. Her thick, damp hair hung loosely around her face making her look even more beautiful to him. Exotic.

He cast a slow gaze over her, "Well, I see you didn't need my help after all."

"I take it you approve then?" she asked, intentionally flirting with him.

"Approve? That's an understatement."

She chuckled and looked into her purse for her wallet.

"No, this dress is my gift to you," he insisted, pulling a white flower from a basket on the counter and placing it in her hair.

"No, you've done so—"

"I want to," he interrupted, "you know, as sort of a keepsake commemorating this special day."

She hugged him and forced back the urge to tell him that she loved him. "Thank you."

"You're welcome." He turned toward the shopkeeper and placed his check card down onto the counter, "We'll take the flower, too."

On the drive back to the hotel, Lola gazed at Mike several times and patted his leg to make sure that he was real and not merely a creation brought forth from her fantasies. Still, she found it hard to believe that this man was in her life, adoring her.

While Mike parked the Jeep, Lola walked the flowered path to the hotel doors where she met Sheila sitting on the bench beneath the awning. Sheila stood up, smiling. "We were hoping that you two were still going to join us tonight."

"Yes, I'm glad we made it back in time." Lola took a seat on the bench. "It's amazing how fast time goes here," she shook her head in wonder.

"It has a way of doing that," Sheila giggled and sat back down beside Lola.

"We had a picnic in the most wonderful place. It was awesome." Lola's eyes sprung wide open. "And I didn't even mind the rain."

"You got caught in that storm?"

"Yes, we did, but check out my new dress." She stood up and twirled. "Mike gave it to me."

"It's gorgeous." Sheila's eyes lit up.

"Thank you," Lola sighed, almost feeling guilty for being so happy.

"I've missed you," said Nora, walking up the path toward them.

Lola hugged the elderly woman, "I've missed you, too."

"I hear you've been taking in all of the sites."

"Yes, I have and I'm having a wonderful time." Lola smiled at Nora, hinting to her that she'd taken her advice.

The three walked toward the limousine where Mike and Eddie were already waiting with the others. Nora stopped and looked at Lola, "I like your dress."

Lola grinned, "It was a gift from Mike."

Saying nothing, Nora smiled and turned back toward the limo.

"Sheila, it's me," Lola announced, tapping on Sheila's door the next morning.

"Come in."

Lola pushed the door open that was propped open with a shoe. Sheila was standing in the bathroom pulling her hair up in a ponytail.

"Well, do I look ready to go Christmas shopping?" Lola twirled in her shorts and sandals.

"You're really enjoying the climate here, aren't you?"

116

"Yes, I am," Lola replied, sitting on Sheila's bed. "It's a beautiful day and I'm determined to finish my shopping by lunch time."

Sheila popped her head around the door, "You really think you can?"

"Of course! I made a list." Cheerfully, she waved a page that she had yanked from her planner. "And with you and Nora as my guides, I won't waste any time at all."

Sheila smiled and worked some hand cream into her hands before turning off the bathroom light. "Have the guys left to play golf yet?"

"Yes, a while ago."

"That's a sport I should really try some time. It just never looked appealing on TV, so I never considered it. But, now, I'm thinking I'm interested...it's a healthy activity."

"Well, I know Eddie sure enjoys it," Lola teased.

"I see...you're on to me."

"I am," she grinned. "If you want, I'll take lessons with you and when Eddie invites you to golf with him, you'll look like a pro."

"Would you? That's a great idea." Sheila hesitated for a moment, thinking. "All right, when we get to New Zealand, you and I are taking those lessons. But let's not tell the guys."

"Never!"

After visiting every store within walking distance of the hotel, Nora was spent and decided it was time to call for the limousine. She spotted a sidewalk bench, placed her bags down beside it, and planted herself in the center of the bench before phoning the driver. "We'll wait here for the limo," she said, puffing slightly from fatigue.

Sheila opened a new pack of gum and sat down next to Nora.

"I've been wondering, what are the Christmas plans?" Lola asked.

"We reserved a gathering room in the hotel for the festivities." Nora's eyes brightened as she spoke. "They always prepare such a nice banquet during the holidays."

"That sounds really nice." Lola leaned back and allowed the sun to rest on her face.

"Next Christmas, you'll have the opportunity to meet my entire family. This year they are spending Christmas with their in-laws. But next year, they're all mine," she laughed deviously.

Lola and Sheila laughed at the endearing woman. "I'm looking forward to meeting them." Lola was careful not to divulge the fact that she'd already spoken to one of Nora's daughter's. Together, they were working in secret on gifts for Bill and Nora.

The chauffeur pulled up and loaded their bags into the trunk. Lola stood beside the automobile and studied the driver, noticing that it was always him on duty, both day and night. Broad shoulders carried his tall frame while spikes of gray hair sprouted from his temples. Dark glasses always concealed his eyes, creating more mystery. His few words were deliberate and woven together tightly with a heavy accent. Lola wouldn't consider him rude, but she wouldn't call him friendly either. Something about him disturbed her, but she couldn't put her finger on it.

"Goodness, Nora, are all of those yours?" Bill poked his nose into one of the bags as the ladies entered Nora's suite.

"Now, get your snout out of that bag, there just might be something in there for you." Nora huffed.

They all laughed and looked at Bill adoringly.

"Well, I guess I'd better get to my wrapping." Lola picked up her bags.

"I'm sure Bill would love to help you wrap all of those gifts," Sheila grinned, gently nudging Bill in the ribs on her way out the door.

Lola and Shelia rode the elevator together until the floors separated them, sending each to their suites.

"Hello, Mom? It's me," Lola's fingers played with the telephone cord.

"Lola!" Her mother sounded excited.

"Did I wake you?"

"No, I'm just watching an old movie. It's so nice to hear your voice. Are you having a good time?"

"I am having the most exciting time of my entire life. This island is glorious."

"I'm so happy to hear that," Lola could hear the cheer in her mother's voice.

"I sent you a package yesterday, so you should be receiving it soon."

"I just got it this morning. Thank you, they are the most extraordinary cookies I've ever had. I'm going to try and figure out the recipe and make them for the folks at the senior center."

"*Huh?* Cookies? I didn't send any cookies. Does it say who sent them?"

"Well, the card reads, 'From Mike, Lola and the rest of the gang.' By the way, who's Mike, again?"

Only the most wonderful man in the world. "Oh, he's the captain's first mate," she said casually.

"Oh, that's right. Pardon me," she giggled, "it's hard to keep up with everyone."

"No problem. I'll tell Mike and the gang that you liked the cookies." They chatted for nearly an hour before Lola wrapped up the conversation with plans of meeting her mother in New Zealand in the coming months.

When Lola hung up the phone, she turned on the radio clock and fidgeted with the dial until she came to a station that played Christmas music. Satisfied, she looked over the gifts that she had spread out across the bed while talking with her mother.

Chapter Eleven

"Silver Bells" played on the alarm radio the next morning, pulling Lola out of a heavy sleep. Merrily, she hummed along with the popular tune as she made her way to the shower.

When he arrived, a half hour later, Lola swung the door open and eagerly invited Mike in with a kiss.

"I see you're wide awake and bushy tail this morning."

"I am," she beamed, happy to see him. "So, where are we going today?"

"Paradise."

You are paradise. "I've never been there before. Is it far?"

Mike chuckled at her joke. "Maybe an hour and bring a jacket this time…a waterproof one."

"All right, I'll go get it." She headed toward the bedroom, "Come with me."

He followed her into the room, "They're not calling for any rain today, but where we're going, you might need it."

"It sounds intriguing." She pulled a jacket from the drawer and tossed it over her shoulder. His striking image reigned inside the mirror, gripping her heart when their eyes mingled inside the reflection.

"Stop being so irresistible," he warned, "we've got things to do today and you're seriously threatening my good intentions."

"Am I?" she asked playfully.

"Yes," he said, directing them toward the corridor.

She laughed and took his hand.

White water rushed down a massive hillside dividing an emerald blanket of foliage that surrounded a few jagged cliffs. At the base of this grandeur was a natural pool of water that churned with ferocity, spraying a mist upon Lola's face. She looked at the scattered ferns and wild flowers that wandered aimlessly throughout the flourishing terrain. Softly, she spoke so as not to bruise nature's majesty, "Mike, you *have* discovered paradise." She spun around in all directions to capture nature's abounding gifts. "I think I've seen this waterfall in a picture somewhere," she whispered. "And here I am beside it."

"I knew you'd love it." He took in the scenery around them.

"It's magnificent." Her eyes couldn't take it all in fast enough.

He smiled back at her and found a clearing where they could see the tumbling water spill from the earth's mouth. He spread the red blanket on the ground and emptied the picnic basket. This time he brought turkey on wheat bread sandwiches, fruit and soda. "And for dessert," he announced, rubbing his belly, "we have chocolate chip cookies with macadamia nuts." He waved the hand-wrapped package of cookies in front of her eyes.

"They're huge!" Lola reached for the cookies to inspect them. "Where did you get these?"

"There's a little bakery in town that specializes in cookies. These are my favorite, but I warn you, they are addicting."

She peeled the plastic away from a cookie and took a bite. "Oh, these are deadly." Lola brushed the crumbs from her lips. "Thanks for introducing me to my new weakness."

"My pleasure," he grinned.

"These are the cookies that she was talking about."

"Who?"

"My mother. Last night she told me about the cookies you sent. Are these what she was talking about?"

"Yes, they are. She already got them?" He seemed surprised.

"Yes. And she went on an on about them, telling me how great they were. Thank you." Lola leapt across the blanket and showered him with kisses.

He looked up into her eyes, again lost in her magic. Mike knew he couldn't resist her another second, so he rolled over and invited her to eat with him. "Here, have a *sanger* before we get into trouble," he countered.

"A *sanger*?"

"Yeah. A sandwich."

"Of course...I knew that." She rolled her eyes and took the sandwich out of the paper wrapping. "With you, everything looks better, smells better, and tastes better. That could be disastrous for me. I could gain a ton of weight."

121

"I wouldn't care."

"Well, thank you, but I used to be rather large. I lost some tonnage before coming here and I intend to keep it off. So, if you don't mind, please stop making everything so wonderful," she begged in jest.

"All right, I'll try." He thought for a moment. "Tonnage?"

"Yes, I lost over forty pounds before I arrived in San Diego." She waited for his reaction.

"Really?"

She nodded with some reluctance.

He snapped another bite off a cookie, "You are one strong woman and that makes me a very lucky man."

Lola smiled, feeling better than she had ever felt in her entire life. "Thank you."

A few hours had passed when Mike looked at his watch, "I have something else planned, so we'd better get moving."

Lola looked around her newly found paradise, almost sad to leave it. "What did you have in mind?"

"Nope, you'll have to wait and see."

After returning to the hotel, Mike ordered a pizza from room service while Lola went to her room to change her clothes and check in with Sheila. On the third ring, Sheila picked up, "Hello?"

"Hello, Sheila?"

"Hi!"

"I just wanted to check in and see how things are going…with Eddie." Lola clarified in a softer voice.

"Just fine," Sheila turned away from Eddie's glimpse. "We're just fixing to leave for dinner right now."

Lola could hear the smile in Sheila's voice. "Are just you and Eddie going?"

"Yes, that's right."

Sheila's short answers indicated that she was trying to camouflage the topic of their conversation.

"Is he with you now?" Lola whispered into the phone.

"Absolutely."

Lola giggled, "I'll let you go, but call me later."

"I will."

Lola hung up the phone and moved over toward the dresser. With Eddie and Sheila going to dinner alone, she felt more hopeful. Perhaps they'll finally put their political differences aside and admit that they are crazy about each other.

Mike met Lola in the hallway with a steaming box of pizza propped in his left arm and a six pack of RC COLA dangling from his right pinky finger.

"Looks like fun. What are we doing?"

"We're having dinner on the beach and I've arranged for the sunset to be our guest."

"Oh, you have?" She was charmed by his whimsical side. "You are just full of surprises," she told him, relieving his pinky of the soda.

From the blanket, Mike and Lola gazed into the distance, pleasuring in nature's sweet opulence. Salmon-colored ribbons spanned across the painted sky as the sun slowly melted into the diamond-studded waters. She leaned against his shoulder as the tide rippled toward her, unthreatening. "Thank you for sharing all of this with me and for showing me the way." Lola turned in his arms and kissed him as the final ray of light disappeared beneath the horizon.

"I love you," he whispered.

She held her breath as if to hold his words inside her forever. "I love you, too," she released with a gentle breath.

"When I first saw you," he said, looking into her eyes, "I instantly knew that my life was going to change course and that you were at the helm. Your pretty smile triggered something powerful in me. It's like you woke me up from a long sleep." He brushed her cheek with his hand and smiled, "Thank *you*."

They basked in their tender proclamations for a while before Mike looked at his watch and presented an idea. "There's a Christmas Eve service going on at the church in just a little while. You had mentioned that you used to do that with your parents, so I thought it was something we should do. You know, keep the tradition."

"I'd love to." He was everything she needed. Her heart nearly burst with happiness as so many good things kept coming her way.

"Good evening, Mike. What can I do for you?" Bill spoke in his jovial voice, welcoming Mike and Lola into his suite.

123

"We'd like to invite you and Nora to the Christmas Eve service at St. Peter's tonight. There's still time to make it, if you would like to join us."

"Sounds like a smart idea, Mike," Nora quickly interjected, grabbing her purse. "I'm ready right now. Come on Bill."

Bill laughed at his adorable wife of forty-five years. "Let's go."

"Everyone is meeting us in the lobby," Lola explained, taking Nora's hand. Moments later, the entire group, including Pascal, whom Lola once considered a heathen, was strolling down the sidewalk toward the old cathedral.

Hundreds of candles flickered inside the beautiful sanctuary while the choir sang traditional Christmas hymns from the balcony above her. For a moment, Lola returned to her childhood where she remembered sitting beside her father on Christmas Eve in their favorite pew. He would sing loudly, deep from his soul. Though he could never carry the proper tune, it never stopped him. At the time, Lola snickered at her father's inadequacy, but she had since grown to cherish the special memory. She looked around the church noticing all of the people around her singing along with the choir. She wondered if they were all as happy as she was. She hoped they were.

Very early the next morning, an urgent knocking on Lola's door stirred her from a sound sleep. She staggered to the door and opened it without thinking to put on her robe. Still groggy, she blinked her eyes to focus on the blurry figure at her door.

With a cup of coffee in his hand, Mike stood beaming at the beautiful image standing innocently before him. Her hair was tousled and stiff with hair spray. Dark smudges of makeup, articulating distinct characteristics of a raccoon, circled her eyes. And to complete the lovely ensemble, she wore only a drowsy smile and an oversized t-shirt.

"Merry—"

"*Agh!*" She shrieked, slamming the door in his face after suddenly realizing her appearance.

"Too late," he called out through the door, amused.

Lola scrambled around her room searching for her robe when she caught her unsightly reflection in the mirror. Even without her contacts in place, she could see that she was a mess. Horrified, she darted to the bathroom for a washcloth to remove remnants, of the night before, from her face. After a quick brushing to her tangled hair, she slipped on the robe that had been dangling elusively behind the bathroom door.

Again, Mike bared his handsome grin when she opened the door. "Now, what was that all about? I mean, really…shutting the door in my face." He attempted a pitiful expression, but he couldn't pull it off without laughing.

Lola's forehead rippled as images of herself paraded through her mind, mocking her.

He leaned in and kissed her on the neck, "Don't worry, love, your secret is safe with me. I won't tell another soul just how lovely you are in the morning."

His sensual voice in her ear caused her to feel warm and dizzy. She could almost forgive him.

"Merry Christmas!" he finally announced, handing her the coffee that he had brought for her.

"And Merry Christmas to you." She followed him to the sofa. "Thanks for the coffee," I could really use it this morning."

"My pleasure."

She breathed in its robust aroma before taking a sip.

"The reason I'm here so early this morning is that I am hungry and would like to know if you would join me for breakfast." Breakfast wasn't the only thing he had planned, rather, he had something very special to tell her and he couldn't wait a minute longer.

"Breakfast sounds great. Just give me a minute and I'll be ready." Her brilliant eyes smiled back at him. "For the record, I was going to set my alarm extra early and bounce *you* out of bed. But, regrettably, I didn't hit the right switch." Her smile bent.

"I'm not disappointed," he grinned, handing her his key. "Come down to my room when you're ready."

She smiled at him, "I'll only be a few minutes."

When Lola stepped into the corridor, she paused, deciding to take Mike's gift with her. The Christmas party was some hours away and she didn't think she could wait that long.

"Mike?" she called out, entering his suite for the first time. It was just like hers except his was designed in a dark blue and green motif. Out on the terrace was a beautifully arranged table with crystal goblets and platters of food hidden beneath shimmering lids. An alluring bouquet of exotic looking flowers sat proudly in the center of the table, calling her attention. She leaned in toward the many flowers and closed her eyes to fully absorb the aromatic gifts swirling around the delicate petals.

Gently, he kissed the back of her head when he came up behind her. "Those flowers are called Anthuriums," he pointed to a coral heart shaped flower with a distinct stem protruding from the center. "They are known as the heart of Hawaii."

"I've never seen anything like these before. They're so unique, yet elegant."

"Surprisingly, they aren't native to Hawaii. They actually came from Colombia."

"Really?" Lola took a second look.

"*Uh-hum.*" He pulled a chair out for her to sit in as he continued, "An English missionary brought them over during the late 1880s. I just think they are cool flowers and I thought you'd like them, too."

"I do," she nodded, still admiring them.

He took his seat beside her, "You look beautiful."

"Thank you," she laughed, "that means a lot considering my appearance only a bit ago."

"You were gorgeous then, too." He smiled at her with those eyes that looked right through her.

She found it very hard to think clearly when he looked at her that way. His inebriating charm left her feeling loopy. She needed to switch gears. "I've decided to forgive you for catching me in that dreadful state earlier," she declared in a composed manner.

"Oh, you have?" he laughed. "I'm glad to hear that."

She straightened herself in her chair and looked over the table. Something was forthcoming, she sensed, though she had no clue as to what it was. "What do we have under here?" She lifted a lid to reveal a steaming platter of sausages, eggs and fried potatoes. Beneath the other lid was a fruit platter that made Lola's stomach growl loudly.

Mike filled the goblets with orange juice and set the pitcher onto the table. He lifted his glass and, following his gesture, she lifted hers. "Here's to us," he said, "and a very Merry Christmas." Their glasses chimed together in harmony, just as their souls did.

When they finished breakfast, Mike cleared the dishes from the table and placed them on the tray out in the corridor. He returned to the table where Lola was seated and he reached inside his pocket. "Lola, I know we've only—" Suddenly, his telephone rang harshly, bringing his plan to an abrupt halt. "Excuse me," he said with an awkward grin. "Hello? What? Are you messing with me? All right, Captain, I'll be right there. Remember, don't touch anything." Mike dropped the phone back into its cradle.

"What's the matter?"

"Somebody has broken into the yacht. The captain doesn't think anything was taken, but we should get down there right away."

"All right, you head down there now and the rest of us will meet you there."

He kissed her goodbye and dashed out the door.

Lola returned to her room and placed Mike's gift back into her drawer before picking up the phone. "Sheila? Did you hear?" Lola listened carefully as Sheila shared the details regarding the break-in. Have you spoken to Bill and Nora yet? All right, we'll meet you in the lobby."

Within a half hour, Lola and the others arrived at the harbor. "Nothing appears to be taken or vandalized except for the broken window to the salon," Eddie explained.

"I want you all to check your quarters to make sure that your things are in place," Captain Andre advised as he moved farther out on deck. "It's obvious that somebody has been here, though we're still not exactly sure what the purpose of their trespass was. Everything appears to be fine."

"Maybe it was just some rowdy kids looking for a place to party or something," Sheila suggested.

"Yeah, well they'll rue the day they stepped onto this boat when I catch them," Pascal growled.

"I'm sure they were just some bored kids," Lola interjected, trying to shrug off the disturbing thoughts that arrived with the alarming news of the break-in.

Bill and Nora returned to the deck stating that all was fine in their suite. Lola observed them protectively and decided that they had taken the startling news quite well. In fact, better than she had.

Before finishing his report, Officer Luna turned to Captain Andre, "You stated earlier that all firearms are accounted for?"

"Yes," Captain Andre reaffirmed, "and the cabinet was still locked when I arrived."

"All right," said Officer Luna. "Don't hesitate to call me if you make further discoveries or have anymore problems. Sorry about the fingerprint dust. My men were all over this boat." He placed his card in the captain's hand before leaving.

"Well, there's nothing more we can do here. Let's go back to the hotel and celebrate Christmas as planned, the captain suggested.

A few hours after the discovery of the break-in, Bill and Nora greeted nearly all of their guests at the door to the banquet hall. Dozens of candles flickered merrily throughout the room and evergreen centerpieces sprawled the tables, accentuating the festive theme.

When Lola arrived, only a few minutes late, she was wearing her new black dress with green embellishments. Her hair was done up in a classic twist and a faux diamond necklace sparkled around her neck, adding to her elegance. She stood near the doorway talking to Bill and Nora while Mike sat at the table engaged in conversation with Eddie and Sheila. In the background, he heard Lola laugh and his gaze found her. She was stunning, again stopping his breath. Patiently, he waited for her to join him as he tried to catch up to the ongoing discussion at the table.

Sheila wore the blue dress that Lola had given her. She was striking, Lola thought to herself, taking her seat. Apparently Eddie thought so, too as his eyes remained steadily on Shelia. Lola also noticed that Eddie seemed different. Perhaps even, exuberant. His enthusiasm had illuminated the whole table, causing Lola to ponder his lighter mood.

Conversation and laughter filled the room as they ate their Christmas dinner. Lola was in love with all of them. She had come to trust every one of them and she couldn't imagine her life without them.

When first arriving in San Diego, Lola realized that Pascal was the hardest to get to know. He was a pleasant fellow, but he never had much to say. Prior to setting sail, Pascal and Lola hadn't much in common and their conversations were few, but on the ocean, he flourished. While teaching her to fish, he inadvertently revealed more of his congenial nature. He was entertaining and shared fascinating stories about his nomadic life. His next move was always random, never planned, though he remained fully committed to Captain Andre and the crew for the time being. Contentedly, Pascal lived his life minute-by-minute and he was comfortable with himself, not caring what people thought about him. He had taught Lola how to fish off the boat and she treasured the days he had spent with her, patiently baiting her hook until she finally got the nerve to do it herself. When she made her first big catch, he was more proud than she was and offered to remove the hook himself, sparing her the unpleasant task.

Eddie was friendly, but oftentimes distracted. His periods of solitude suggested mystery, always piquing Lola's curiosity, but she liked him. She didn't consider him moody, but he would disappear for significant blocks of time, usually at least a couple of hours each day and several times she observed him working by flashlight on deck scribbling in his journals when he was supposed to be sleeping. It was an unspoken rule that seemed to be understood by all that no one should disturb him during his quiet episodes. Lola respected his privacy, but harbored hope of unfolding the mystery some day.

Her reflections turned toward the ever compassionate Captain Andre, a very wise man, who possessed an innate desire to help others. His unending kindness, uninterrupted by his profound wealth, inspired Lola. She knew that she was, truly, in good hands.

When the staff came to clear the dishes, everyone gathered on the large sofas near the Christmas tree to share their gifts. Saving Mike's gift for last, Lola gave Pascal seven brand new baseball caps with new fishing lures fastened to each—to replace the ones she had lost during her first few days at sea. For Eddie, she wrapped tablets of paper that matched his journals and included a pack of his favorite style of pens. Captain Andre was the most difficult of all, she discovered early on. What do you give a man who has everything? She had wondered, but the answer came to her one morning in November when she saw a stylish frame inside a shop window. A group photo of his current crew would look nice in the frame, she had decided. Lola found a complete DVD collection of culinary classes from French cuisine to backyard barbeques for Sheila and for Bill and Nora, who were smitten with their ever-growing family, she had photos of all their grandchildren printed onto several t-shirts. Lola smiled as she looked around the room, realizing the magic of Christmastime had returned.

Eddie handed Sheila his gift while the others watched.

"Wow, this is heavier than it looks," Sheila commented, taking it from his hands. She tugged on the gold ribbon and loosened the lid. Inside the box was Eddie's mystery about to be revealed.

"Eddie? You want me to read your journals?" She appeared most bewildered.

"Yes," he chuckled, "actually, they aren't journals as I've led you all to believe," he cleared his throat. "It's a novel."

"Are you serious?" Sheila pulled the tablets from the box. He nodded.

"Thank you," Sheila clutched the tablets. "What's it about?" she asked, opening the top tablet.

"You'll find out soon enough."

"See? I told you, Sheila." Lola blurted excitedly.

"Yes, you did." She turned back to Eddie, "We were trying to figure out what the heck you were writing in these things."

"I'm sure I caused a bit of conversation," he laughed. "Well, now you all know what I've been up to. I couldn't have you all thinking that I'm the dark and brooding type for too much longer," he joked.

Sheila and Lola looked at each other and burst out laughing and then Sheila burrowed her eyes into the handwritten words scribbled across the opening page.

"Hey, Eddie, when do the rest of us get to read it?"

"I didn't know you could read, Mike." Pascal teased.

"Ignore him, Lola." Mike shook his head in mild annoyance.

"May I take a quick peek at it?" Nora asked.

"Certainly," Eddie gestured with a tip of his head.

The captain shifted on the sofa so he could read along with Nora.

All eyes rested on Nora, awaiting her initial feedback. The room was quiet, only the shuffling of a few pages and "Carol of the Bells" were heard.

Nervously, Eddie sat like a cold stone with his hands folded tightly, nearly cutting off the circulation to his fingers as fresh eyes scrolled the first few pages. Regret for publicly introducing his novel toyed with him as he immediately began to question his literary ability. Eddie hadn't anticipated everyone's interest and he suddenly felt naked among them.

Finally, Nora looked up and slowly removed her glasses.

Eddie held his breath and hoped the others didn't sense his unease.

"Eddie, I think you should have someone take a look at this. And, it just so happens, that I have a friend in the business. If you'd like, I could arrange a meeting for you. Of course, after Sheila's done reading it." Nora smiled.

"I'd like that very much, thank you."

Lola reached for Mike's gift and placed it in his hand. "This is for you."

"What could possibly be in here?" He gently shook the box with wonder-filled eyes. "I have a prezzy for you, too, but I forgot it in my room." He lied. It was tucked safely inside his jacket pocket, but he decided not to put Lola on the spot in front of everyone. "It's just a little something that had your name all over it." His eyes flickered with mystery.

She smiled back at him, wondering what it could be.

Mike looked down at the blue box in his hands, untied the silver ribbon, and peeled away the paper. Inside was a handsomely crafted sextant with an inscription that read, "*May*

131

Your Journeys Always Lead to Health, Love, Happiness and Prosperity, Love Always, Lola." His eyes focused on the fine instrument and then he read the inscription again. "Lola, this is ace," he said sincerely. He held it up to his face and peered through a small hole. "Captain, you've got to take a look at this." Mike turned to Lola and hugged her.

Captain Andre reached for the gem and after reading the inscription; he smiled and nodded approvingly at Lola.

Chapter Twelve

Torrential rains arrived the morning after Christmas, leaving Mike and Lola to wait out the storm in his suite. "Want some more coffee?" he asked, rising from the sofa.

"Please," she handed him her cup.

A gleam appeared in his eye when he returned. He was imagining bringing her coffee every morning for the rest of his life. He liked the idea and he could hardly wait to give her his gift, but he had decided to wait until New Year's Eve.

"What are you up to?" she asked, noticing the extra glimmer in his eyes.

"I'm just very happy." He blew into his coffee cup and took his spot beside her.

"Me, too," she sighed, leaning up against him. The ocean churned with intensity as another round of thunder rolled through the room. "That storm is pretty angry about something." She was glad that she wasn't out on the boat.

"It just looks meaner than it really is."

"Have you been in worse storms at sea?"

"Sure, many times," he stated with a bit of pride. "You don't have anything to worry about," he added, eyeing her concerned expression. "We're all quite acquainted with Mother Nature's temper."

His confidence was comforting, but something was still bothering her.

"Are you worried about storms while we're out at sea?"

"Maybe...I'm not really sure what's bugging me today. Have you ever had that feeling that something bad is about to happen?"

"Sometimes. Do you feel that way now?"

"I think so," she said, confused by her thoughts.

"Maybe the break-in caused you to feel unsettled," he suggested.

She nodded, thinking. "Actually, I've had this feeling for a few days, but it does seem stronger since the break-in."

Mike glanced at the window, considering what she had told him.

"It's probably nothing," she shook her head, deciding to dismiss her worry.

"Well, just in case, we'll be extra cautious." He took her hand and held it.

"Thank you for not thinking I'm crazy or anything."

"I could never think that." He leaned in for a kiss and grumbled when his phone rang. "Hello? Hi, Sheila. Yes, she's here. Hold on a second."

"Hey, what's up?" After a moment, Lola hung up the phone and explained to Mike that Sheila was ready to clean the ship and buy the rest of the supplies.

"Duty calls," he said, somewhat reluctantly.

"That's right," she giggled, stealing a kiss on the run.

The storm had cleared by the time Lola and Sheila arrived at the yacht with the food and other supplies. After they had cleaned the entire vessel, Sheila made a pot of coffee and poured two cups. She sat down in the galley and released a long sigh. "I'm wiped out. With the shopping and the extra cleaning from the fingerprint dust, I'm really spent."

Lola leaned against the counter, "Yeah, I'm feeling it, too." She sipped her coffee and stirred a teaspoon of sugar into her cup. "So, tell me about Eddie's book."

"The only thing I will tell you is that I love it. I don't want you to have any fixed ideas about it, so that's all I'm going to say about it right now."

"I understand...sort of."

"We were up until midnight talking about it," Sheila yawned. "He said that I was his muse. Imagine that! And, apparently, I'm pretty good at it."

Lola chuckled, "I'm not surprised." Her eyes reflected her happiness for Sheila. A patrol boat sped through the water, catching their attention. "It's kind of eerie being here knowing that a stranger was here." Lola looked around warily, wishing she could forget the break-in.

Sheila stood up and refilled her cup. "Yeah, I know. Captain slept here last night. He had hoped to catch the little monsters in case they returned. This whole thing has set him off pretty good. Do you want some more coffee?"

"No thanks," Lola put her cup down. "We'll be leaving day after tomorrow, so we won't have to worry about intruders

134

much longer." Her eyes wandered to the newly replaced window in the salon. "I'm sure having a great time here."

"Me, too. I'd have to say that this has been the best trip ever." Sheila rinsed her cup and looked at her watch. "Bill and Nora are joining us for dinner in a bit. We're going back to THE ORCHID."

"I love that place."

"You should wear that black dress. You know...the one that held you prisoner with the clasp? Mike won't be able to keep his eyes off you. Not that he can now, but this will truly punish him." Sheila flashed a fiendish grin.

"Sheila!"

Early next morning, Mike knocked on Lola's door and when she opened it, he stood gleaming in the corridor, "Good morning, love, we have a full—"

"Good morning to you," she interrupted, leading him in with a long awaited kiss.

Her zealous greeting left him dazed for a moment before his faculties fully returned, "As I was saying," he sputtered, "the boat is all ready for launch, so we have the entire day together."

Her beauty captivated him again, leaving him in a daze. He liked it.

"What are we doing today? And whatever it is, I'm paying," she stated.

"No, ma'am. It's my privilege to pay for such pleasures."

"No, I think I should share in that as well," she protested more firmly. "I won't go anywhere with you unless I get to pay." Stubbornly, she stiffened and folded her arms.

"Now, isn't this delightful?" he declared in his best charming manner.

"Isn't what delightful?" Lola was suddenly confused.

"Our first quarrel. I'll remember it always." He placed his hand over his heart in dramatic fashion.

"Oh, Mike," she laughed, thrusting herself into his arms.

"I thought we'd have breakfast down in the restaurant, then head to the beach for a bit and then the captain has arranged for all of us to go snorkeling later."

"Good, then I'll pay for breakfast," she giggled.

Mike smiled back in defeat.

"Let me just get my bathing suit on." She dashed to the bedroom for her white one-piece and skirt. "I've never snorkeled before!" she called out from the bedroom. "I've always wanted to do that."

"You're in for something special."

After breakfast, they wandered to the beach where Mike demonstrated his creative abilities with sand and water. When his castle was finished, it stood nearly three feet tall and four feet wide. With a stick, he carefully applied architectural details for the windows and doors to his monument. "There," he said with hefty satisfaction, "it's done."

Lola studied his castle with a pleasing but careful eye. "It's magnificent. But it needs one thing." She jumped to her feet and grabbed a pale.

Inquisitively, he looked over his masterpiece, "What else could it possibly need?"

"You'll see." From the green patch, just yards away, she collected a pale full of weeds and other scattered variants of wild vegetation. "No castle is complete without a garden of some sort," she stated upon returning. She knelt down into the sand and thoughtfully placed sprigs of greenery around his castle. "There, now it's done."

"Yes, much better." He surveyed his castle. His head bobbed up and down and then from side to side, examining every angle of the castle.

Lola looked on curiously. "What are you doing?"

"This here," he pointed to the highest tower of the castle and studied her face like a child does when they have something important to say, "will be our room."

Her stomach spun with the meaning of his statement. "I think that's the best place, too."

"He stood up and brushed the sand from his hands and knees. "What time is it?"

"Eleven."

"The captain will be ready to go soon. You're going to love snorkeling. It's an entirely different world down there."

"I'm looking forward to it." Lola picked up the blanket and folded it before gathering up their *toys*. "Wait, I want to take a picture of the castle. Go over there and stand right next to it. Nope, a little closer," she instructed with a wave of her hand. "There, that's better. Ready?"

"Stop!" he blurted. "Set the timer and we'll both get in on the shot."

Captain Andre had enlisted the expertise of a local snorkeling association to guide Lola through her first underwater expedition. She listened carefully as the tour master stood upon the rugged beach explaining the dos and don'ts of marine exploration. He led Pascal, Sheila and Eddie into the water and then Captain Andre, Mike and Lola.

A new world gracefully emerged when Lola slipped below the azure surface into a fluid tapestry, rich with electric color that revealed some of nature's prized assets. Calming ripples trailed her movements as a dead silence filled her ears. Schools of friendly fish swam past her face, undisturbed by her presence. Their swiveling fins lured her to follow until they vanished inside the cerulean empire. Cautious sea creatures, with bulging eyes, studied her as she floated past their modest dwellings and thriving below her weightless body was another variant of sea life that brandished sturdy blossoms of vibrant yellow, pink and red tendrils. Using her new underwater camera, a Christmas gift from the captain, she collected several mementos of her first underwater adventure. As she swam farther out, curious black-and-white striped fish popped in and out of hiding to get a better view of her, while other bashful sea critters sped away quickly. Mike reached for her hand and pointed out a lonely turtle wandering aimlessly near the ocean's surface. Probably searching for a mate, Lola decided. Her eyes followed the roving turtle until the murky distance swallowed him.

The hour-long excursion expired when the tour guide pointed to his watch, indicating that it was time to return to shore. As part of a marine conservation effort, snorkeling at this particular site was strictly limited, allowing only one-hour adventures, five times a week. Everyone returned to shore chattering excitedly about their experiences while the guide gathered up the equipment and passed out warm towels.

Lola and Mike walked alongside the captain as they headed toward the van. "Captain, that was awesome," Lola said, still excited by the event.

"I'm glad you enjoyed it." Captain Andre bent over, picked up an oval shaped seashell and placed it in her hand, "Here's another souvenir to go along with your pictures."

Lola studied the small trinket crafted by nature and then looked into the captain's eyes, "Thank you."

The captain nodded and smiled back at her.

"You know what I'm going to do?" Lola was just a step behind the captain.

"No. What?" Captain Andre slowed his pace and turned to her.

"I'm going to collect one seashell for every time I visit a beach. It will be a lifelong collection, complete with a brief history for each." Lola smiled as she protectively clenched her first shell.

"That's a nice idea," he said, pleased by her willingness to enjoy the simple things.

"When we get to New Zealand, you can go snorkeling as much as you like. I've got a few good spots that I think you'll especially enjoy."

"She's going to love it there, aye, Captain?" Precariously, Mike balanced on one foot to rid his water shoe of grit while the entire group looked on, waiting for him to topple over. Finally, he gave up, removed both shoes and took to the rough beach with bare feet.

"Better now?" Lola laughed.

"Yes."

"So, Captain, tell me more about this place in New Zealand." Lola squinted from the sun as she looked up into his face.

"Well, it's not far from my house. In fact, it's right off my beach. The snorkeling equipment is always ready and there's no need for reservations."

"Snorkeling from your own back yard...that's just unbelievable," she said, trying to comprehend such available pleasures.

Again, the captain was amused by her enthusiasm. "Lola, there's a good reason why I had you endure those irregular accommodations back at the motel in San Diego," he said, almost apologetically.

"No need to explain, Captain. I understood your strategy from the second I stepped into that old motel. Well, it was more like a few minutes after I stepped into the motel," she clarified. "I was just so thrilled to be considered for the position that I didn't care where or how I lived."

"That pleases me," he stated proudly of his youngest *protégé*. "It's that kind of ambition that I was seeking in a new crewperson. I know you've endured some pretty tough times." He dared to reveal his knowledge of her unfortunate history. "Anyone surviving such adversity belongs on my crew. You're invincible, though I don't think you've quite realized that yet." Lovingly, he patted her on the back as a father does following a child's victory.

An empowering moment of love and acceptance came over Lola, filling her heart and giving her more strength. "Thank you for giving me this second chance at life."

He knew what she meant. "You're welcome."

Mike followed the captain into the oversized vehicle and sat beside Lola. He studied her cheerful face for a moment, thinking. "What does one do in Miller Lake, anyway?"

Lola laughed, "Not much. Let's see, there's skating in the wintertime, high school football in the fall and sometimes the movies…and reading and…biking in the summer. Yep, that's about it," she sighed, realizing how limited her old life was compared to her new life. "Today, I met a fish….and his family! You can't do that in Miller Lake," she said with a serious tone.

Everyone inside the van laughed.

The soothing water of the shower rinsed away the ocean's salty residue while the day's images played out in Lola's mind. Something was in the works, she knew, as the guys had begun acting strangely. With plans of meeting Mike in his room in half an hour, she would finally learn the mystery behind the secret conversations that had kept them grinning all day. She straightened the collar to her blue blouse and couldn't help but wonder what Mike had in store for the evening. He brandished a wild eye when he promised her a "thrill later." His presence was thrilling enough; she thought to herself and hoped that he didn't feel the need to lavishly entertain her to win over her affections. Lola was happy to be with him anytime, anywhere. She would clear that up with him later, she resolved turning off the table lamp.

Voices penetrated the door to Mike's suite when she arrived. Pascal opened the door and waved her in. Everyone, except for Bill and Nora, lounged comfortably on the furniture inside Mike's suite. "What's up?" Lola looked around the room.

"Well, I promised you sightseeing and one of the best ways to see Hawaii is from the sky. I've arranged for a helicopter tour. And you know those waterfalls you loved so much, well there's more and they are waiting for you. How do feel about seeing a real volcano?" Mike nearly burst from his own excitement.

"Wow...from the sky? You're always up to something." Quickly, she searched her mind for more words. "My goodness, a helicopter!" was all she could come up with in response to his kind gesture.

"I've never been in a helicopter either," Sheila said, with bug eyes. "This will be a new experience for both of us." Her attempt to be positive was futile. Lola had already picked up on her true impression of the aerial endeavor. Sheila was, undoubtedly, petrified.

"No worries, ladies, this company has the safest record on file," Mike nodded in confidence. "Nationwide," he added.

"Good to know." Lola blinked several times, still standing in the same place as when she first heard the news.

"After you get over the butterflies, you'll love it," Mike encouraged.

"Wonderful." Still, Lola hadn't budged. "A helicopter," she repeated, with an on-the-spot manufactured smile.

"I told you, Mike, you should have checked with them before committing to the flight," Pascal reminded.

Captain Andre chuckled, knowing Lola and Sheila would come around after the bomb had settled.

"It's not much different than the plane ride that you liked so much," Mike pointed out, looking at Lola and then to Sheila.

Lola nodded, considering the opportunity. "Well," she started slowly, "I have always wanted to ride in a helicopter and here's my chance, right now, in Hawaii." She looked to

Mike and then to Sheila and back to Mike again, deliberating.

"Ladies, it's all right if you don't want to go. Nobody will force you and nobody will be upset if you choose not to do it," Mike said kindly, realizing that perhaps he'd made a mistake.

"No...I think I'm ready to do this. How about you, Sheila? Are you with me?"

Sheila took in a deep breath, "Yes." Her answer sounded more like a question than an answer to the affirmative.

"All right, let's do it!" Lola was coming around. "I'm still scared, but I'm more sick of being scared."

"That's the spirit," Captain Andre arose from his chair.

"You'd kick yourself later if you didn't go. I can promise you that." Clearly, Eddie was speaking from experience, Lola concluded.

Eddie draped his arm around Sheila's shoulder and steered her out of the room before she could change her mind.

The elevator door slid open inviting everyone aboard. "I am starting to look forward to this," Lola smiled with building excitement.

"So am I," said Sheila, yielding to her giddiness.

"I arranged this little jaunt before we even left San Diego," Mike explained. "I figured you all needed a thrill, something different than the same old routine."

"Well, you surely accomplished that. This is as far from the same old routine as you can get," Sheila laughed.

"And the timing is perfect," Eddie interjected, "We'll see the sun set, which is totally awesome up there."

Lola buckled her seatbelt snugly and checked it three more times before she was satisfied. "I'm in," she called out.

"I can't believe we're doing this!" Sheila squealed in a nervous pitch, squeezing Lola's hand tightly.

"I know!" Lola's eyes equaled the size of golf balls.

"In just a few minutes from now, you're going to be so glad that you did this." Eddie shouted over the whirling propellers.

With everyone's headsets and life vests on, the helicopter scooped them up into the sky, whisking them off to see the island's coveted jewels.

Lola pressed her hands firmly over her mid section with the helicopter's swift aerial movements and Sheila slammed her eyelids shut, holding her breath as the helicopter swooped down inside a valley.

"Open your eyes, Sheila!" Eddie coaxed, not wanting her to miss anything.

Lola gasped in wonder when rushing waterfalls appeared in her window. Earth's natural faucets poured white rivers into a pool of bubbly rainbows below while lush forests climbed the rising landscape and rugged cliffs. Green, wooly valleys and robust peaks jetted out from meandering jungles beneath the sky, thrusting Lola in a state of awe. She and Sheila were lost in the magnificence, each forgetting her fear.

Mike's endless grin stretched across his face as he watched Lola marvel at God's living canvas. "You love it. I told you that you'd love it!" Mike could hardly sit still.

"It's amazing!" Her eyes continued to scan the stunning landscapes all around her.

Mike was so in love with her that it nearly pained him. The inescapable sensation pounded with each beat of his heart. He knew that Lola was sent to him. She was a gift from God. Tenderness surrounded him as he watched the reflection of the sun highlight her beautiful face. New Year's Eve was just a couple of days away and he could hardly wait to show Lola how much he loved her.

"Look over there!" Pascal pointed to Kilauea Volcano as it flickered in the distance with its small curtain of fire and blazing fountain.

"It's funny how something can be so angry and yet so beautiful at the same time," Lola observed, impressed by nature's fury.

"Yeah, I find that most women are like that, too." Pascal shot a grin toward Eddie who limited his comment to a discerning smile.

With the setting of the sun, the tour came to an end, leaving Lola's head full of the day's colorful images. The limousine carried the group back to the hotel where they joined Bill and Nora for their last evening meal on the island. Afterwards, Mike walked Lola to her room. "Aren't you coming in?" She held the door open for him.

"No, I shouldn't. You still have to pack and I have some things to finish up tonight." Another reason kept him from stepping through her doorway. He knew that if he did, he wouldn't leave the respectable man he wanted to be.

"Are you all right?" Lola pulled her jacket off her shoulders and sat down on the edge of the sofa, studying his face.

He looked at her, thinking how beautiful she was. Her entire essence fueled his desire and ruled his heart. "Yes, I'm more than fine." His smile revealed that he was telling the truth.

She stood up and kissed him passionately, unknowingly furthering his quandary.

"You see, that's the problem," he backed away with a restless smile. "I'm just getting so lost in you that I'm afraid my manners will diminish, especially with you kissing me like that." He blushed at his honesty.

She smiled back at him in admiration.

"So, you see why my immediate departure is necessary." He took a step back and then stopped. He was conflicted. Part of him wanted Lola to pull him into her chamber and lock the door, but he willed himself to make a hasty retreat. "I'm going to say goodnight, now."

Chapter Thirteen

It was New Year's Eve, just three days since the Big Island became a tiny speck in the distance. The sails flapped mightily in the ocean breeze, carrying the *Clarisse* unto new horizons. Nora knitted a sweater for one of her many grandchildren under a straw hat that she had purchased in Hawaii and Lola, Eddie, Mike and Pascal fished off the boat, under Bill's *supervision.* Sheila donned her sunglasses and read Eddie's manuscript on deck while the captain watched the horizon and listened to the laughter erupting from his ocean family below. A small boat in the distance caught his eye, so he grabbed the binoculars to get a better look at the approaching craft.

"Ouch!" Lola yelped when a fishhook snagged in her left index finger, anchoring deep inside her flesh.

"Holy dooley, Lola! What did you do to yourself?" Mike leaned in for a better look at Lola's injured hand.

"Is everything all right?" Captain Andre looked down toward Lola.

"Oh, I just got a stupid hook in my finger...I'll live," she said, infusing a bit of humor to her uncomfortable situation.

Mike reached for his knife inside his pocket and opened it. "Lola, hold the pole, you're still tethered to it."

She held the pole firmly, not allowing it to tug on the hook that was implanted in her finger.

"Be sure to get it cleaned right away," Captain Andre suggested when his eyes returned to the sea.

"Will do," she replied, wishing the ordeal was over. Everyone had gathered around and watched Mike tend to her hand.

"Hold on," Mike cut the fishing line with his knife.

"Thank you," Lola smiled and prepared to stand.

"You'd better let me help you get that hook out of there."

"Oh, I can take care of this little thing myself," she told Mike, downplaying the whole incident. Lola was more embarrassed than anything else. All she wanted to do was privately remedy the problem and get back to fishing without anybody making a fuss over her. "I'll be right back."

Mike looked at Pascal and grumbled before shouting, "Lola!"

"Yes?" She stopped quickly and turned back toward him.

"Wait," he said sternly. "I'm going to remove that hook. Now, sit down here and behave yourself and we'll have it out of there fast." His sturdy voice and gentle smile calmed her, which is what she needed at the moment. "You can trust me."

Sheila handed him the wire cutters.

"I've done this a thousand times." Mike brought the cutters up to the hook. "Just be still for a minute and it'll be out of there before you know it."

Lola welcomed his confidence and swift intervention, realizing that she had no idea how to properly remove the menacing hook without causing further damage.

"Done." He looked over her finger and admired his work.

Surprised, Lola looked at her finger in amazement. "That's it?"

"Yep, that's it." Mike kissed her hand sweetly and noticed that she was trembling.

She assessed the wound once more, "I don't think I would have had the nerve to pull it out myself after all," she admitted. "Thank you. I'll be right back. Don't let anyone else catch my prized fish while I'm gone!"

"We'll save the big one for you, I promise," Mike smiled back at her and grabbed his fishing pole.

Meanwhile, Captain Andre's attention rode steadily on the approaching vessel. His guard had heightened and his voice was heavy with urgency when he called out to the rest of his crew.

Immediately, they reeled in their lines and tossed their poles aside to answer the captain's call.

"What's up?" Mike asked, interpreting the captain's uneasiness.

"I've had my eye on that boat for a while." His voice was laden with suspicion. "They are approaching mighty fast and I just wonder what they're up to."

Swiftly, Mike went into action heading over to the munitions cabinet. All crewmembers wore a chain around their neck with a key to the gun cabinet, a stiff requirement imposed by Captain Andre. Mike reached in and pulled out the loaded weapons, discreetly passing them out to Captain Andre, Eddie and Pascal. He kept one for himself and shoved it inside the band of his shorts.

"Nora, I want you and Bill to stay in your quarters for a bit. I just want to see what those folks on that boat want. Sheila, you and Lola stay below, too."

"All right, Captain." Sheila spun around and left the deck.

Nora collected her things and hurried with Bill to their suite. Mike took the helm while Captain Andre tried to contact the small boat. "This is the *Clarisse*. What is your situation?"

The occupants of the small boat answered back. A slightly distorted voice came over the radio asking if any antibiotics were onboard.

"That's affirmative," Captain Andre replied.

The rugged voice explained briefly that there was an accident aboard their boat and they were in dire need of some medical attention.

"What is the extent of the injury?" Captain Andre asked.

The speaker squawked and then a distressed voice came over the radio, "A large gash to hand while cleaning fish yesterday. It's badly infected."

"Permission granted for one to board the *Clarisse*," Captain Andre advised.

Guardedly, Mike's eyes shifted from the small vessel back to his concealed gun. He nodded at the captain, signaling that he was ready. Pascal positioned himself as if to be relaxing in a chair while he steadied his pistol under Sheila's towel. Eddie stood next to Captain Andre with his pistol stuffed inside the waist of his trousers, hidden.

Bill and Nora waited quietly in their suite while trying to calm their excitement. They were aware of modern day pirates, but they also knew that the captain wouldn't let any harm come to them. He was a clever man and was certainly wary of sea crimes.

Sheila caught up to Lola in the lower head, "The captain says we are to stay below for a bit until he gives us word to come back up on deck."

"Why?" Lola's face wrinkled in concern.

"No biggie, there's just a boat nearby and he isn't sure what they need yet. So, he just wants us to stay here for a few minutes until he gets a response from them. Like you learned in training, remain on guard, listen for signs of trouble, and be ready for anything. I know this all sounds a bit alarming, but it is just routine. Remember, the captain just wants to ensure safety among his passengers and crew."

Lola nodded and tried to ignore the nervous flutters in her stomach.

In an effort to ease Lola's concerns, Sheila offered a brief story about the first time they were approached by a mysterious boat. "I was terrified at first as I hid, waiting for all hell to break loose. And of course, all turned out to be just fine. But I know how you feel right now. It will be fine— really. Just remember, fear is your worst enemy and it will not help you out in any situation. Just keep your wits about you and everything will be all right." She looked at Lola's newly injured finger. "Gosh, that's nasty. How did you do it, anyway?"

Lola rolled her eyes, "It's quite humiliating, really. I was showing off in front of the guys, you know, trying not to be a girl about baiting my hook and it just happened so fast."

Sheila cringed and handed Lola a tube of antibiotic cream. "Use this. It speeds up the healing."

"Sheila, will you or Lola bring the first-aid kit to me?" Captain Andre's voice startled both of them as it came sharply through the intercom. "Meet Eddie in the salon with it." His voice sounded calm, without alarm and that put Lola's uncertainties to rest.

"Sure, Captain." Sheila released the call button. "Someone on that other boat must have gotten an *owie*, too." Sheila giggled.

"*Oops,* I just used the last of this antibiotic stuff. I'll go get another tube from storage. I know right where it is." Lola swiveled her hips past Sheila in the tiny doorway and headed for the storage room.

Meanwhile, Sheila gathered up the rest of the first aid kit and hurried toward the salon.

Lola found the bin that held the necessary items and grabbed a package of bandages just in case there weren't enough in the first aid kit. Suddenly, she heard gunfire. Several shots rattled above on the upper deck and then there was complete silence. Confusion shrouded her as her heart slammed inside her chest. She panicked and ran up the ladder to see what had happened. Then, remembering what she had learned in training, she turned back and hid inside the storage room to gather her thoughts. Fright engulfed her entire mind and body. She trembled uncontrollably. *I have to get to the radio!* Lola stood on her quivering legs and attempted the ladder again. She felt very heavy. Paralyzed. An unseen force was pushing her back down the ladder. She recognized the force. It was fear. Her worst enemy! With all her will and bravery, she climbed the rungs again and peered around.

Above, the air was frighteningly calm. No shuffling footsteps. No voices. Nothing. Carefully, she wobbled on her shaky legs to the radio to put out a distress call. She didn't see any of her crewmembers at all. Lola refused to resort to panic and made her way to a radio. Quietly, she spoke into the microphone. "This is the *Clarisse*. Gunshots on board! We're under attack from another vessel. We need help! This is the *Clarisse*, we are under attack. Gunshots onboard. We're under attack." On the chance that someone heard her on the other end of the radio, and was maintaining silence for Lola's safety, she gave approximate coordinates of their position several times. She crept to the galley to look through the small window and to her horror, she saw her crew, including Bill and Nora on the other boat. *Dear God! What happened? Where's Mike?* Her mind raced with questions and then she saw a slumped over body that Sheila was madly attending to. *Mike's been shot!* Lola nearly fainted from the shock. Keep your head clear, a voice inside her mind instructed.

A tall man stood guard near her friends holding what appeared to be a large automatic weapon. Another guard stood opposite him with the same type of gun. Captain Andre was speaking fiercely to both of them. The guards kept shaking their heads angrily in protest. The taller guard finally struck Captain Andre with the butt of his weapon, knocking him down. Lola's heart ached at the horrible sight. Then her eyes fell upon a man that she knew she had seen somewhere else. It was the limo driver! She shuddered as she watched him throw what appeared to be radio equipment over the edge of the small boat and then he tossed several crates into the sea that quickly sank.

She rushed back to the radio and on her way, sent fragments of prayers toward heaven. She grabbed the radio microphone when, all of a sudden, two unfamiliar voices approached the salon, interrupting her second rescue attempt. For a split second, she froze, unsure of her next move. But their voices were coming closer. She had to leave immediately. Her heart pounded so fast that it ached inside her chest as she tried to replace the microphone back into its slot before being caught. The radio device slipped through her sweaty fingers and crashed against the cupboard. She gasped in fright, but her hands automatically retrieved the radio piece and she replaced it in the proper slot, barely escaping the sight of the evil savages.

Stealthily, she slunk back to the storage room—her only escape. Jumping ship had entered her mind but she'd only be left behind to die alone in a watery grave and if she was dead, her friends would have no chance for survival at all. Abandoning ship was not the answer, she knew. *Think, Lola. They need you!*

The storage room was the best place to hide, so she scurried down the ladder into the cargo pit. There, she could better form a rescue plan. She hoped. Panic loomed, ready to swoop in and destroy her mission, but she forced herself to think through it.

A trunk over in the corner caught her eye. She hurried over to it and opened the lid. Immediately, she removed its contents and scattered the items around the room in an organized fashion, so that it didn't appear that the trunk had recently been emptied in a frantic moment because Lola had decided to hide inside the trunk. She knew her time was limited as the men would search every square inch of the yacht very soon and she could only hope that they wouldn't look inside the trunk.

Desperately, her eyes roamed the small room in search of anything that would deliver a deadly blow. Finally, her eyes landed on an old fishing knife that dangled above the trunk. She lunged toward the knife and yanked it from its hook before taking temporary refuge inside the old trunk. The knife was not enough, she realized and then she remembered the spare flare gun. Gently, she climbed out of the trunk and quietly rummaged several shelves until her hand fell upon it. She grabbed it and then searched the shelves for extra charges. She took those, too. Fully armed, Lola returned to her dungeon with a knife, flare gun and extra charges tucked securely in her waist band.

The powerful surge of the yacht's engine began to roar. Lola knew that the opportunity to rescue her friends was diminishing. Alone, she was stranded with the dreadful men while her beloved was seriously injured and left to die on another other boat with the others.

Suddenly, a series of muffled gunshots sounded again, robbing her of all hope. Her dear friends had been shot; a prelude to her own demise. Now, confined by despair, she waited inside the trunk. What she was waiting for, she didn't know. Perhaps death. Only scant pockets of air remained, slowly sucking the life out of her. She felt herself slipping away as she sobbed quietly, mourning the loss of Mike and her treasured friends. She took in her last breath when her eyes sprang open, depriving her of death. She wouldn't allow herself to die, not without trying to save them first. And like a volcano about to scorch the land with all its fury, Lola's terror turned to rage. A deadly wrath that promised to counter all evil swelled from the small untapped resources of her soul.

Immediately, she began to plan her assault. First, she had to figure out how many men there were in all. She remembered seeing three on the other boat and she had heard two voices on the captain's yacht. Could there only be five? And were they aware of her existence? Lola couldn't worry about the latter, she had to remain in attack mode.

With every passing moment, her friends were inching closer to death…if they hadn't already perished. She had to carry out her assault with haste and precision. She looked around the small room searching for other forms of weaponry in case the knife failed. Her very last resort would have to be the flare gun as it could certainly result in a fire onboard. She remembered seeing a package of syringes along with other medications in the storage bin just moments before the attack. An idea emerged when she spotted the bottle of bleach in the corner of the small room. Realizing that she had very little time before her temporary asylum was discovered, she quickly ripped the package of syringes open and filled three with the potentially noxious fluid and then unscrewed the light bulb from its socket, rendering the tiny room black as pitch. Darkness would be her ally.

Coarsely, her heart drummed inside her chest as the anticipated footsteps approached. Mightily, she gripped the knife in her right hand and in her left, she held a lethal syringe. Slowly, the door opened where he appeared in a subtle mist of light that swirled around him. He peered down into the black pit and then entered her lair. His feet shuffled on the floor as he went for the light switch. In the meager light from above, she saw his hand move up the wall and flick the switch, but darkness, her sweet accomplice, continued to shield her. A chorus of loud, vulgar words streamed from his mouth, shattering the silence they shared.

She remained still and would only attack when the moment was right. Too many people were depending on her, she couldn't blow it with haste or miscalculation. The opportunity to strike was suddenly upon her. From behind him, she crept forward and plunged the knife deep into the back of his neck. Instantly, he dropped to the floor. She knelt beside him with monstrous determination and thrust the knife into him again, making sure he wouldn't survive. *I've just killed a man!*

Somewhere in the scuffle, she inadvertently dropped the loaded syringe. Perhaps they would serve more as a danger to her, she thought, pulling the remaining syringes from her back pocket and tossing them behind the trunk.

Quietly, she pulled the trap door closed and crept back down the ladder where the evil lump lay dead at her feet. Fierce with adrenaline she dragged the body across the floor and heaved it up into the trunk that had nearly become her own coffin. When the legs were completely stuffed inside, she covered the limp body with a blanket while exhaustion loomed, threatening to impede her valiant efforts. Suddenly, a heavy set of footsteps thumped over her head. They were coming. She hurried to her corner and waited in silence as she prepared her knife. The small door opened and the mysterious shadow made its descent. When the light failed him, he cursed in his tongue, startling Lola to a perilous measure. She held her breath and hoped that he hadn't heard her gasp. Cursing again, he grabbed the ladder and angrily climbed back up the rungs and out of her sight.

In silence, she waited in the blanket of darkness worrying that precious time was evaporating. She had to do the kill and get on with the rescue, but waves of panic arose, aiming to unravel her. *I can do this.* Lola brought her hands up to her temples and massaged her scalp to calm the chaos that was whirling around in her head. Anticipating his return made her ears hiss. When she opened her eyes, she was startled to see that he was already hovering above the ladder. Something was in his hands, but she couldn't make it out and then, to her horror, she realized it was a flash light. Her traitor!

As he descended the ladder, the sturdy beam of light whipped across the floor, just missing her. Her eyes followed the treacherous ray as it bounced around the room, ready to expose her. She had to act quickly as a surprise attack would be her only means of escape. As soon as his foot touched the floor, she lunged forward with all her strength and sank the knife deeply into his neck. He thrashed around the room before collapsing to the floor where, again, he met her fury-driven dagger.

Unaware of her blood-smeared face, Lola pulled the body toward the trunk and struggled for several minutes, heaving until the larger corpse rested quietly on top of the other. Grabbing another blanket, she covered the two foul heaps and closed the lid, making sure to secure it with a padlock.

With the flashlight, Lola took a quick inventory of the room and realized that she had to somehow conceal the bloodstains. Surprisingly, there wasn't as much blood on the floor as she had expected, but there was certainly enough to alert the others of her actions. She found old linens that were stored for rags and draped the remnants over the stains. The blood quickly soaked through, clearly defining a fresh kill. With her foot, she swiped the linens over the stains to wipe away the blood. When the floor was mopped clear, she piled the sheets together in a corner and tossed another heap of linens on top of the blood soaked bundle to conceal the evidence.

Stopping only for a moment to catch her breath, Lola rubbed her throbbing head again and reeled in her scattered thoughts. Too much time had passed and she worried she was too late in helping her friends. Decidedly, there was no time to wait for another unsuspecting victim, she had to go up and initiate the attack. Carefully, she inspected the flare gun making sure it was loaded and then tucked it securely inside her waistband beside the extra flares. She looked up toward the opening and reached for the ladder. During her daring ascent, she noticed a sticky substance on her hands. It was blood. She needed to escape that knowledge. *Just finish the job!*

Lola collected herself and prepared for the violent storm that awaited her. She envisioned shooting the remaining savages right through their hearts with white-hot flares. Searing flame would split their chests wide open, scorching their insides while they screamed in terror begging for her mercy. After several deep breaths, Lola reached the top without making a sound. She listened for voices to get an exact locale of each member belonging to the evil clan and tiptoeing ever so slightly, she spied two men on deck.

Cautiously, she advanced deeper into the salon near the deck and situated herself behind an overstuffed chair, so she could listen for a moment and assess the situation. The glass doors leading out to the deck were still open, that would be her only advantage. Her heart stirred in pain when a mild breeze carried a whiff of Sheila's lingering perfume into the room. *Don't think about that now.*

Briefly, she looked beyond the deck and into the horizon. The sun had gone and darkness fell. She tried to figure out how much time had expired since her friends were cast out to sea, but her mind remained on the task, not allowing her to venture into the dreaded possibilities.

From her remote position, she could see two men who appeared to be talking to another man above, presumably at the helm. She hoped there were only three men remaining. Their conversations were difficult to understand as they alternated between scant English and their foreign tongue, which was quite similar to Spanish. Lola's three years of Spanish class came in handy because she was able to put the broken pieces of language together and figure out that they were selling Captain Andre's yacht to an established buyer.

Her hate for the evil criminals continued to fester as disturbing images of her friends' suffering infected her mind. The thought of the wicked men selling Captain Andre's boat tortured her as visions of the beloved captain standing proudly at his controls replayed inside her head, mixing her thoughts. *Focus!*

Lola secured her position and cautioned herself to wait for the right moment. Any undue haste could result in grave consequences for her and her friends. Mentally, she reviewed her plan, but was still concerned about catching the boat on fire with the flare gun. Missing her targets and not reloading her weapon in time would surely guarantee a swift and agonizing death.

She figured with the first strike that the men would be dazed only for a second, but enough time for her to reload. For the final man, she was just going to have to take that chance and hope she reloaded before she was discovered. She had no choice, either way she would die and so would all those poor souls who might still be counting on her.

Lola drew in a deep breath and prepared to aim. Her hand trembled. She brought the gun back down to her side when Sheila's prophetic words returned, "Fear is your worst enemy." Again, she took aim, remembering to gently squeeze the trigger while holding the gun steadily. The fireball surged from the barrel of the flare gun and slammed directly into the chest of her first chosen target, fatally wounding the chauffeur. With a *thud*, he hit the deck, colliding with a fiery death. His companion bolted from his seat and drew his gun aimlessly as he sought the elusive assailant hiding in the shadows. The other man joined him on deck and, together, they fired a stream of bullets into the salon. When they stopped to reload their weapons, she squeezed her gun and thrust a small inferno into the groin of her second mark. His brief cry was muffled by instant death as he crumpled over the table where Lola and her friends had just played poker the day before.

From the dark recesses of the salon, Lola quickly reloaded the flare gun and spotted her prey. His fast approaching footsteps mingled with her labored breathing in the whirling shadows. With pointed gun, he fired several times and she responded with perfect aim, releasing all of her fury with a quick grasp of the trigger. She focused her eyes and saw his head disappear inside a raging blaze upon his wilting shoulders. There were no screams before death pulled him overboard into his grave. She could only hope that there weren't any more of the heinous men cowering in the darkness aboard the yacht. Had she gotten every one of them?

Heavy smoke loomed over the smoldering bodies, emanating a foul odor of baked flesh. Her eyes, stinging from smoke, strained to look past the gruesome scene to see if the yacht had erupted into flame. Weak and unable to rise to her feet, Lola realized something was holding her down. Again, she tried to stand, but scorching pain radiating through her left thigh hindered her attempt.

Dancing flames swirled around the bodies on deck and in the fiery glow she saw blood pooling beside her. *I've been shot!* Frantically, she dragged her body toward the extinguisher to douse the encroaching flames. With all of her strength, she hoisted the canister in position and drowned the blaze before it spread.

She was safe and could now make her way to the radio. "Hello, can anyone hear me? This is the *Clarisse*, we went under attack today. Several are dead and injured. Does anyone copy?"

"Yes, I copy," came a welcomed stranger's voice.

Lola nearly cried, "Hello? My name is Lola, I'm aboard the *Clarisse*. We were attacked today. My crew has been shot and dumped onto a small, disabled vessel at sea. You have to hurry, it's sinking!"

"We're already on our way."

His words were comforting to her and she felt herself relax.

"Are you still in danger?"

"I think I've gotten them all. There was a fire, but I put it out," Lola managed, feeling woozy.

"Stay with us," the voice instructed. "We don't want to breach communication with you again."

Lola leaned against the cabinet with the radio still in her hand, fighting shock and exhaustion. Across from her was part of Eddie's manuscript sitting on the table next to a spool of Nora's yarn. "Stay awake," she told herself.

Chapter Fourteen

Intense light penetrated the fleshy lids to Lola's swollen eyes. Gradually, she opened them to find a stranger beside her. "Lola?" His gentle voice fully summoned her from the heavy state of sleep that had seized her for two days. She focused on the fuzzy figure as he slowly came into view. "Hello," he said gently, inspecting the centers of her eyes with a small, lighted instrument.

"My friends, did they find my friends?" Lola's voice cracked.

"Let's first talk about you. We had to operate and repair the damage the bullets caused, but you're going to be fine."

"Bullets?"

"Yes, you suffered two gunshot wounds. One to your abdomen and the other lodged in your leg. Do you remember what happened?"

"Yes," she answered solemnly. "Where are my friends? Did they find them? They were shot and left on a small boat."

Dr. Andrews responded hesitantly. "Yes, we know about your friends and they did locate the boat."

Lola looked into his face, trying to decipher what his words weren't telling her. Clearly, he was avoiding her question. His expression could no longer hide the devastating truth.

"They didn't make it, did they?" Tears rushed from her eyes as her mournful wails reached the far ends of the hospital. Her beloved was gone forever, along with her dear friends. In an instant, they were all ripped from Lola's life where each suffered a horrific death on the sea. Her cries were embedded with grief and the familiar pain instantly devoured her soul. "Why did I have to live?" Small hoses inserted in her arms whipped back and forth as she thrashed in her bed, "No!"

"Lola, please, you're going to hurt yourself. Please calm down." His voice sounded in desperation. "I'm truly sorry about your friends." Dr. Andrews struggled to calm her as he held her arms down against her. "You tried desperately to save them, but there was nothing you could do." He tried to console her, but her anguish was impervious to his attempts.

157

During the struggle, he pressed the nurse's call button and in mere seconds, a nurse arrived, ready to assist him. "We're going to have to sedate her, or she'll rip herself to shreds," he told her.

The following morning, Detective Blake sat beside Lola's bed waiting for her to wake. "Good morning, Miss Wilson."

She responded with a groan as she tried to pull herself up in bed. Her head felt as though it had been filled with foam.

"I have some questions to ask you and I know it's very hard, but we need your help in getting the rest of these evil men. Your attackers were involved in a large crime ring and any information you can give us will certainly aid in the capture of their leaders." The detective sat up straight in his chair, eager to hear Lola's recollection as he pulled a pen from his shirt pocket.

Tears spilled onto her pillow as she opened her mouth to speak. He pulled a tissue from the box sitting on the portable bedside table and gently swabbed her face. He then lifted the small pitcher of water and filled her cup. After a half hour, the kind detective thanked Lola for her information and promised to keep her informed regarding the case.

Three hours after hearing the horrifying news regarding the heinous ambush at sea, Mrs. Wilson jumped a plane for Hawaii and arranged for Dr. Lee, the very best psychiatrist on the island, to help Lola through the trauma. She rented an apartment near the hospital where families of patients could stay during their loved-one's recovery.

Nearly a week had passed since Lola learned the fate of her friends. Once again, anguish owned her soul. Her body would heal, but her heart would not.

"Mrs. Wilson, it's just going to take some more time. We're going to have to be patient," Dr. Lee explained, sitting across from the desperate mother in the hospital cafeteria.

"Yes, I know," she sighed heavily. "From Lola's past experience, I know we've got a difficult road ahead of us. I just hope she can recover from this."

"I believe she will," Dr. Lee nodded, convincingly.

Without realizing it, Lola's mother glared at a young woman who sat at a nearby table contentedly reading a magazine, unaware of the distress she caused every time she stirred her iced tea. Rising exasperation whittled harshly against Mrs. Wilson's nerves every time the young woman's spoon clanked against the glass. Lola's mother was on the verge of screaming. While her own daughter was lying in a bed on the third floor, possibly withering away to oblivion, this young woman had the audacity to flaunt her life.

"You know, I would like to spend some more time with you as well. Perhaps together we can better help Lola," Dr. Lee offered, observing Mrs. Wilson's agitation.

"Yes, you're right," Mrs. Wilson acknowledged her own condition. She would first have to get her own head in the right place before she could help Lola, she admitted to herself.

Haunting images of her friends drifting away on the small boat continually tormented Lola, leaving her shattered. She kept seeing Mike's smiling face, the last time she saw him. She felt as though she died with them on the desolate ocean. Her joy was gone forever. Where would she go after leaving the hospital? Back home to Miller Lake? And then what?

The taxi driver loaded Lola's bag into the taxi while she stood staring off into the horizon seeking refuge from the anguish that had suffocated her for two weeks. She closed her eyes hoping to escape the agony, but there was no relief. Her torment had become her every breath.

Mrs. Wilson slid into the taxi beside Lola and reached for her hand. "We can keep the apartment for another week and I can exchange the airline tickets for a later departure, if you'd like." Deliberately, she fused her words with a ring of cheer. "Perhaps you can show me some of your special places before we return home."

Lola looked blankly out the window of the taxi and then she turned to her mother. "I just can't, Mom. This place is different now. It just hurts too much."

Mrs. Wilson patted her daughter's hand. "I understand, sweetie." The drive to the small apartment was silent. Neither wounded soul could speak. Rampant words filled Mrs. Wilson's head, but she resisted them, fearing she could further damage Lola's emotional state by possibly saying the wrong thing.

The taxi came to a firm stop in front of the apartment. Lola looked vacantly past the small building and uttered a few words, "I'll just wait here."

"Sure, honey, I'll only be a few minutes. I just have to settle up with the manager and get my bags."

As if a cruel hoax had been orchestrated, the taxi crept past the grand hotel where Lola and her friends had stayed during Christmas. Lola held her breath with fixed eyes on the rambling estate. Silent tears streamed down her face nearly bringing her to collapse.

"That's your hotel, isn't it?" Mrs. Wilson asked intuitively.

"Yes," Lola sobbed.

Mrs. Wilson moved closer to Lola and squeezed her lovingly. "I know this hurts. Embrace the good memories here and love them."

Lola nodded and held her mother.

"We'll get through this, I promise. Just take one day at a time and just know with each new day, a little more of the hurt will go away."

"Mom, I loved him," said Lola, between sobs.

"Who, dear?"

"Mike. And he loved me. I wanted to tell you about him before, but I was afraid I would spoil it by speaking too soon about it. He was so wonderful and I couldn't wait for you to meet him. Now, you'll never know what a grand person he was." Her sobs became heavier, drowning her words.

"I'm so sorry," was all she could say for the moment as she was holding back her own tears, further understanding Lola's enormous loss. She reached inside her purse and pulled out a wad of tissues and dabbed Lola's face. "I want to hear all about him," she encouraged, resisting the urge to cry out loud. Strangling with her own emotions, she asked, "What did he look like?" Her innocent question suddenly sounded reckless to her as it boomeranged inside the taxi. What *did* he look like? She replayed the question inside her head, realizing that it served nothing but to emphasize Mike's former existence. Immediately, she wanted to yank the words back into her mouth, but it was too late.

The taxi driver offered a subtle smile of compassion as he looked at Mrs. Wilson in the rear view mirror. She smiled back in response.

Lola sat quiet for a while and then she started talking, "He was very handsome with little blond curls and he had the most beautiful blue eyes," she sniffed. "He was from Australia and he was very good to me," she sniffed again, looking down at her healed finger that he had tended to that day. Hot tears poured down her cheeks as she thought about their final moments together.

Mrs. Wilson pulled her daughter against her and caressed her head, smoothing away the hair from her tear-soaked face.

Lola slept most of the flight home to New Hampshire, as did Mrs. Wilson. When they arrived at the Manchester Airport parking lot, Lola's mother guided them to the old Buick she had left a few weeks earlier.

"You kept Daddy's car," Lola said sensitively.

"Yes, I couldn't part with it. I leave mine in the garage and only use his car or his old truck. It helps me."

With her mother's words came a sharp revelation. "Mom," Lola began to cry, "I've been so wrapped up in me all this time that I never really considered what you went through when Daddy died. I've been so selfish! I'm so sorry." She was truly ashamed of herself. "How did you ever get through it alone and then having to deal with me on top of your own sorrow?"

"You needed me and, honestly, you saved *me*," her mother answered gently. Together they sat quietly, allowing the familiarity of the old sedan to comfort them.

Lola ached for her mother and, suddenly, it occurred to her that she had purpose again—to avenge those who ruined her mother's life as well as her own. Decidedly, she would resurrect her old companion *revenge* and make her enemies pay for their crimes.

Two months had passed since Lola returned home to Miller Lake. Tulip sprouts at the left side of her porch hinted to winter's end. A new season was coming and so was a tumultuous storm.

While having breakfast one morning, Lola flipped through a magazine that had been delivered a few days earlier.

She was drinking her coffee when her eyes landed on a startling image. It was Sara Parkins' nauseating face staring back at her. "Mom!"

Mrs. Wilson jumped in alarm with the sound of Lola's desperation. Hurriedly, she finished tying her robe on the way to the kitchen. "What's the matter?"

"What is she doing in there?"

"Oh...I heard she's modeling now," Mrs. Wilson rolled her eyes. "That must have been quite a shock to see her there." She leaned over the magazine and shook her head, unimpressed.

"She always said that she was going to be a model or something." Lola bitterly scoured the page with a scornful eye and drew the page in closer, inspecting every grain within the photo. "She hasn't improved any."

"No, she bloomed early and I'm afraid it's all down hill for her now." Mrs. Wilson smiled at her beautiful daughter who had gone away a humble caterpillar and returned home a beautiful butterfly.

Lola sipped her coffee and glared at the photo in the magazine. According to the clock, it was still too early to visit the private investigator. She would have to wait at least an hour.

When Lola had fallen in love with Mike, she awakened unto a new life, free from the binding chains of hate. But Mike and the others were gone now, having been savagely ripped from her life and leaving her broken. Destroyed. If it wasn't for Sara Parkins, Lola would never know such excruciating pain. Solemnly, she looked into her mother's tired eyes, aged far beyond their years. Sara will pay for that, too, she thought, heading to her bedroom.

"I need to use your car today, if that's all right," Lola explained when she came back into the kitchen wearing a black skirt suit. "I've got a few errands to do, but I won't be long." She leaned over and kissed her mother who was still reading the paper.

"Yes, that's fine. Will you pick up some bread on your way home?"

"Sure. Is there anything else you need?"

"No, that's all."

Lola drove down Asbury Street, completely avoiding Main Street where her family's bakery used to be situated. Since Mrs. Wilson sold the business, Lola avoided that particular part of town because she couldn't bear the thought of another person operating her parents' bakery. Too many wonderful memories were born there and she wanted to preserve them.

When she was young, she and her father took long walks down Main Street during the summer. On one of those excursions, Mr. Wilson carried Lola on his shoulders after visiting the ice cream shop. Just as she licked her ice cream cone, it toppled over and landed on his head. Together, they laughed until their stomachs ached. With a long sigh, Lola filed the cherished memory back into her heart for safekeeping.

She drove a few more miles and reached the neighboring town where she had previously met the private investigator. The sign above his storefront read, HANSEN'S CLOCK/WATCH REPAIR, but he also did investigative work on the side. In front of his small store, she parked her car and entered, jingling the chimes as she pushed through the door.

"May I help you, miss?" It was clear that he did not recognize her.

"Yes," she stepped toward the counter wearing a timid smile. "I commissioned some work from you a while back regarding Sara Parkins and a few of her friends?"

"Oh, yes," he hesitated for a moment, "you're Lola?"

"Yes, that's me."

He peered over his glasses to get a second look at her, "You look different."

"Yes, I've been busy making some changes."

"Well, it looks good on you," he smiled. "Let me go get the file. I'll be right back."

Lola leaned against the counter and casually browsed his shop from her stance. Several clocks, new and old, twitched with perfect time on the walls. Across from her, on a small table, was a black marble clock that displayed a lion's face. Intrigued, she wandered over to the table and stroked the handsome piece, admiring its age and artisanship. Beside it were two keys, one for winding the chime and one for winding the timing mechanism.

"Thank you for waiting," he said, coming through a black curtain.

"No problem." She was very eager to get her hands on the bulky file because not long after her first picnic with Mike, she purged all of the files the investigator had emailed her. "I appreciate all of your fine work," she told him.

"Certainly," he nodded, "I just pulled this out of a magazine yesterday." He pointed to the top page in the file.

"Yes, I saw that, too." Lola did her best to mask the hatred she held for the figure shown in the magazine.

"I was beginning to wonder if I'd ever hear from you again."

Lola tried to think of a comfortable response.

"From your last email, it sounded like you wanted me to cease updating this file, but since you paid me such an exorbitant amount in advance, I kept at it, just in case. Now, I'm glad I did," he smiled, pleased with his decision.

"I'm glad you did, too," deviously, she grinned. "I've been doing some traveling for quite some time and I didn't think I would need this file anymore. But it appears that I do after all." She hoped he wouldn't ask her any probing questions regarding the information or her need for such. He hadn't asked before and she hoped he'd maintain the same discretion.

"Honestly, I enjoyed this assignment. It became more of a hobby for me like a crossword puzzle or something of that nature," he admitted.

"I'm happy to hear that. I'll definitely keep you in mind for future projects."

"I'd appreciate that."

"Do I owe you anything?"

"Nope, all is paid for. Do you want me to continue, or is this enough?"

"No, this should be fine." Lola shook his hand and commended him on his work after peeking inside the file. She turned toward the door and then paused, "That clock over there on the table…is it for sale? I didn't see a price tag."

"Yes, it is. I just finished repairing it and haven't had a chance to place a price on it yet. It's a gem, isn't it?"

"It certainly is."

"It's a SETH-THOMAS, crafted in 1904. Recently, I picked it up at the estate sale at Green Gables before they renovated the old mansion. Apparently, the property managers didn't realize its worth when they cleared some of the things out of there. Sure, it was broken, but I was able to repair it. Personally, I think it should have remained with the old estate. Don't you?"

"Yes, it belongs there," Lola agreed with the same sentiment.

"I was going to ask six-hundred for it, but I'm going to give you a better deal seeing that you are smart enough to appreciate things of this nature. How does three-hundred and ninety-five sound?"

"I'll take it."

"Fine, let me just put it in a box for you." He lifted the antique from the table and headed toward the back of the store.

A few miles down the road, Lola pulled her car into a parking lot where she could privately review the juicy details contained inside the file. "The man is articulate, I'll give him that," she mumbled as she pored over the documents.

Some of the details she was already familiar with due to the investigator's past emails, but some new and surprising information kept her reading for a long while. "So, Sara is still living with her parents in Miller Lake. That's no surprise," she scoffed, flipping to the next page. "Let's see if you haven't flunked out of Addelbrooke yet, Joya." Hungrily, her eyes followed the investigator's notes to the bottom of the page. "Well, well," she hissed, "it looks like college suits you, Joya. And you're only an hour away."

Her eyes darted to the next page where she continued to read the file's contents aloud, "Debbie is still in New York; a small challenge, but definitely worth the effort." Another page confirmed Nick's entry-level position at Sara's father's company. "How perfectly convenient for you, Nick," Lola sneered as she read about his recent engagement to Sara. "Now then, what are Billy and Todd up to these days?" Lola scanned the pages and stopped when she came to Billy's name. "Billy is still in town…didn't figure him to go too far." Her eyes drifted to another page. "And what about you, Todd? Oh, that's right, you're dead," she said without emotion, dismissing his obituary.

Todd, who was drunk at the time, smashed his car into a tree a month after Lola left for San Diego. She lingered in thought for a moment, "I guess we could call it poetic justice?" Callously, she turned her attention back to Sara, never giving another thought to Todd's unfortunate end.

On the drive home, she stopped at the local grocery store to buy the loaf of bread for her mother. Three people were ahead of her in line, so she grabbed an entertainment magazine and grazed the pages while she waited. A voice called out from the express lane, "I can take you over here."

Lola replaced the magazine in the rack and joined the cashier at his stand where she dropped the bread onto the counter. She gasped when a familiar set of eyes met hers. Holding her breath, Lola looked directly into Billy's face when he announced the total of her purchase. Blankly, he looked at her, expressing not even a hint of recognition. *He doesn't even know me.* The power of her anonymity could play a vital role in her plan, she thought. Smugly, she stood before him disguised in her beauty and handed him her cash. He turned back toward her with twenty-seven cents and offered her the receipt. Lola stared into his eyes, again tempting him, but still he didn't know her. "Thank you," she said, taking her leave.

She hurried to her car, encouraged by the many rewards her secret identity would provide. On the seat beside her, was all of the key information she needed to carry out her mission. She reminded herself to pay better attention to the smallest of details to avoid surprise encounters with her subjects. Although her brief reunion with Billy was fortunate, she preferred to plan the meetings.

Lola gathered the mail from the box at the curb and found a letter from the insurance company that insured Captain Andre's yacht. Instantly, the small reminder brought everything to surface. The devastating memories were heavy, hardly allowing her to breathe as she made her way into the house.

166

For three days, the unopened letter remained on her bedside table, antagonizing her. "You should really open it," her mother encouraged, sitting down on the foot of Lola's bed. "It could be important."

"I know what it is," Lola sighed.

Mrs. Wilson nodded. "Honey, you have to get on with your life. Mike wouldn't have wanted you to suffer like this," she dared to mention his name. "You said that he and the rest of your friends had given you so much. Please take what they have given you and live your life well and find happiness again."

"I know," Lola nodded slowly, looking at the envelope that served as a bridge to the recent tragedies. She tore it open and found a check written to her for five-hundred thousand dollars. "What am I supposed to do with this?" She shook the check in her hand, upset by the colossal reminder.

"You take it and make a life for yourself, Lola. That's what you do with it."

Lola fought her tears and leaned back into the pillows that aligned her wooden headboard.

Mrs. Wilson soothed the hair from Lola's face, caressing her. "Why don't you start your own business doing interior decorating? You always loved that sort of thing and were very good at it."

"That's a good idea. I'll think about that," Lola forced herself to say.

"You rest while I make us lunch." Lola's mother got up and headed toward the kitchen.

A cold rain spattered the window above Lola's bed. She pulled the patchwork quilt over her legs and listened to the soothing rhythm. On the pale green wall across from her bed, a bulletin board displayed pieces of her life. In the center of the cork surface, a photograph of her father smiled back at her and just to the right of that was a worn page from an old atlas that indicated places she'd someday visit. A blue ribbon dangled from the wooden border, reminding her of the fourth grade spelling bee. Her thoughts wandered back to the day she received the ribbon. It was a happy time in a world that still held promise. It was a world of hope, contentment and innocence...before Sara entered.

A scathing plan for her vengeful assault came to her while she slept. Instead of becoming a home decorator, Lola would be a wedding planner. Strangely though, her one and only client would be Sara Parkins. Lola laughed wildly as detailed images of the suffering Sara danced inside her head. She would make sure that Sara's wedding would be a miserable disaster and certainly the talk of the town for years to come.

Beneath Lola's mattress was the all-important file to begin her work. The investigator's comprehensive notes included information so astonishing that it guaranteed a successful *coup*. While Lola sat at her desk scribbling on a yellow tablet, a scrupulous catalogue of ideas emerged below her swiveling pen, promising overdue retribution. Happily, she looked up from her work and noticed the sun had returned and dried up all of the wet clouds.

One of her first tasks would be to meet Mrs. Parkins and charm her way into her good graces and then shrewdly persuade the Parkins women into using Lola's contrived wedding service. Certain that Sara and her mother had already secured another wedding planner by this late stage in the game, Lola was still very confident that she would win them over, entirely. She knew how the Parkins women operated and what motivated them.

Lola chewed furiously on her pen, devising the first element to the plan. "What am I going to wear?" She headed over to her closet and opened the doors, "Nothing here will do." In order to present herself as a prominent wedding planner from Los Angeles, she would have to acquire a new, expensive wardrobe. Careful thought and fashion knowledge was an absolute must. The Parkins women could smell a designer rip-off from miles away, not to mention, a single strand of synthetic fiber. Whatever she wore in the company of the Parkins women had to coincide with her charade because Sara and her mother were all about current fashion and labels.

Lola would also have to assume a particular persona, sleek with style and sophistication to support the sham or they would see right through her.

From the investigator's file, she learned that Sara and her mother had standing appointments every Saturday morning at the MILLER LAKE VILLAGE SALON AND SPA. At the same time, Lola would also be a customer where she would stage an accidental meeting with Sara and her mother. "If all goes well, I can launch my plan from there," Lola cackled to herself.

With the phone firmly in her hand, Lola entered the key numbers to block her phone number before dialing. After a deep breath, she shook her body to rid herself of the nervous jitters to prepare for the role she had rehearsed. "Hello? This is Lola Sorenson of Los Angeles," she announced in an ostentatious tone. "I will be in your little town this week for a very important wedding and I will need to have my hair done on Saturday morning. Will that be a problem?" Before the voice on the other end could answer, Lola quickly interjected, "I will be in your charming town preparing for a rather large wedding coming up next weekend and my hairdresser that usually travels with me on these excursions has suddenly taken ill with appendicitis. I am in a desperate situation as this wedding is for very prominent clients of mine." Lola cleared her throat, "They are huge Hollywood celebrities," she emphasized with a hard whisper. "Do you think perhaps you could fit me in this Saturday morning, say around nine? Oh, thank you. I do so appreciate this. Now, please don't utter a word of the special wedding that I just mentioned. My clients wish to keep their wedding secret from all of the media. We wouldn't want circling helicopters to ruin their special day, so mum is the word." Triumphantly, Lola tossed the cordless phone onto the bed. Her first performance went well, she decided.

Chapter Fifteen

On Friday, Lola drove to Clawson, a neighboring town, to work out a deal with a private car rental agency. At almost twenty years of age, she would need some serious collateral to procure a car. After a bit of negotiating and a twenty-thousand dollar deposit, Lola drove away in a silver Mercedes, a crucial element to her charade.

When Saturday morning arrived, Lola pulled the elegant automobile into an empty parking space in front of the salon, hoping to draw attention from the curious onlookers inside the shop. With a rented sable coat draped sinuously around her shoulders, Lola sauntered inside the chic salon where inquiring glances immediately fell upon her, scrutinizing every inch of her being. Subtle whispers whirled around the facility as she made her way to the reception counter. Thoroughly engulfed by her role, Lola announced with self-importance, "I'm Lola Sorenson and I have a nine-o'clock with Lisa."

The bleached-blonde straightened her posture as if Lola was a celebrated icon. "Yes, follow me, Ms. Sorenson. I'll take you to see Lisa right now. Can I get you a cappuccino or something?"

"No, thank you," said Lola, preparing for the next phase of the plan. She was well acquainted with the wagging tongues of women, especially in small towns, and had counted on the fact that gossip traveled quickly in Miller Lake. She presumed that everyone inside the salon was already familiar with who she was or, rather, who she was pretending to be.

Swift glances and soft murmurs indicated there was, indeed, a buzz among the patrons. Gossip, her trusty accomplice, had fulfilled its mission.

An icy shrill raced up Lola's spine when her eyes landed on Sara who was reading a fashion magazine. Sara looked up and greeted Lola with an overly zealous grin. A paradox, Lola thought in amusement. Never in her entire life had Sara smiled at her in a greeting. Lola savored the moment and then employed the next facet of her scheme by tossing her purse to the floor. "Oh, my goodness!" she exclaimed with added drama. "I swear this bag jumped right out of my hand."

Strategically, Lola's expensive GUCCI prop fell directly at the feet of Sara's mother who was all too happy to assist the renowned wedding planner from Los Angeles. Elated by the fortuitous event, Mrs. Parkins eagerly retrieved the spilled items from the purse and kindly handed them to Lola.

As planned, one of Lola's phony business cards was cleverly planted among the items that had fallen to the floor.

"Oh, I see that you are a wedding coordinator," Mrs. Parkins smiled shrewdly, pretending not to already know that Lola was an exclusive wedding planner who regularly consorted with Hollywood's elite.

Lola wanted to slap the smug right out of Mrs. Parkins' smile, but she remained composed. *Idiot woman. She has no idea that she's being played and yet she thinks she's playing me.* The stupidity of the Parkins women brought a smile to Lola's face. "Yes, I am a coordinator," she finally answered, taking the card from Mrs. Parkins' hand. "Well, I mustn't keep Lisa waiting," Lola nodded at the receptionist and walked past Sara and her mother.

Sara huffed at her mother and cast a commanding glare after slamming the magazine down on the seat beside her. In a snit, Sara huffed again, "Mom," she whispered loudly, prompting her mother to initiate their rehearsed plan.

"Yes, I know!" Mrs. Parkins snapped back sharply. "Excuse me, Ms. Sorenson."

Lola stopped and turned. "Yes?"

"My name is Shaundra Parkins and this is my daughter, Sara." Both women stepped up to Lola. "Sara is going to be married very soon and we were just now thinking that perhaps we needed a new wedding planner for the grand event. We have some doubts about our current coordinator." Shaundra donned a look of concern and leaned in closer to Lola, whispering cattily, "I think she has a bit of a drinking problem." Shaundra nodded slightly with her lips pressed together.

"Oh, I see. You do have quite a predicament on your hands. With regard to the wedding, what is her progress thus far?"

"Not much, I'm afraid. We've only just initiated her services a little more than two weeks ago. And I'm just not impressed. You understand—the drinking thing," Shaundra reemphasized with a subtle raise of her eyebrows.

"I see."

Nervously, Shaundra adjusted her blouse collar before launching her question. "I was wondering, Ms. Sorenson, are you taking new clients at this time?"

"Well, I usually only do—" Lola deliberately interrupted her sentence as if to be exercising courteous discretion and then she rephrased her answer. "Well, do you have any references?" Lola nearly laughed at Shaundra's dumbfounded expression.

"References?" Shaundra stammered.

"Well, yes, I usually require references in my line of business, you understand, of course." Lola cut her words short and left Shaundra on the edge of unimportance.

The mother of the bride was nearly drooling at Lola's feet as she desperately wanted to enlist the services of a fancy socialite from Los Angeles whose clientele was so famous that it had to be kept secret.

Sara's demanding eyes darted back and forth between Lola and Shaundra.

Lola maintained her poise and resisted the urge to laugh at the simple-minded women. The most important element to Lola's plan was upon her and she didn't want to blow it by coming off too eager or too *blasé* about the matter. "I'll tell you what," Lola hesitated, "since your little town has been so good to me, I'll make an exception and forego the references. When did you say your wedding is?"

"April 30th." Sara blinked several times, awaiting Lola's response.

"And, of course, that's next year."

"Well, no," Shaundra corrected, "it's actually next month."

"Goodness!" Lola blurted, drawing more attention. "That only gives us about four weeks. And you just sought a wedding coordinator only two weeks ago?" Lola then paused for dramatic effect. "*Ahh*, is there a special reason why we're hurrying this wedding along?" she asked in a sugary tone, not resisting the unsavory jab at Sara.

The bold insinuation hovered over Sara and her mother for all those nearby to hear. Each of the patrons, at least those who weren't planted under hair dryers, was heavily interested in the conversation among the three ladies. The customers listened intently, awaiting Sara's response to the loaded question as Sara's eyes bulged at Lola's inference. Immediately, Sara and her pretentious mother struggled for a respectable answer, knowing full well that all of the nosey regulars were hinged on every word.

"Oh, we're just dying to get married," Sara responded with a hint of rile in her voice.

Revealing her suspicion, Lola took a quick glance at Sara's belly. "I guess we should get busy with all of the details right away then," Lola stressed. "Have you already sent out the save-the-date cards?"

"Oh, yes," Shaundra thrust in her answer.

"Good, that's a guarantee of a larger audience at your wedding." Lola chuckled, "Did I just say audience? I meant to say attendance, please, pardon me," she smiled and prepared to join Lisa who was still waiting. "I'm staying at the Green Gables Estate. Are you familiar with the place?"

"I am. And what a lovely place it is," Shaundra nodded.

"Splendid. Why don't you and Sandra come around nine tomorrow morning and we'll discuss the wedding over coffee and pastries? My treat!"

Sara's face flushed, "My name is Sara."

"What did you say?" Lola looked annoyed.

"*Uh*, my name is Sara."

"Oh, my apologies," Lola said dismissively. "We'll have to conclude our meeting by ten-thirty as I have an important event to attend later in the afternoon."

"That will be fine. And again, thank you, Ms. Sorenson. We'll see you at nine." Shaundra beamed as if she'd just won a trophy.

Lola was grateful that she was able to secure a short-term lease at the newly renovated Green Gables Estate. It was a magnificent structure, cradled in white clapboard with enormous dark green gables that crowned the stately manor. Everything was running perfectly, according to her plan.

While she waited at the estate for Sara and her mother to arrive, she stood in the library, admiring the old clock she had purchased from the private investigator. It looked regal sitting on top of the old mantle and she was glad that she had bought it.

As soon as the clock chimed nine, Sara and her mother drove up the long driveway beneath a budding canopy of cherry blossom trees. They rang the doorbell and waited. Deliberately, Lola left them standing on the porch for several minutes before answering the door. "Hello, ladies. I'm sorry. I was caught on the phone, long distance to Paris. I hope I didn't keep you waiting too long," Lola used her rehearsed voice.

After a round of niceties, Lola showed them to the parlor and invited them to take a seat on a luxurious floral sofa. "Let's get started, shall we?" She offered her despised guests a tray of baked goods.

Sara and her mother made their selections, neither aware of the unique ingredient Lola added earlier that morning, which consisted of a sprinkling of toilet water. "Since I won't be spending a year working on your wedding, I've decided that I'm only going to charge you twenty-five-thousand for my services," she casually announced while placing her contract on the sofa beside Shaundra. "I require half down to begin and, of course, you will be responsible for all of the wedding expenses."

Shaundra swallowed a bite of pastry over an instantly parched throat, "That sounds acceptable," she forced herself to say through strained composure, knowing her husband was going to flip out over the rising costs. Shaundra's powerful need to flaunt Sara's wedding that was conducted by a world-renowned wedding coordinator drove her to proceed with the outrageous arrangement. She was bound by her own pride and relished the idea that the entire town would be profoundly envious over her daughter's wedding. Somehow, she would make her husband accept it, she thought...she hoped.

"Your guests will always remember this extraordinary wedding," Lola nodded. "And your groom will never forget it. I promise you." Lola's eyes flashed with excitement. "I will take care of everything and I assure you, there is not another person in this world that can do for you what I can." She smiled and watched Sara take another bite of the soiled Danish. "Is all this agreeable to you, Shaundra?"

"Yes...yes, that will be fine." Shaundra lifted her cup.

The cost of the wedding wouldn't be such a problem for Mr. Parkins if he actually liked Nick, but he couldn't stand Nick at all. He had hoped that they would elope, saving him the expense because he expected the marriage to last no more than a year.

Suspecting that her mother had some reservations regarding the costly affair, Sara stiffened on the sofa and callously ignored that possibility. Quickly, she shoved a box of photos and fabric swatches toward Lola. "I'd like to have these photos of us projected onto a large screen during our reception."

"Marvelous. I think that's a delicious idea. Don't you?" Lola cast a tainted smile in Shaundra's direction. "You know, Ben and Jen...the first Ben and Jen," she clarified, "considered using their photos the same way at their wedding." Lola dropped the names for added leverage. "Of course, we all know what happened with them. Anyway, we won't think about them right now. Are the pictures in the order that you would like them displayed?"

"You know Jennifer Lopez?" Sara was very impressed and wanted to hear more about it.

"Yes, I know Jen quite well. Now, about those pictures, are they in order?"

"Yes, they are," Sara was still feeling star-struck.

"Splendid," Lola smiled, hardly able to harness her own excitement over the fact that Sara had just unwittingly contributed to her own demise. "Now then, your bridesmaids will be wearing dresses made from this silver material?" She dangled a piece of cloth from the very edge of her fingertips. "And the blue fabric is for the bows around the waist. Is that right?"

"Yes," Sara said softly, sensing Lola's indifference. "What do you think of the colors?" She searched Lola's face for her crown endorsement.

Wise to Sara's colossal need for praise, Lola avoided expressing too much enthusiasm. "All right then, these will do," said Lola, with a hint of deprecation. "Now, as I understand it, the dresses are nearly complete. Is that correct?"

Sara squirmed against the plush sofa, regretting her choice in colors. "Yes."

"Well, there's no time to make any changes, but I think what you have chosen will be fine." Lola liked toying with Sara. "How many bridesmaids?"

"Three. My cousin and my two friends, Joya and Debbie."

This is almost too easy, Lola laughed inside, enriched by the fact that Joya and Debbie would be members of the wedding party. Certainly, Sara couldn't resist rubbing her friends' noses in her grand wedding. Lola could read Sara like a book and it pleased her thoroughly to know her enemy so well.

The short meeting reached its conclusion when the old clock in the other room chimed at ten-thirty. "Well, I think we have discussed everything we need to for today. Don't worry, ladies, leave everything up to me. I'll create the most unforgettable wedding for you. You're just going to die when you see all that I have planned for you."

"Oh, I'm sure it's going to be lovely, with all of your expertise and such. Sara and I are very excited to be working with you." Shaundra lifted her purse from the floor and prepared to leave.

"I assure you, ladies, the pleasure is all mine." She cast a pleasing smile. "We'll meet again in a couple of days and, at that time, I'll reveal my luscious designs for your wedding. Like I said earlier, the ideas coming out of Paris are simply going to knock you over! Let me just collect your down payment and we'll be ready to launch this glorious wedding."

"Oh, my goodness, I nearly forgot." Shaundra grabbed her checkbook from her purse.

Lola took the check and showed Sara and her mother to the door. The gravel driveway crackled beneath Shaundra's blue Mercedes as she drove away from the estate.

Relieved to be rid of Shaundra and Sara for the day, Lola's appetite returned. She wandered into the kitchen, pulled a wedge of cheese from the refrigerator and opened a box of crackers that was sitting on the table. While eating an early lunch, she looked around the kitchen, appreciating the old-fashioned features that remained. Just above her was a brass chandelier that still used candles and scattered around the room were several sconces that also used candles. Below her feet were stone tiles that rested firmly in mortar, adding to the antiquity. Her favorite, among the historic relics, was a large fireplace that was positioned in the center of a massive red brick wall. Iron utensils used for stoking the fire sat ornately beside the gaping fire hole. And left of the fireplace, a window displayed a sweeping forest behind the manor where a stone structure remained, presumably former servants' quarters. It was covered in ivy and nestled among many large trees. It was as enchanting as the main house.

Lola tried to visualize what life was like in the grand home one-hundred and forty years before her birth. At the sink, she imagined a proud cook preparing fresh vegetables for the prominent family in which she served. Later, that family would enjoy an elegant meal in the formal dining room that was located down the hall. And outside in the special lawns, Lola projected children playing in the gardens, squealing with laughter. She fondled a ring of skeleton keys that dangled from a nail beside the rustic pantry door and wondered how many hands had held those keys and what stories those keys could share with her.

Lola washed her plate in the sink and placed the dish back into the cupboard before heading into the library that was next to the dining room. In there, she would work on her sinister plans until nightfall.

"Lola, how was your day?" Mrs. Wilson took Lola's coat and hung it on a coat tree inside her foyer.

"Well…it was very productive," Lola cheerfully replied, stomping fresh spring snow off her feet.

Mrs. Wilson's eyes sparkled with delight, encouraging Lola to elaborate.

"I've worked out some strategies for the decorating business." Lola lied behind a counterfeit smile. "And I should have it up and running within a month or so," she said, forcing another fabrication. She walked over to the fireplace and stirred the glowing logs, hoping to kill the conversation because she hated lying to her mother. She needed to get away for a while. Her lies were enormous and eventually her deceit could be tracked by her mother if she stayed in her mother's house much longer. Lola chewed on her lip as she pondered her predicament.

"I'm very excited for you." Mrs. Wilson's voice rang with hope as she sat down on the sofa ready to hear more of Lola's plans.

"Well, I'll be traveling a lot, beginning tomorrow," Lola announced, making an on-the-spot decision to reside at Green Gables Estate for the duration of her secret operation. She would simply let her mother believe that she was away traveling, all the while, running her covert mission from the extravagant estate.

Some time after midnight, Lola sat at her desk, reflecting on recent conversations with Sara and her mother. She was convinced there was more behind Sara's sudden rush to the aisle, because Sara's expression in the salon had revealed plenty. Lola assumed that there was a baby on the way and that Sara was hoping to be married as quickly as possible. Rich thoughts flowed through her mind as she continued to spin her web, wondering how a baby would affect her plan, if there were a baby.

The following morning, two bulging suitcases sat on Lola's bed as she explained to her mother that she would return in a couple of weeks. "When you want to reach me, Mom, just call me on my cell phone. I'm not exactly sure where I'll be staying. I'm just leaving it up to fate and where my ideas lead me." Lola hugged her mother goodbye and made her way through the door.

Among the many luxurious rooms inside the magnificent mansion, the grand library was Lola's favorite. Cherry wood paneling lined the entire room with one wall fully dedicated to an enormous bookcase that housed at least a thousand books. An enormous brick fireplace, boasting an elegant marble mantelpiece, accentuated the stylish furniture inside the room. Long curtains of red velvet filled the tall windows that reached fifteen feet high and positioned between the two soaring windows was a solid cherry desk where Lola would perfect her designs toward justice.

Before sitting down, Lola ran her hand across the fine wooden surface on the desk, recognizing its worth while piles of bridal magazines, notebooks, DVDs and floral books awaited her attention beside a Tiffany lamp. She chewed on her pen while going over intricate details to her just designs.

Like a venomous spider awaiting her *dinner guests*, Lola would linger patiently inside her web. Her plan began with Billy Elders, a solid member of Sara's twisted clan. Because he brought the booze that fateful night, he guaranteed himself a place at Lola's table. *The Feast of Reckoning*. With his lust for women and drink, he was an easy mark. And with that, Lola's mission was underway.

Concealed by sunglasses and a platinum blond wig, Lola prudently deflated the rear tire on the Mercedes and waited in the grocery store parking lot for Billy's shift to end. "Excuse me!" she shouted from her car when she spotted Billy walking toward his old truck. "I've gotten a flat tire and could use a gentleman's assistance." With a sultry smile, she baited her hook. "Would you be able to help me?" The red knit dress hugged Lola's sensuous form, rendering him helpless inside her trap.

"Sure. Do you have a spare?" Billy leered at the voluptuous figure standing before him.

"I'm not sure. It's a rented car," she said, pressing the trunk release button.

Billy hurried around to the back of the car and gaped around the side of the trunk to steal another peek at Lola. Next to the spare tire was a fifth of Jack Daniels she had cleverly planted for him. "Do you like to party?"

"Well, honey, of course I do. Doesn't everybody?" A noxious giggle followed Lola's rehearsed drawl.

Willingly, Billy tugged on the bait. "Hey, I'm off work now. Would you like to go and party somewhere? Maybe my apartment?"

Lola wanted to wretch, but kept to her charade, "Sure, but not at your apartment. I know where we can go," she hesitated briefly, "it's private and out of the way."

Billy's lecherous grin nearly caused her to vomit from repulsion. She was nervous and hoped that her scheme would not fail her. If it backfired, Lola could be in a serious heap of trouble.

When he was finished, he dropped the jack back into the trunk along with the flattened tire. "Are you ready to do some major partying?" The bottle was hardly in his hand for a second when he cracked the seal. Once more, he leered at her and then took a long, greedy drink.

What a louse, she thought. He hadn't even been invited to drink yet. She withheld her scowl as she watched whiskey drip from his chin before he wiped it away. "You just follow me in your truck, doll, and I'll take real good care of you."

Billy followed the Mercedes to an abandoned warehouse where they both parked behind the old building. Cleverly, she chose the old warehouse for its seclusion. Several large trees and overgrown bushes near the edge of the parking lot provided a private setting for the impromptu rendezvous. She wanted no witnesses to the set-up. With a flask that she pulled from her purse, Lola clanked his bottle of Jack Daniels, "Cheers."

"What's that you got in there?" Billy tipped the bottle of *Jack* to his eager mouth.

"Oh, this is special. It's what ladies drink." She cast an alluring gaze in his direction.

"Well, then, drink up," he grinned, winking with his left eye.

Lola tried to ignore how revolting he was. She didn't smoke, but she bummed a cigarette from Billy for effect and also because a lit cigarette to the eye could serve as a handy weapon if Billy got out of control.

She tipped her flask several times, portraying herself a seasoned drinker. Little did Billy know, but her flask was filled with herbal tea. "I didn't figure you to be a lightweight," she challenged.

"Lightweight? I'll show you who's a lightweight!" He gulped more of the brown fluid down his throat, which promptly made him more senseless. In mere moments, Lola watched him stagger as he approached her with another lusty grin.

"I've got an idea," she quickly interjected, stepping on another cigarette. "Follow me to my house, I'm sure we'd be more comfortable there."

"Now, you're talking," he slurred. "I'll follow you, cause I don't know where you live." He laughed and stumbled over to his truck.

"All right, stay close," Lola told him. "I don't want to lose you." She jumped into her car and prepared her cell phone to dial.

Like a fish on a lure, Billy followed closely behind the silver Mercedes in his old Ford. Slowly, his truck swerved back and forth over the centerline in the road making Lola anxious. Going no faster than fifteen miles per hour, she still felt nervous, hoping not to endanger other motorists, even though she had wisely chosen an isolated road. Without any delay, she dialed *911*. "Hello? There is a man driving dangerously on Old Range Road and it appears that he is really drunk or something. I thought I should report it to you right away. Yes, he just passed the old paper warehouse heading north. All right. You're welcome. What was that? Oh, my name is Debbie. Thank you and goodbye."

In the distance, Lola could already see the blue and red flashing lights approaching her. "You're about to get yours, Billy." She laughed hard and accelerated to the proper speed, leaving Billy in her vengeful wake. The cruiser sped passed her car, whipping around in a U-turn behind Billy. "Yes!" she shouted, looking into the rear view mirror, "that should mess up your life for a while."

Chapter Sixteen

The following morning, Lola made herself a cup of coffee and opened the newspaper to the local crime section to see if Billy's name had made an appearance on the PAGE OF SHAME. She laughed in triumph when she spotted his picture and read the brief description of his despicable crime. Her plan was a success and because this was Billy's second traffic arrest involving alcohol inside of a year, she was certain that a mandatory jail sentence would follow the appalling incident.

Humming all the way down the hall to the library, Lola retrieved her yearbook and opened it on a specific page. For a moment, she studied Billy's photo and then she drew a black X through it.

She was now free to focus on Debbie and Joya who were equally responsible for all of the sorrow in her life. Their silence regarding Sara's tampering with the fountain had betrayed the truth, which ultimately led to Mr. Wilson's death. And for that, they would surely pay.

For Debbie's punishment, Lola had to carefully fashion a plan that would accommodate the distance to New York. She had only a small window of opportunity, so her technique had to be quick and methodical. Luckily, Debbie's supreme vanity provided the solution.

It was early in the morning and Lola could smell spring at its best. She loaded the Mercedes with her luggage and set out for New York City, which was about a six-hour drive. Her first few hours driving were spent alternating between music and talk radio. Finally, she turned off the stereo and listened to the dull rumble of the tires while her mind ran through the plan.

Rising in the distance, she could see the legendary pinnacles that articulated the magnificent city. A glorious architectural empire with dignified buildings that dominated the famous New York Isle openly welcomed her. She was so impressed by the extraordinary scene that she pulled her car over to the side of the road to fully absorb it.

Immediately upon entering the city, she realized that she should have arrived by other means, perhaps by plane and taxi. Navigating the overly congested grids was a slight oversight on her part, leaving her a bundle of nerves as she had not fully anticipated the difficulty of driving through New York City traffic. After barely escaping one crash after another, and missing several turns, she finally figured out that if she abandoned her proper driving habits and simply assumed the way of the people, she would successfully make it through the chaotic maze. "When in Rome," she chuckled nervously, steering through another near-miss.

Two hours later, she circled the same block three times until she was able to turn into her hotel's parking garage. A bit rattled, she sat quietly in her car for a moment and collected herself.

Debbie's office was across the street from Lola's hotel and having just driven through hell, Lola was grateful that she had chosen the pricey, yet convenient accommodations. She gazed through her hotel window, surveying the wandering citizens on the street below her. It was *4:34 p.m.*, when an exodus occurred, flooding the sidewalks with weary workers in front of Debbie's office building. The meandering crowd began to divide while Lola sorted them with her eyes. "Where are you, Debbie?" She picked up the phone and dialed Debbie's office.

"Biggs and Stadler," came a small voice on the other end.

"Is Deborah Harrison available?"

"Hold on a moment and I'll check for you. No, I'm sorry, she has already left for the day. But she'll be in tomorrow morning at eight."

"I'll just get in touch with her then. No message. Thank you." Lola hung up the phone and sat down on the bed, glad to know Debbie still worked there.

Her many unscheduled detours while driving in the city's labyrinth caused her to arrive too late. She'd have to carry out her mission the next day, but that was all right with Lola because she had prepared for an overnight stay.

With nothing else to occupy her time, she turned on the television and leaned back against the headboard. Details of specific New York attractions paraded across the television screen, encouraging her to explore the mighty city, but she was hesitant because before the death of her father, her parents had planned to take her to New York as a graduation gift, but Sara's menacing hands crushed that dream.

She flipped through the channels, but boredom loomed, forcing her to make a decision. Her eyes landed on her suitcase when an idea emerged. A new disguise awaited her, permitting her to venture out into the city. Beginning with a long mane of blond hair, she stuffed all of her hair inside the wig and then she grabbed a pair of sunglasses. "I'll just do a little sight-seeing and dinner out," she told herself before heading to the door.

The congested sidewalk along SIXTH AVENUE swallowed Lola up in a bustling swarm of New Yorkers and wonder-struck tourists. Eventually, she slowed her pace to take in all of the intriguing storefronts and impressive architectural compositions that were planted along the popular avenue. "Oh, pardon me," she politely offered, after being spun into a window by an overzealous pedestrian. The large man kept his fierce stride, hardly even noticing her. She percolated on the offense for a moment when a whiff of baked bread kindly intervened. Considering it an invitation, she made her way to the small deli across the street.

Seven people waited at the counter in front of her, giving her plenty of time to make a decision from a menu that held at least a million possibilities. A bit overwhelmed, she decided on a Reuben sandwich, a safe choice, "with a pickle on the side." When she turned from the counter, she spotted a table that had just become available. Immediately, she claimed it, already adapting to the New York style. She wiped the table with her napkin and then feasted on the long overdue meal.

Through the window, she noticed that New Yorkers didn't saunter down sidewalks as folks did in Miller Lake, rather, they moved briskly, appearing to be heading to a very important engagement. When a few interesting passersby caught her attention, she projected herself into their lives, wondering what it would feel like. Some, she imagined, were rushing home to be welcomed by their families, while others were heading off to an all-important meeting. And, perhaps, some were even going out on a romantic date with their beloved. She sighed at the latter.

184

The next morning, the revolving doors on Debbie's office building swallowed worker after worker while Lola watched from her window, hoping for a glimpse of Debbie. It was nearly eight o'clock when she looked at her watch and at *7:58*, Debbie arrived where she was engulfed by the corporate abyss. "I'll see you at *4:30*, Debbie."

Lola slept the day away while the television played through the network schedule. When the time finally came to execute her plan, she rolled eagerly out of bed and stepped into the shower. Later, with a towel wrapped around her head, she stood at the foot of the bed, surveying the scattered items on the white comforter. Her eyes flickered with excitement as she hovered over the collection, which included a wig, magazine, duct tape, a pair of leather gloves, sunglasses, scissors and an electric razor. Carefully, she assessed her tools. "*Oops*, almost forgot." She reached into her suitcase and wrapped inside a green scarf was her gun; a firearm she had borrowed from her father's collection of antique weaponry.

Moments later, with the wig snug on her skull, she adjusted the sunglasses on her face and closed the suitcase. Inside her coat pocket was the gun, awaiting its role for the mission while the rest of the paraphernalia remained hidden in her purse. Three more times, she searched the room, making sure she had gathered up all of her belongings. When she was satisfied, Lola placed the hotel key onto the dresser and headed for the parking garage to leave her suitcase in her car.

With plenty of time to spare, Lola decided to have a light meal in the hotel café before her surprise reunion with Debbie. Blankly, she stared at the menu. Distracted.

"Have you decided yet?" A friendly voice broke through her thoughts.

"*Uhm*, yes, I'll have the turkey sandwich on wheat, hold the mayo, no fries and a glass of tea, please."

"All right then, I'll be right back with your tea."

"Thank you."

Rowdy patrons that were sitting in a nearby booth began to pluck at Lola's nerves. Among them a woman who kept cackling in an obnoxious pitch, each time bringing Lola closer to screaming. The disruptive woman intercepted Lola's biting glare when their eyes met. Immediately following the silent, but stern exchange, whispers circulated the boisterous group of friends and soon a string of daunting glances trespassed Lola's table. She ignored the woman and her companions, not yielding to their deliberate intimidation.

"Here is your tea and I'll have your food out in just a minute." The waitress placed the glass of tea onto a coaster and hurried over to another table.

Lola concentrated on her plan and forced herself to avoid nagging concerns of something possibly going wrong. Her act would be criminal, punishable by law, but she remained true to her operation.

Outside of Debbie's office building, Lola sat on a bench pretending to read a magazine. A casual glance at her watch signaled that at any moment her unsuspecting prey would arrive. The ever-spinning door continued to churn out pedestrians while she waited. When she finally spotted Debbie, Lola was ready to swoop down like a vulture and claim her victim. Casually, she placed the magazine in her bag and slowly fell into step behind Debbie.

They walked only a few blocks to the subway where a crowd of people had already formed a line on the platform waiting to board. A few passengers trickled past, allowing a comfortable distance between Debbie and Lola. When Debbie chose a seat on the subway, Lola carefully selected a seat three rows behind her. Nonchalantly, she pulled a pair of leather gloves from her bag and slipped them over her hands. Adrenaline fueled her desires and dissolved any hint of doubt.

Lola slithered along in Debbie's vigorous stride and still, no one was suspect of Debbie's unwelcome shadow. Gently, Lola halted her pace when Debbie dropped her keys in front of her apartment building. From the information gathered by the private investigator, Lola knew that Debbie lived on the second floor in apartment *203*. She would allow Debbie a little time to settle into her home before paying her a much deserved visit.

After climbing a flight of stairs, Lola planted her hand on the gun inside her pocket. She took a deep breath and prepared to storm Debbie's apartment, but as soon as she gripped the doorknob, she heard voices through the door. Immediately, she yanked her hand off the knob. Debbie was not alone!

Daringly, Lola leaned in and pressed her ear against the door to listen to a series of soft mumbles alternating inside the apartment.

"All right, sweetie, I'll see you tomorrow morning after work," said the man on the other side of the door. "I love you."

Lola quickly spun around before he came through the door. Cleverly, she stepped in front of the neighboring apartment, portraying herself as an arriving guest. Debbie's unexpected roommate swept past Lola, leaving her in a wake of his cheap cologne. Her heart thudded inside her chest as she stood frozen in front of apartment 204 debating whether she should proceed with her plan or not. When he had been gone for several minutes, Lola decided to carry out the day's mission.

She hoped Debbie's door was still unlocked, otherwise, she'd have to knock and pretend to be a lost visitor. She didn't care for that scenario. The idea of bursting into Debbie's apartment, uninvited, was more gratifying.

Again, she took hold of the doorknob and turned it gently. Debbie was sitting on a green sofa staring at a television inside an oak cabinet. A small lamp, sitting on the table beside her, cast a subtle glow inside the room. Several boxes were scattered, some full and some empty. Lola presumed that Debbie's boyfriend was in the midst of moving in with her.

The blaring television provided a stealthy entrance. Debbie had no clue that a stranger was standing a mere four feet behind her, staging an attack. Lola locked the door and then charged the scene, pointing her gun at her target. Debbie jumped to her feet, hardly making a squeal as she stared at the small barrel of the pistol that was aimed directly at her face.

"What do you want? I don't have very much money, but I'll give you what I have." Her words were frail, exposing her fear. "My purse is over there on the table," she instinctively offered.

Lola pulled the duct tape from her bag. "I don't want your money. I have more money than you can count. Just sit down in that chair over there and shut up," Lola ordered, pointing at the straight back chair beside the kitchen table. "Just do what I say and I won't hurt you," she warned.

"Please! What do you want?" Debbie pleaded.

"Let me just ask you something," Lola glared, "have you ever done anything in your life that you now regret?"

"What?" Debbie looked confused.

"Are you stupid?" Lola snapped. "All right, since you're a moron, I'll ask my question again. Is there anyone you've ever wronged in your life?" Lola was thinking of her father lying helplessly on the living room floor...dying. And it was Debbie's shared cowardice that put him there.

Debbie remained still, staring blankly. "No, no, I've always been a good person."

"Really?" Lola looked at her harshly through her dark glasses. "Are you sure about that?" The eerie pitch in which Lola spoke sounded foreign to her ears.

"Yes, I'm sure," Debbie answered with a quake in her voice. Obviously, she was shaken by the harsh intrusion and bizarre questioning.

Lola shook her head in disgust, "I don't think so."

Debbie could feel Lola's piercing stare behind her glasses and, yet, she dared to speak, "I *am* a good person."

Saying nothing, Lola planted Debbie's legs firmly against the chair slats and wrapped them with duct tape. Surprisingly, Debbie was cooperative, but Lola didn't drop her guard. At any moment, Debbie could resist, resulting in a dangerous struggle.

"Please! Tell me what you are going to do," Debbie begged.

"You already had your chance to speak, but you blew it. Now shut up and I mean it," Lola strongly advised, waving her gun in Debbie's face.

Debbie's tears splashed against the hardwood floor. Lola began to tape Debbie's wrists together behind her back. Flashbacks of the many years' torment flooded Lola's mind along with the knowledge that her mother would probably die a lonely widow.

"Please...I don't know why you're here or what you are going to do. Please stop," Debbie pleaded softly.

A swift slap of gray tape across the mouth instantly quieted Debbie and only a soft moan was audible. Lola took the razor from her purse and plugged it in before making brutal swipes across Debbie's skull. Her body shuddered every time the cruel instrument scraped her tender scalp, dropping layers of her lovely mane to the floor. In just moments, Debbie's fuzzy scalp was revealed except for a few remaining strands of hair left dangling at the base of her skull; a cruel reminder of what she once treasured. Lola leaned back and studied her subject, fully enjoying the moment. The bound creature in the chair sobbed, bringing Lola to a bout of maniacal laughter.

Lola looked around the dreary room, searching for a mirror. Basic white curtains hung dismally in the window and the stark walls continued to reflect Debbie's lack of creativity. The room was cluttered with misplaced magazines, discarded clothing and dirty dishes. "You wait right there," Lola joked, spotting a mirror on the wall. "Have a look!" she demanded. Her voice was thick with hatred for the coward sobbing in the chair. "Now, flaunt that, you little witch."

Debbie turned away in stern protest. Her defiance was met with a hard slap across the face, leaving a solid handprint on her cheek just above the tape. With a raised hand, Lola hovered ominously over Debbie and then she slapped her a second time. "Look!" she demanded again, forcing Debbie to examine her naked scalp. "I want you to see how lovely you are."

Soft whimpers filled the room as Debbie looked briefly into the mirror to satisfy the crazy woman who had just invaded her home and assaulted her. She was horrified by her reflection and quickly turned her head. There was no escape from her reality. On the floor was a large pile of her hair and on her chest and shoulders were mere remnants of her legendary locks that glistened in her tears.

"How dare you cry?" Lola nearly shouted and turned to gather her things before she lost control. "By the way, the guy who claims to love you has another girlfriend." Her tone was glazed in venom. The spontaneous jab, serving as a bonus, brought Lola to laugh. Her few words had simply destroyed Debbie's perfectly good relationship with her new boyfriend.

Lola laughed again and grabbed a dirty coffee cup from the table and headed toward the bathroom. When she returned, she had a dripping cup in her hand. Debbie's eyes swelled with dread as Lola's disturbing grin approached her. Clearly, she interpreted Lola's intentions. Without wavering, Lola reached up and poured an entire cup of toilet water over Debbie's head, leaving her soggy in filth.

Debbie jerked fiercely and wailed behind the tape that muffled her cries.

"Have you seen that toilet? That's disgusting," Lola scolded. "You wish now that you had cleaned it, don't you?" Before leaving, Lola twisted the heat thermostat on the wall to eighty degrees. "Have fun!" she taunted, slipping through the door.

Lola's champion mood quickly dimmed to a state of fear when she drove slowly past a seamy motel that she had earlier flagged. Twice she went around the block before getting up the nerve to proceed with the cryptic task that awaited her.

The shabby motel hosted a wide range of undesirables that lurked in the darkened doorways and shadows of the corrupt facility. If anything went wrong, grave consequences could develop, leaving her either dead or imprisoned, but fear wouldn't stop her.

Inside her car, she observed the happenings on the street and when she spotted her target, she made her move. Within a few short minutes, Lola was safely back in the Mercedes and headed back to Green Gables.

The roads to Miller Lake were dark and nearly empty with only a few travelers making their way in the night. Lola sped down the highway while entertaining images of Debbie's naked white skull bobbed in and out of her thoughts, making her giggle.

Later, her mind ran busy, fine-tuning the next phase to her plan when tender memories of Mike began to penetrate her thoughts. Fatigue, perhaps the isolation, was getting to Lola as she drove the lonely highway. She forced him to the far recesses of her mind, not allowing herself to tread where his memories dwelled. She occupied her mind only with vengeful schemes and resisted the urge to reach out in his memory. Guilt was playing its hand, ready to interfere, but Lola enforced her own will until she could feel no more.

She turned into the long driveway toward the old estate and parked the Mercedes in the garage. "Oh, I forgot the store," she grumbled, dragging her tired body out of the vehicle. Though the brief excursion to New York was most rewarding, it was also exhausting.

The refrigerator was bare, equaling the stark condition of the pantry. Defeated, she leaned against the refrigerator, ready to succumb to starvation when an idea popped into her head. A moment later, she was perched over the desk, flipping through piles of papers and magazines until she found the menu from the local pizzeria that delivered until *2 a.m.*

In the midst of a deep yawn, Lola flicked on the television using the remote control and switched the channels until she came across the re-broadcast of the nightly news. And, just as she sank her teeth into the pizza, she heard the anchorwoman announce an upcoming story about "a bizarre home invasion that occurred in New York City early this evening." Lola was thrilled that her plan was so despicable that it made it to the news.

Chapter Seventeen

The alarm on her cell phone buzzed, stirring Lola to wake at 7 *a.m.* As soon as she switched it off, she remembered that she had to call Shaundra first thing. Repulsion invaded her body as she picked up the house phone, dreading the sound of Shaundra's voice so early in the morning.

"Hello?"

"Hello, is this Shaundra?"

"Yes."

"This is Lola Sorenson, I've just gotten back into town and would like to schedule a meeting with you some time today?"

"Sure. Today is fine. What time?"

"Is ten convenient for you?" Lola drummed her fingers on the desk.

"Absolutely. We'll be there at ten."

"All right, see you then." Lola hung up the phone and began preparations for the morning meeting. She glanced at her planner and caught a glimpse of Shaundra's check peeking out over a page. She paused for moment, pondering her history with the Parkins family. The threat of a slander suit still burned inside her mind and so it gave Lola immense pleasure to spend as much of the Parkins' money that she could get away with.

When the door chimes rang inside Green Gables, Lola left her guests waiting outside for a full minute before leading them to the parlor. "Goodness, I just haven't had time to get your check into the bank," Lola declared, after letting Shaundra's sizable check fall insignificantly to the floor as if it was something of a petty nature.

The sting of her husband's disapproval over her passing over that amount of money still resonated in Shaundra's expression as she stared at the check. She hadn't mentioned to anyone that her husband was furious with her for entering into such a lavish business relationship without his consent and knowledge. He was angrier with her than he had ever been in their twenty-three years of marriage. It was no secret that Mr. and Mrs. Parkins were wealthy, but even they had to impose limits. Mr. Parkins wasn't willing to part with his money so easily, especially for a wedding that he hardly believed in. Shaundra had risked a lot, she realized, but she and Mr. Parkins were legally bound to Lola's contract. In secret, Shaundra worried that her husband would throw her out into the street, but she was under Lola's stiff agreement and there was no escape clause, she had explained to him. "Foolish woman!" he had shouted while slamming the door in her face during an angry argument. He didn't speak to her for nearly two days.

Lola hoped that the exorbitant costs of the wedding were becoming a hot issue inside Sara's family. She smiled at the fantasy. "Please, have some iced tea, Shaundra." Lola passed a tainted glass to the unsuspecting woman.

By noon, the wedding invitations were on their way to the printer for rush service. The bridesmaids' dresses were ready for pickup and the flowers had all been ordered. The church had already been reserved before Lola came onto the scene, leaving one less burden for her to tackle. All of the table decorations and romantic lighting essentials were ordered and scheduled for setup. The band, along with the photographer and bridal limousine, was secured. All that was left to do, that day, was visit the baker and caterer's facility for samples and place the orders.

The bride and her mother followed Lola to the rear of the baker's shop where he had a room especially designed for tasting and selecting wedding cakes...expensive wedding cakes. Crisp white linens covered a round table that was elegantly decorated with white candles and a beautiful floral arrangement. His presentation was almost as delicious as the cake he offered. He poured champagne into crystal glasses and then opened his book of wedding cake masterpieces.

Shaundra's eyes shifted from the portfolio to the champagne in her glass. Yes, he'd have to get you tanked to get you to pay these prices, she thought.

"Oh, Sara," Lola gasped dramatically, pointing to a ten-thousand-dollar cake. "This cake is extraordinary and I've never ever seen anything else like it!" Lola exclaimed. "Just look at the intricate detail. It matches the lace in your wedding gown. Isn't that amazing? And have you ever seen frosting so white?" Lola feigned wonder. "I must say, Los Angeles has never seen anything so fine. Honestly, Shaundra, this cake is a steal at this price. A cake like this would cost you fifty-thousand dollars in L.A. Easy."

Shaundra's eyes glazed over.

"Sara, your wedding will be legendary," said Lola, feeding the bride more bull. "Why, even *Cinderella* would be jealous."

A faraway look came to Sara's eyes. She was deep in fantasy, picturing the fairytale cake at her wedding where she and Nick danced around it looking so elegant and noble.

"You know, this has me thinking," Lola paused for effect, "I just might submit some photos of your wedding to *Bride*…if that is acceptable to you and your mother." Lola cleverly cast her line, knowing they would lunge for the bait.

Sara nearly fell out of her chair and the baker beamed, puffing his chest up with pride. "Here, have some more." He bent over the table to pour more champagne into their glasses.

"Easy there," Lola cautioned with a smile, "it's pretty early in the day for that much champagne."

He bowed graciously and reached into his pocket, still grinning. "I'll leave you ladies alone to discuss your preferences. When you are ready for your samples, just ring this bell." He placed a small bell onto the table.

Sara's eyes fogged over as she imagined her wedding appearing in *Bride Magazine*. "Mother, wouldn't that be awesome?"

For the moment, Shaundra couldn't answer her daughter as she was already deep in her own thoughts, calculating the many benefits to the magazine exposure. The positive publicity for her husband's company would be considered a smooth business maneuver, she dared to think. Hoped. Then, he'll have to forgive me she decided.

Sara browsed the book one final time before deciding on the cake that Lola had insisted was the best for her wedding. Shaundra hoped that her husband would offer a reprieve if the wedding was covered in the magazine. But the growing dollar signs still worried her.

Sensing that Shaundra wanted to speak privately with Sara regarding the steep cost of the cake, Lola considered politely excusing herself from the table, but it was more fun watching Shaundra squirm inside the confines of pride and a non-negotiable contract. Lola wouldn't make it easy for Sara nor her mother and she banked on the fact that Shaundra was too proud to openly discuss financial matters in front of Lola and would, therefore, proceed with the staggering costs.

Lola's thoughts drifted for a moment. Sara killed Joe, though not intentionally, she did it and Lola's father paid the ultimate price. Never did Sara fess up about the whole ordeal, instead, she left the burden of her crime to fall on Lola and her family. The Parkins family deserved what was coming to them. For her crimes, Sara would suffer. And for the parents who raised and protected a monster, they, too would have a painful dose of justice. "Shall I ring the bell?" Lola asked with a thread of antagonism, daring Shaundra to suggest a more inexpensive cake. A bead of perspiration appeared on Shaundra's forehead, bringing Lola to smile even wider.

"Yes," Sara interjected, not taking heed to her mother's signs of distress.

Shaundra nodded, though her enthusiasm was wavering.

The baker's assistant arrived with an elegant tray that carried a wide variety of wedding cake flavors. Under other circumstances, Lola might have been tempted to try some of the fine confections, but her companions were becoming increasingly nauseating. *How do these people stand each other?*

"Oh, this looks divine." Lola smiled and thanked the assistant. She waited for Shaundra to fill her mouth will cake before asking, "Do you have your checkbook with you today?"

"*Uh-hum.*"

"Splendid. We'll need to put down a deposit on the cake. Just to make sure, you still want the cake that Sara adores, correct?"

"Yes," Shaundra forced a smile.

"He requires half down to make the order and final payment two days before the wedding. Is that acceptable?"

"That will be fine." Shaundra dabbed her mouth with a linen napkin.

After all of the samples had been tested, Sara decided on a white cake with raspberry cream filling.

"All right then, go ahead and write the check and I'll give it to him while you and Sara finish the rest of your champagne." Lola waited politely as Shaundra filled out another check.

Within the hour, Lola met Shaundra and Sara in front of the caterer's establishment. "This place comes highly recommended," said Lola with a tug on the door. "It smells heavenly in here." Immediately, the savory aromas swirled around them, clearly defining the chef's ability and reputation.

"Mr. Parkins and I have always enjoyed this restaurant," Shaundra stated, looking around the place.

"Good, then you're familiar with it." Lola smiled.

Shaundra nodded, looking like a snob.

"Oh, Mother, I'm so hungry!" Sara rubbed her growling stomach.

"Normally, we do the cake samples after the caterer, but, Simon, the head chef, wasn't available any other time, so I jumped at his first availability." Lola led the two ignorant sheep to the back of the restaurant where they gathered at a small table, not far from the kitchen. Each of the ladies was given a menu with a price breakdown relative to entrées and number of guests.

Lola kept peeking over her menu to watch a symphony of varying expressions mounting on Shaundra's face as she considered the options for the wedding feast. Every kink and ripple revealed her stress and even her eyebrows had taken on a language all their own. Lola snickered behind her menu and for a moment, she could almost swear that she saw Shaundra's bleached hair turn grey.

"I know this place is a bit pricey, but I've searched all over town and even neighboring communities for a caterer that was available to service your wedding. I've also had my assistant working on it, but nothing, sad to say, is available during your special time of need." Lola lied without batting an eye. "So, what do you think? Or…we could order up some of those fancy trays from the local grocer?" Lola's eyes sparked with shrewdness, "those are always nice."

That notion was appalling even to Shaundra who was still suffering from sticker shock and possible eviction from her own home. The veiled insult prompted Shaundra to proceed with the expensive caterer, which is precisely what Lola had expected. Pride can be costly, Lola lectured them inside her head.

Small portions of salmon, lobster, shrimp, chicken and prime rib were delivered on silver trays for the three women to sample.

Sara searched her mother's face, seeking input regarding the wedding supper. Shaundra's expression was that of a stone, leaving Sara unable to decipher her mother's thoughts. "Mother, I'll let you decide. Which do you think should be served?"

"Well," Shaundra began, happy to be a part of the decision process, "I want all of our guests to be happy." She was stalling, hoping Sara would pick up on her quandary and suggest the chicken.

"May I help you out here, Shaundra?" Lola swooped in to help.

Shaundra bit her lip and huffed quietly into her napkin.

"You mentioned earlier that you have some special people coming to the wedding who are in talks with your husband regarding a paramount merger. Is that right?"

"*Uh-hum*," was all Shaundra could muster up, knowing where Lola was headed.

"Well, the way I see it is…you want to astound these people with your success and impress them with your high caliber. So, may I recommend that you go with the lobster and prime rib? I think it's the ideal business strategy." Lola produced an endearing smile, "And your only daughter will always cherish this fine wedding that you have given her."

"Mother, the lobster is wonderful and the prime rib simply melts in your mouth. I really think Daddy would approve. After all, it's for him, too," Sara urged. "And the most beautiful wedding in the world for me." She spoke in her baby voice, attempting to manipulate her mother. Lola thoroughly despised that tactic and she suddenly felt the need to poke Sara with a fork.

Slowly, Shaundra nodded, working up to a smile.

"All right then…have we all agreed?" Lola rushed the verdict, not giving them a chance to reconsider. "I think you have made a very sensible decision and I believe that your husband will be amazed at what a savvy businesswoman you really are, Shaundra."

A simple wave of Lola's hand signaled Simon to return to their table and discuss the pertinent arrangements. And at the conclusion of that meeting, Shaundra left another hefty deposit in the amount of ten-thousand dollars. The entire wedding banquet, not including the three-hour open bar, was around forty-thousand dollars.

Lola waved goodbye and shouted to Sara and her mother as they walked toward their car, "The invitations will be arriving soon, so we'll get those sent out the day they arrive."

The entire day spent with Sara and her mother left Lola feeling drained. Besides being evil-natured and a killer, Sara had the personality of a wet dishrag. Lola loved toying with them, but even that was taxing.

Finally, the Parkins women were out of her hair and Lola was on her way back to the lovely Green Gables Estate. She passed Martini's Restaurant and circled the block while she dialed in a take-out order of spaghetti and salad.

Two days later, a large box arrived at Green Gables. It contained two-hundred and fifty invitations, corresponding envelopes, elegant napkins and personalized labels for the gift wine. The thought of all those people attending a very expensive wedding thrilled Lola to the core, which provided endurance to spend another long day with Sara and her mother.

When Lola's only clients arrived, she placed a pot of tea and a tray of cookies on the dining room table where they would prepare the invitations. "I think it's cheap to send wedding invitations that have not been hand-addressed. It's unsophisticated," Lola reminded Sara, after Sara had complained about her cramping hands.

"Yes, you're right," Sara agreed.

"Sara, tell Lola about what happened to your friend," Shaundra suggested while placing another completed envelope into the basket.

"Oh, my gosh!" Sara put down her pen, eager to share gossip. "My friend, Debbie, was recently attacked in her home and the crazy woman shaved off all of her hair!"

"What?" Lola pretended to be shocked. "That's terrible! What happened?"

"Well, she was at home and all of a sudden a woman busted in to her apartment with a gun and tied her up. The lady asked Debbie if she was a bad person and all this other weird stuff about her boyfriend. And then...she shaved Debbie's head completely!" Sara's eyes were huge.

"I've never heard of such a thing!" Lola silently applauded herself for the Oscar-worthy performance she'd just given.

"And then she beat her up!"

Two slaps to the face is hardly beating somebody up. Lola was thrilled to hear the story from another perspective. "Oh, that is simply monstrous! Why would somebody do such a thing?" Lola shook her head. "Tell me, is this the same Debbie who will be in your wedding?"

"*Uh-hum*," Sara nodded, excited by the conversation.

"And she is all right? She'll still be in your wedding?"

"Yes," Shaundra interjected, "I've talked with her mother and she said that Debbie is doing better and has been talking with a therapist about the ordeal."

Lola could feel herself smiling inside and hoped it wasn't obvious to her guests. *Better shift gears.* "On a lighter note, where will you be spending your honeymoon?" Lola forced herself to engage in small talk with her reviled guests.

"We're going to Hawaii. It's my father's wedding gift to us. Isn't that great?"

"Yes." Dollar signs filled Lola's head. Hawaiian honeymoons aren't cheap, she giggled to herself. *Add that to over-inflated wedding costs and...*Suddenly, her thoughts were jumbled as an explosion of uninvited memories burst inside her head. "Hawaii," she repeated, immediately excusing herself from the room.

Lola stood in an upstairs bathroom and tried to collect herself as images of their first picnic swarmed inside her head and visions of their sunset dinner, where he first proclaimed his love for her, crashed against another tender memory. Her head was under attack. She resisted his memory and closed her mind tightly. "Focus!" she reprimanded herself and turned on the tap to splash water on her face. Angrily, she looked at herself in the mirror, "Finish this!"

When the invitations were completed, Lola stuffed them into a commemorative wedding box and sent Sara and her mother on their way. "Don't forget to mail them on your way home!" Lola called out to the blue Mercedes in the driveway.

Lola tried to keep her mind on the operation and suffocated any lingering memories that threatened to jeopardize her mission. While organizing her paperwork, she added up some of the wedding costs aloud, "Let's see here, about forty grand for catering, plus twenty-five for my services, ten for flowers, seven for table decs and lighting, ten for the cake, three already spent on her dress and with her honeymoon, open bar and other essentials...Wow! They're hitting over a hundred-thousand on a sham wedding!" She was very pleased.

As dawn moved quietly over Green Gables, Lola sprung out of bed, ready to launch another element to her plan. Eagerly, she loaded the Mercedes with supplies for her cunning endeavor and then made the hour-long trek to Addelbrooke College to pay Joya a special visit.

An alleyway that aligned the rear portion of several stately homes caught her attention when she first arrived in the small college town. Lola turned into the secluded alley and turned off the engine. Nearby, a lone dog barked, but all else was quiet and seemingly free from nosy neighbors.

On the seat beside her was a new disguise waiting to be deployed. Generously, she applied liquid ivory to her face and robust red lipstick to her lips. Thick black liner contoured her eyes, reshaping them while her eyelids were painted light green. After brushing on a thick coat of mascara to her long lashes, she penciled on a beauty mark just to the right of her mouth. The curly red wig needed a little persuasion, so she fussed with it until it took on the character she desired. Lola enjoyed wearing the disguises as much as she liked putting them together.

From the glove compartment, she prepared a few strips of sturdy tape and lightly stuck them to the interior of her coat pocket for easy access that would be needed later in her plan. And hidden beneath her seat, was a half-pound of marijuana that she had discreetly acquired from the sleazy New York motel. Carefully, she plunged the contraband deep into her other coat pocket and started the engine. Two blocks from the dorm, she parked her car on a street in a quiet neighborhood.

A brisk walk led Lola to Joya's dorm. She stood outside of the locked doorway awaiting passage from an unsuspecting resident. Finally, a young man arrived on his bicycle. "Excuse me, sir," Lola called out in another fabricated drawl. "I'm here to visit with Cindy Smith and I'm afraid I can't call her. My cell phone just died," she shook her head as if to be annoyed with herself. "I'm such an idiot," she admonished herself, adding to her ploy. "Anyway, I was supposed to call her when I arrived."

"Well, in the future, there's a pay phone right over there, but I'll just let you in," the friendly young man offered.

"Oh, my goodness! I didn't even see that phone over there," Lola giggled. And I've been standing here, mindlessly, for over ten minutes."

"I know how that goes," he smiled as he prepared to lock his bike to the rack.

"So, you know Cindy? Are you a relative or something?"

Lola gasped and quickly searched for an answer while he fiddled with his bike chain. She hadn't expected a real Cindy Smith to reside at the dorm.

He didn't seem to notice that she didn't answer his question. "I'll just take you to her room. This place can be kind of confusing at first."

Lola froze for a moment, stalling. "Oh, aren't you the gentleman. I do appreciate that, but I don't want to bother you any further and I'm sure I can figure it out from here."

"Oh, it's no problem. She's just on the floor above mine."

Lola's mind spun in all directions. She couldn't think her way out of the complicated mess.

"Excuse me," he said, opening up his cell phone, "I have to take this call. I'll be real quick."

The roaring inside Lola's ears drowned out his phone conversation. For a moment, she could hear nothing else outside of her own head.

"I'm sorry for ditching you like this after I offered to take you up to Cindy's room, but I just got word that I can finally meet with my advisor right now," he apologized. "It's so hard to get in to see him. I hope you understand." His smile was sincere as he opened the door for Lola.

"Goodness, that's not a problem at all. I just appreciate you getting me out of the fix I was in."

He nodded and climbed onto his bike.

"Good luck!" she shouted, relieved that he was pedaling away.

It took her a minute to recover from the close call and when she did, she made her way up two flights of stairs to Joya's floor. After a sturdy rap on the door, Lola waited for Joya to answer. A soft rustling on the other side could be heard and then a thumping sound, which indicated that someone was coming to the door. Quickly, Lola reached inside her pocket and positioned the tape at her fingertips. The door opened with a subtle creak and there they stood, face-to-face. Joya's hair was disheveled and dark makeup smudges were smeared across her upper cheeks. She rubbed her eyes with the backs of her hands and yawned.

"Oh, my! I'm afraid that I have woken you up. Please forgive me," Lola begged, in a very friendly manner.

Joya's drowsy body hardly moved, managing only a slight nod of her head.

"Is this Gertrude Dunlop's room?"

"No, it's not." Joya's hoarse voice was shrouded in a dense fog of bad breath that reeked in booze, presumably from a recent party.

Lola cleared her throat and held her breath. Casually, she surveyed the door, ready to make her next move. Unfortunately, Joya was leaning against the door thus precluding Lola from placing the piece of tape over the recessing device alongside the edge of the door. "I'm so sorry to continue to bother you, miss, but would you know where I could find my sister? She is in room *319*, too. I guess I have the wrong dorm. Isn't this the Canterbury Dorm?"

"No, it's not."

"Can you tell me where I can find it?"

"Yeah, hold on a minute," Joya mumbled.

Lola assumed that she was trying to remain in a sleepy state, so she could return to her bed when Lola was done bothering her. But Lola had other plans. When Joya turned away from the door to look at the campus map that was fastened to the wall, Lola swiftly pressed the tape over the door's metal locking device.

"All right, you take the same road that you used when you came here, but go down two more blocks, turn left and it's the third building on the right."

"Oh, thank you so much. I was really lost. Once again, I'm sorry to have bothered you."

Joya nodded with a half smile, pushing the door closed.

Relieved that the door didn't pop back open and alert Joya to her illicit actions, Lola quickly scurried down the hallway to the fire alarm that she had already located upon coming through the stairwell door. With her hand firmly on the handle, Lola yanked it downward, setting off a deafening shrill throughout the corridor. A blinding confusion blurred her thoughts as the brain-piercing siren continued to scream. Lola scrambled to the bathroom where she remained hidden until the proper time. Not bringing ear plugs to this operation was a big mistake, she thought to herself, wedging her gloved fingers into her ears.

Suddenly, dozens of scantily clad bodies hurried from their rooms in a flurry toward the stairs. Through a small crack at the bathroom door, Lola watched the chaotic scene. Finally, she spotted Joya inside a rushing stream of girls that was moving toward the exit.

When the hallway was empty, Lola burst through the bathroom door and ran into room *319*. Two beds were situated inside the messy room. Which one was Joya's? She wondered. Lola yanked off a glove and rested her hand on the bed that she suspected was Joya's. It was still warm. She felt the other bed and it was cold. Quickly, she gloved her hand again and reached into the table beside the warm bed and pulled a single strand of hair from Joya's hairbrush. She opened the bag of marijuana and stuffed the wavy string of hair into the bag and kneaded it deeply into the weed, believing it would build a stronger case against Joya. Lola knelt down and shoved the illegal substance under Joya's bed to the farthest corner, out of sight.

When Lola prepared to leave, her trembling hand struggled to peel the tape from the door. The alarm continued to blare, further rattling her nerves. She had to hurry, but the stubborn tape wouldn't come loose. She was nearly in a panic when she ripped her right glove off and used her fingernail to loosen the tape. Finally, she was able to remove the entire piece of tape. She replaced her gloves and peered into the hall. It was still empty except for the penetrating siren. She hurried through the exit and made it to her car without any trouble.

Though she was hungry for revenge, the planted stash would have to remain under Joya's bed until the conclusion of Sara's wedding day. It wasn't imperative to the plan, but it would serve as a delightful bonus if Joya was a part of the *grand finale*.

Before reaching Green Gables, Lola stopped at the hardware store to pick up a few items that she needed for Sara's *special* wedding gift. And later in the afternoon, she relaxed on the sofa with her yearbook in her lap. Billy and Debbie had a black X drawn through their senior pictures and soon Joya, Nick and Sara would have the same comment assigned to each of their photos.

Chapter Eighteen

The most expensive florist that Lola could find delivered the flowers to the church the evening before the wedding. For an extra commission they would also decorate the entire cathedral and reception hall, sparing Lola the strenuous efforts. Lola strolled around the church and adjusted some of the arrangements making sure that everything was looking spectacular. Some blue and silver bows still needed fastening to the pews, so she assisted in that effort while the minister ran through the ceremonial procedures.

Several boxes of candles needed tending to as well, so Lola placed them in appealing locations. It was coming together wonderfully, she decided. Too bad it's all wasted on them, Lola thought as she marveled at her impressive creation made from candles, imported lace and flowers.

"Lola," Shaundra called out as she approached her in the foyer. "I'd like you to meet Nick's parents. This is Frank and Leslie Evans."

"It's nice to meet you." Lola tried to attach sincerity to her forged greeting. They, too, had raised a monster, she thought with festering hatred, but soon enough Nick would get his along with the others. A peculiar smile mounted on Lola's face as she looked ahead to the upcoming events.

"And these are the bridesmaids," said Shaundra, pointing at three young ladies who were coming down the aisle near the rear of the church. "This is Joya, Debbie and my niece, Shelly."

"I'm very pleased to meet you all. I've heard so much about you that I feel I already know you." Lola nearly laughed at her own statement.

Joya and Debbie merely smiled while Shelly properly shook Lola's hand and said, "It's very nice to meet you, Ms. Sorenson."

"Likewise," Lola smiled, returning the sincerity.

"Excuse me, Lola, we need to speak with the minister. We'll catch up with you in just a few minutes," said Shaudra.

"Certainly," Lola nodded, thinking it was a welcomed departure as she watched Frank and Leslie walk away with

Shaundra. "Well, Sara, it appears that everything is in order. Do any of you have questions for me? Any concerns?"

"No," Sara answered blandly.

"All right. We'll all meet here at *1:30* tomorrow. That should give us plenty of time since the wedding isn't until *3:00.* You all have hair appointments in the morning, right?"

"Yes. Well, not Debbie. I mean, Debbie has an appointment, but it's not for her hair," Sara explained without using any tact.

Incensed, Debbie glared at the back of Sara's head, wishing that the insensitive bride's hair would suddenly fall out.

The pointed exchanges between Debbie and Sara were certainly added perks. Lola relished her handiwork as she studied Debbie's cheap wig. "So, Shelly," said Lola, turning away from Debbie, "who is doing your hair?"

"I am," Shelly replied cheerfully. "Sara said the salon was over-booked, so I'm going to curl my hair and use some barrettes my mother bought."

"I see," Lola smiled at Shelly and then cast a sharp look in Sara's direction, realizing that Sara was up to her old tricks. It then occurred to her, for the sake of family relations, Shelly was appointed maid-of-honor by meddling mothers and not by Sara at all. Lola knew perfectly well that the salon would have made room for Shelly, if asked.

"Shelly, I also have a hair appointment in the morning, but I have some very precious matters to tend to as well. I just don't feel that I will be able to keep my appointment and accomplish all of my tasks for Sara's wedding. Would you be a love and take my appointment for me? I would consider this an enormous favor," she smiled, glowing with empathy.

Shelly's face lit up, "Sure, I'd be happy to." She smiled as if she'd just been invited to the prom.

"Thank you." Lola ignored the snide expression mounting on Sara's face. "Excuse me, ladies, I'll be right back. There's something I need to take care of."

Lola dashed away from the group and slipped into the restroom where an ongoing conversation rolled back and forth between two occupied stalls. Lola listened for a moment before identifying the two voices. It was Shaundra and Leslie

Evans. Apparently, they were already done speaking with the minister. She nearly laughed as she listened in on their gossip.

"Darling, she's got to be at least thirty-five. I can tell that she's already had some work done on her face. Living in Los Angeles and dealing with all those celebrities, of course she's compelled to keep up her appearance."

"*Hmm*, yes," Shaundra agreed. "Well, I'd like to have the name of her plastic surgeon because she looks fantastic."

Again, Lola struggled not to laugh and then she heard the sound of rustling paper behind the stall doors. Quickly, she stepped through the door and turned around, pretending to be entering the restroom. Shaundra and Leslie moved toward the sinks where Lola joined them and washed her hands, too.

Discreetly, Leslie surveyed Lola's complexion in the mirror. "How long will you be staying in Miller Lake?"

Lola flaunted her youthful face and beamed, "My client is sending his jet for me at the airport tomorrow after the reception." Lola's statement left Shaundra and Leslie in a dense state of curiosity.

"Oh, I see. You're pretty busy?" Leslie attempted to extract more information from Lola.

"Enormously. I have three weddings coming up. Two in Paris and one in the Cayman Islands." Lola politely excused herself, stating she had some things to tidy up for the wedding.

She walked out into the parking lot and called the hair salon. "Hello? This is Lola Sorenson and I have an appointment for tomorrow morning, but I would like my very special friend to take my place, instead. I want this young lady to get the works, including a professional makeup job. Assign your very best artist to work with her and spare no expense. Her name is Shelly and she'll be arriving at nine tomorrow morning with Sara Parkins."

When the conversation was over, Lola dropped her phone inside her purse and returned to the bride and her maids. "All right, it's all set. Shelly, you are to be at the salon tomorrow at nine. So, I guess that is it for today. Now, I don't want any of you staying up past eleven o'clock tonight. Get good rest because tomorrow is going to be a big day." Lola winked at Shelly and left the church.

All of Lola's belongings at the estate were packed except for a few remaining items needed for the wedding. She loaded her own car and, under the cover of night, drove it to a predetermined hotel.

The posh suite that she had reserved would be her refuge where she would privately bask in victory and hideout for a few days after fleeing Sara's wedding. Lola locked her car in the parking lot and took a taxi back to Green Gables where she ordered a pizza for dinner.

On the floor, beside the desk, was a very special package that awaited Lola's attention. While she waited for her dinner to arrive, she opened up the parcel and dumped the contents onto the desk. The work of the private investigator and greedy New York photographer pleased her immensely as she examined the articles.

Later, she nibbled on her pizza and cleaned the massive estate from top to bottom, making sure that it was just as pristine as it was when she first moved in to the manor.

Having paid in advance with cash for her entire stay at the old estate and using a phony name, Lola felt pretty safe that she would be untraceable for those angry persons who would soon be coming to pay her a hostile visit. But Lola wouldn't be there. She cleaned until midnight eating chunks of pizza on the run while swilling bottles of water. After midnight, she declared the home to be in immaculate shape.

A brand new slide projector sat on the floor beside her. Lola pulled it up to the desk and loaded all of the slides, cleverly, adding a few of her own. With that being the last task of the night, her eyelids grew heavy and stung from fatigue. Longingly, she looked at the sofa and plunged herself into its rich, abiding comfort.

Dawn's gentle glow crept through the fringes of the window shades, summoning Lola to wake. With a deep stretch and an everlasting yawn, she sat up and rested against the back of the cushions until her vision strengthened enough to read the old clock on the mantle. It was only six-thirty. With a few hours to kill before the reception hall opened, Lola decided to treat herself to a full breakfast. The café down the street offered everything imaginable for breakfast and it was a day for celebrating. Lola stood up and gathered her clothes.

The café was already busy by the time she arrived at seven. Lola sipped her coffee and waited for her French toast and sausage. The local newspaper could not hold her interest; she was too distracted with excitement for the upcoming events.

"Would you like some more coffee, ma'am?" the server offered.

"Yes, please," Lola smiled graciously at the lady holding the pot of steaming brew. She inhaled deeply as the wonderful aroma swirled up around her face. Giggling children in the next booth caught her attention and for a while she watched the young family. Fragments from their conversations indicated they were on a long road trip. Lola imagined their cheerful father bouncing them all out of their hotel beds earlier that morning, just like her own father had done. And after breakfast, the father would whisk them down the road toward their next destination.

The scene reminded Lola of a time when she and her parents laughed all the way to Florida in her dad's old Pontiac. It was a magical time in her young life and she had always hoped that they would do it again some day. She sighed heavily as a single tear splashed onto her hand, "No more vacations like that."

Memories that were once free to roam Lola's mind were swiftly strangled by the interminable hate that churned within her. Because of Sara, Lola had no father and her mother had no husband. A young man was buried in Miller Lake Cemetery at the hands of Sara Parkins and, finally, because of Sara, Lola found the love of her life and then had to bear the excruciating pain of losing him along with her dear friends. Indeed, Sara was the master architect to Lola's suffering and she deserved what was coming to her.

Outside of the café, dark clouds loomed in the distance. It appeared to be a nasty storm in the making. "How appropriate for you, Sara, a dark and stormy day for your wedding." Contentedly, Lola opened the door to the Mercedes and was on her way.

The parking lot in front of the reception hall was empty except for two cars. Lola pulled the Mercedes around to the back where delivery trucks unloaded their goods. She tugged on the heavy doors, braced them open with two sticks of wood and waited for a special delivery that she had previously arranged with a local courier service.

Within the hour, Lola labeled the gift wine, set up her special surprise for the newlyweds and strategically positioned the slide projector in such a way that every wedding guest would be sure to enjoy the spectacular show. She was careful to keep the power cord to the projector with her at all times because she didn't want anyone previewing the show before the proper unveiling.

On her way back to Green Gables, Lola stopped at the salon to pay for Shelly's hair and facial treatments. Inside, she found it busy and slightly chaotic from all of the wedding fuss. She didn't find Shelly in her search, but Sara's annoying voice could be heard over the fluttering conversations inside the shop. Shaundra's head was planted under a sink alongside Leslie Evans, but still, no Shelly.

"Excuse me," Lola approached the receptionist, "I'm looking for Shelly? Did she make her appointment this morning?"

"She sure did. In fact, come on back and I'll let you have a peek at our new princess." The receptionist hurried toward the back of the shop with enthusiasm, anticipating Lola's positive reaction. She pulled the curtain back and revealed the new and improved Shelly.

"Oh, my!" Lola assessed the eighteen-year old beauty sitting gracefully in the chair. "You look exquisite!" Lola's grin widened, revealing her full endorsement. Shelly's blue eyes were even more noticeable, glistening against her ivory face.

The makeup artist's careful hand had expertly hidden the blemishes that scattered across Shelly's pretty face. It was obvious that, Fred, the makeup artist, had taken special care with Shelly. Her features were soft and pretty. Her long brown hair held gentle curls with tiny white flowers that elegantly adorned her head. "You know, Shelly, it's not polite to upstage the bride." Lola giggled in her sincere compliment.

Shelly blushed and smiled, "Thank you, Ms. Sorenson."

"Please, call me Lola," she said with another approving smile, "and you're welcome."

"This was really nice of you," Shelly looked into the mirror and smiled.

"Believe me, I know exactly how you feel. There was a time in my life where somebody showed me the same kindness." Lola was thinking of Sheila. "I just wanted to do the same for a deserving soul." Discreetly, Lola caught a runaway tear and then smiled again at the young beauty. She hoped that Shelly's newly discovered confidence would counter Sara's evil.

"Again, thank you," Shelly lifted out of the chair.

"Darling, it was my pleasure." She turned and faced the talented stylist, "Fred, you've done a marvelous job and it was just what I wanted."

"Oh, she's a doll and most pleasant to work with." He patted Shelly on the shoulder. "I almost feel guilty for charging you."

Lola chuckled along with him and then she turned back to Shelly, nearly whispering, "Has the bride seen you yet?" Lola's wily grin made Shelly and Fred laugh.

"No, not yet," Shelly replied.

With a gleam in her eye, Lola nodded. "All right, I am off to get busy. Take care of that hair. It looks like it's going to rain."

"Don't worry, sweetie, I've already got that covered," Fred interjected, waving a plastic scarf in the air.

"Superb!" Lola shouted over her shoulder as she hurried toward the reception counter. She leaned on the counter and handed over a wad of cash, which included a generous tip for Fred and even one for the receptionist.

The drive back to Green Gables would be Lola's last trip to the beautiful mansion. She wouldn't be returning. While the tub filled with water, she sprinkled soothing lavender bath salts beneath the faucet and then poured herself a glass of DOM PERIGNON from a bottle she had swiped from the caterer's carton at the reception hall.

After her bath, she stood at the sink and meticulously applied her makeup and then dressed her hair until she resembled a member of royalty. Her new black dress, beaded with diamonds the size of sesame seeds, highlighted every voluptuous curve upon her body. Her beauty was mesmerizing, leaving any man to wilt in her presence, but her intrigue was not to attract a man, rather to stage a revolt so grand that it would completely ruin the newlyweds and their appendages. Lola was beautiful, lovelier than Sara ever hoped to be. "Sara is going to hate you," she giggled to herself in the mirror.

Her last few minutes at the grand estate would be spent relaxing in the library; the room where she was most comfortable. She walked past the window and paused when she caught a glimpse of the horizon. Ominous clouds that echoed her mood tumbled across the darkening sky while thunder rumbled in the distance warning of the progressing storm. Shards of lightning flickered in her reflection as Lola stood at the window sipping expensive champagne from a crystal flute. And long velvet drapes, the color of crimson, twirled in rhythm with the restless winds as howling gusts frantically roamed the room. With another blast of wind, she closed the window and moved across the room to the black sofa where her high school yearbook lay among the cushions.

She sat on the edge of the sofa, careful not to wrinkle her gown, and began sifting the pages that highlighted her miserable past. Hatred, spawned by reigning vengeance, seeped from her pores as she lingered on PAGE 42. "Poor, Sara Parkins, what ever will you do now?" she mocked bitterly and closed the book before tucking it inside her overnight bag with the champagne flute and a half bottle of *Dom.*

A solid chime rang inside the antique mantle clock, announcing the one-o'clock hour. *It's time.* Lola picked up her bag and cast one final glance around the room before heading toward the door.

Inside the grand foyer, she stood beneath a crystal chandelier that served as a crown to the evergreen walls. She lingered for a moment when a gilded mirror beckoned her attention one last time. Emotionless, she stared at the vacant soul inside her reflection. The pleading eyes of the desperate stranger looked back at her and tried to stop her, but Lola's will impeded all reason.

Chapter Nineteen

Rumbles of conversation from the groomsmen and ushers floated upward into the ancient loft where Lola stood overlooking the beautiful sanctuary. The young men in their tuxedos seemed harmless enough, but still, they were friends of Nick and not to be mistaken for gentlemen. She watched them gather around Nick when he arrived and then they all went out into the courtyard.

Suddenly, a gust of wind slammed against the church reminding Lola that a storm was on its way. She turned toward the old wooden door that led into the bridal room and with her hand gripping the knob, she paused briefly with a rising smile. The final showdown was nearly at hand and just before she entered, she heard Sara say, "I don't think Lola likes me, Mother. She's always so cold and I've tried so hard to be nice to her."

"Oh…that mustn't concern you. This is your wedding day. Lola is just a very busy woman who must keep her business head on at all times," Shaundra said coolly, attempting to console the bride.

Lola had to bite her lip hard so as not to laugh at the irony of Sara wanting to be accepted by her! "Hello, ladies. Are we almost ready?" Lola gazed around the quaint room, admiring its timeless appeal.

"Almost," Sara answered, staring at herself in the mirror.

"Wonderful." Lola watched Sara and her mother fiddle with the veil, neither of them looking up to see Lola.

"Mother, stop! I told you I don't like it that way," Sara snapped.

Lola rolled her eyes and swiftly turned her attention toward Joya and Debbie who were quite busy peering through a small window and giggling as they ogled the groomsmen out in the courtyard.

"Dave is so hot," Debbie sighed dreamily.

"Yeah, but he's mine today because he's walking me down the aisle," Joya warned playfully.

"*Hmpf,*" Debbie shrugged her shoulders, dismissing Joya's claim.

"Seriously, Debbie, it's tradition for him to be my date for the duration of the wedding."

"You just made that up."

"No, I didn't. That's how it always is," Joya said smugly. "Let's ask Ms. Sorenson, then."

"All right." They turned to Lola to settle their dispute.

"Wow! You're gorgeous!" Joya's eyes nearly fell out of her head when she looked at Lola.

"Well, thank you," Lola smiled graciously.

"Yes, Ms. Sorenson, you *are* gorgeous!" Debbie was also astounded by the glorious presence.

The bride quickly whipped her head around to survey her traitor. Through the veil, Lola could see malice glowing in Sara's eyes as they studied each other. And in that second, Lola almost wished for Sara's recognition.

"Goodness!" Shaundra gasped, overcome by Lola's arresting beauty. "They're right. You look magnificent." Suddenly, Shaundra realized that she may have just ticked off the bride by acknowledging another woman's beauty on her wedding day. Quickly, she turned to Sara where she promptly intercepted a rapid succession of hostile glares from the acidic bride. "Almost as beautiful as the lovely bride, of course," she swiftly added. "Everyone looks so beautiful today," Shaundra rambled nervously, feeling ambushed.

"Yes, she is most breathtaking," said Shelly, coming into the room.

Lola winked at her new friend and smiled.

Sara huffed and slammed a package of bobby pins down onto the table. "Excuse me! Bride over here!"

"Yes, dear, I'm sorry." Obediently, Shaundra picked up the pack of pins.

Lola moved over toward Joya, giving Sara and her mother more room to work out the issues with the stubborn veil.

"Is everyone nearly ready?" Lola looked around the room.

Sara fussed with her veil and ignored the question while the bridesmaids nodded and smiled.

"You all remember everything that we went over yesterday, right? If you have any questions, let me know now." Curiously, Lola looked upon the operations occurring on top of Debbie's skull. "What seems to be the problem over here?"

"We're trying to fasten this wig, so it will stay on better." Joya was obviously flustered from the task and, without thinking; she yanked the wig from Debbie's head, fully exposing her baldness to everyone in the room.

Sara quickly spun around to see Debbie's naked head.

Mortified, Debbie thrust her hands up over her bare scalp in an attempt to hide herself from Lola, the startling beauty.

Lola studied Debbie's head, silently complimenting herself before asking, "Need any help?"

"Just make sure *that* doesn't happen in my wedding!" Sara hissed.

Debbie's face reddened with further humiliation.

Lola scolded Sara with her eyes, "I'm sure Debbie doesn't want this happening any more than you, Sara. Isn't that right, Shaundra?" Lola raised an accusing brow when her eyes met Shaundra's.

Embarrassed, Shaundra quickly turned to Sara and whispered, "That wasn't very nice."

Lola tuned out the conversation between Sara and her mother and repeated the question, "Debbie, need any help?"

Debbie shook her head and was ready to club Joya for the huge blunder. She probably would have except her hands were busy concealing her stubbly head.

"I think I've got it." Joya placed another thick wad of double-sided tape inside the wig. "I'm sorry, Debbie, about—"

Aggravated, Debbie interrupted the apology with a huff, "Let's just hurry and get it done, but I really don't think tape is going to help," she fretted.

Lola could hardly hide her delight while witnessing Debbie's embarrassment and frustration. It was certainly a bonus. She stepped out of the room for a moment and returned with the bouquets and placed them on the table inside the room. "I have some things to check on. I want you all lined up behind the sanctuary doors and ready to go in fifteen minutes. Don't be late and don't disappoint me, ladies." Lola smiled sweetly at Shelly, wanting to tell her how pretty she looked, but reserved her comment as she didn't want to give Sara any reason to be more unkind to Shelly.

From the loft above the sanctuary, Lola peered down upon the many guests who had arrived for the highly celebrated occasion. The pews were packed full and all who knew about Lola's involvement with the wedding eagerly anticipated the grand event, which was personally arranged by a fancy socialite from Los Angeles. Lola tiptoed down the stairs and made her way to the foyer where she would wait for the wedding party to assemble.

Mr. Parkins was already waiting by the doors, preparing for his fatherly duty. "Well, are you ready to give your little girl away?" Lola asked without sentiment, noticing that he looked much older than he really was. He had thinning hair and it was already all white. His eyes looked tired. The stress of running a large business and having to deal with Sara and her mother appeared on his worn face. But Lola didn't feel sorry for him. Perhaps he was a decent man after all, but he bullied Lola's family with the threat of a slander suit and, for that, he would pay.

"I'm not giving her away, I'm merely adopting a son," he chuckled. "I'm sure I'll see more of her now than before, if I know my Sara."

"I'm sure you will," Lola smiled, surprised by his pleasant demeanor. If he wasn't such a jerk, he could be a nice man. She explored his face, seeking other signs of humanity.

Mr. Parkins reached into his pocket and handed Lola an envelope. "This is your final check, I believe."

"Yes, it is. Thank you, Mr. Parkins." Lola casually stuffed the envelope into her black purse.

The photographer began snapping pictures as the bridal party descended the stairs on their way to the sanctuary doors. Sara stood calmly beside her father while Lola fluffed and straightened the wedding gown, which carried a fifteen-foot train. The bridesmaids were lined up with their groomsmen and ready to proceed down the aisle.

"Canon" emerged powerfully from the mighty rafters in the sanctuary, signaling all eyes to shift to the back of the church. Nick's gaze fell upon Debbie and her escort as they led the procession down the aisle. Nervously, he stood at the altar awaiting his bride.

When "Wedding March" began, all eyes were upon Sara as she made her way to her groom and high school sweetheart. Sara looked prettier than she ever had and Nick actually looked happy. Too bad they're such evil people, Lola thought with abiding contempt. The soft glow emanating from the many candles cast a gentle light upon the young couple who stood at the altar, professing their undying love for each other.

The ceremony was nearing its conclusion when the mighty storm hit. Crashing thunder raged overhead and rain drummed loudly on the roof, drowning out the words spoken by the bride and groom. And, as if it were previously arranged by Lola, the steady roar of the storm eclipsed the poignant words delivered by the minister when he declared Nick and Sara, "husband and wife."

Lola's work was done at the church and it was time for her to tie up one loose end involving Joya before moving on to the *grand finale*.

The reception line quickly formed, thrusting Lola into the mix. She had hoped to avoid the reception line altogether, but decided it would be best to go along with it. "Hello, Nick and Sara, congratulations on your nuptials," was all Lola could bring herself to say as she stood face-to-face with her enemies. The line moved a little more and she was stopped in front of Mr. and Mrs. Parkins. Lola shook their hands politely and accepted their generous praises for the spectacular wedding she had created for their daughter. "I assure you, the pleasure was all mine," Lola had told them many times in the conversation. A grin that held a big secret spanned Lola's face when she reminded them that there was more to come at the reception. "You haven't seen anything yet."

Lola spotted Shelly in the line and made her way toward her. "Shelly, you're a beautiful person. Don't let anyone ever make you feel unworthy." Lola looked into her innocent eyes and nodded for added emphasis.

"All right," Shelly smiled curiously. "Thank you again for what you did for me. I hope that some day you truly understand the depth of your kindness."

"I already know," Lola whispered in Shelly's ear as she hugged her. And with those parting words, she removed herself from the line.

Outside, streams of rainwater meandered through the parking lot forming deep puddles. Lola fastened a scarf around her head and ran to the Mercedes, noticing the soggy decorations on the limousine that was waiting to take the bride and groom to their wedding supper.

It was time to make that all-important phone call to Addelbrooke College and just as Lola dialed, she realized that she was on her cell phone and that the call would be directly linked to her. She would have to wait until she found a pay phone to make that call. "What was I thinking?" she scolded herself.

Before pulling out of the church parking lot, she saw a few guests running to their cars. Lola turned the car out onto the street and sped away from the church.

The exquisite banquet hall that hosted the wedding reception was only two miles away from the church and exorbitantly expensive, much to Lola's delight. She drove directly to a pay phone only three blocks away that would service her needs. Two quarters slipped down the slot and then Lola heard a ringing in her ear and then a crash of thunder overhead. From the investigator's notes, Lola knew that the roommate would welcome Lola's warning.

"Hello? Is this Vanessa?"

"Yes, who's calling?"

"I'd like to remain anonymous, if that's all right."

"All right," Vanessa agreed.

"I have some information that I thought you would find valuable. I was at a party the other night where I overheard your roommate, Joya, bragging to some guys about her secret enterprise. Apparently, she has been dealing drugs out of your dorm room for quite some time."

Vanessa gasped, "Are you sure?"

"Absolutely. She stores her drugs beneath her bed, go check and you'll see that I'm telling you the truth."

"All right, I will," she sounded gravely disappointed.

"The same thing happened to me in my freshman year and I nearly got kicked out of college because my roommate was keeping a large stash for her boyfriend. She blamed it on me, stating that it was mine. I just thought that you'd like to know since the new policy regarding zero tolerance for drugs just went into effect. You could be tagged as an accomplice, or she could simply say it's yours."

Vanessa breathed hard into the phone when she crouched down below Joya's bed. "I think I see something!"

"You should take care of it immediately. Call security to your room right now and don't touch it!"

"Thank you for telling me. I never thought that Joya was into that kind of stuff. She always seemed so focused on her studies except for the occasional parties she attends."

"Yeah, it's always the person you least suspect. I was shocked, too when the same thing happened to me two years ago."

"Well, thanks a lot for telling me. Is there anything else you can tell me before I call security?"

"No, that's about it. Please pardon my anonymity, but I'm sure you understand. The college is a big place and I don't need any form of retribution sneaking up on me."

"Yes, I understand and I'll take care of it right away. Thank you, again."

"You're welcome. Bye-bye." Lola wiped off the phone and slipped it back into its slot.

Genuine marble tiles led Lola through an elegant corridor into the exquisite dining room where guests were beginning to assemble. Massive mirrors hung on the walls, reflecting candlelight and delicate hues of the many bulging flower arrangements. The servers were busy filling champagne glasses in preparation of the arrival of Mr. and Mrs. Nick Evans. In the background, the band played a mix of contemporary and big band music while the guests mingled and consumed large amounts of free booze.

Several folks admired Lola's water fountain that was delivered earlier by courier service. It was an exact replica of the fountain that she and her father had built for the infamous homecoming dance. She was pleased with her personal contribution and the only variations from the original fountain were the color of flowers in the garlands and a hidden inscription that read, "For Joe."

Eagerly, Lola and the rest of the guests awaited the bride and groom's arrival. Lola sat in her chair, which was strategically placed to fully capture Sara's reaction to her fountain.

With anticipation, Lola plucked a champagne glass from a server's tray and watched the doors. Suddenly, the bandleader summoned the attention of all the guests. The room grew quiet as all conversations faded into silence. "Ladies and gentlemen, please lift your glasses and allow me to introduce to you, for the first time, Mr. and Mrs. Nick Evans."

The sound of clinking crystal, followed by clapping hands and cheers, echoed inside the room as Sara and Nick made their first official entrance together as husband and wife. Lola's breath caught in her chest as Nick and Sara made their way toward the wedding table, smiling all the way and then Sara stopped dead in her tracks. Her huge eyes were fixed on the fountain. She gasped in horror as she stood frozen beside Nick. "Where did this come from?" Sara shouted. Her face paled at the sight. Nick looked peculiarly at his new bride, not immediately understanding her odd behavior.

That's my cue. "What's the matter, dear?" Lola sprouted a concerned face.

Sara's tone had become tense and her hands were trembling. "Where did this come from?" she demanded.

"From me. It's my wedding gift to you and Nick. Recently, I met a local artist at a fair and commissioned this wonderful fountain for your wedding. I'm sorry. I thought that you would love it. What's the matter?" Lola donned another contrived look of bewilderment.

"Thank you, Lola." Nick's voice was strained. He took Sara's hand and tried to calm her. He almost appeared human Lola thought in a brief moment.

"Come on, Sara, it's all right. Let's go sit down." Again, Nick glanced curiously at the fountain and shook his head as if to finally understand its eerie message. Sara's eyes were still bulging from their sockets as they remained set on the menacing fountain.

"I thought it was a beautiful piece of art and I knew it would go so nicely with your wedding. What is so upsetting about a water fountain?" Lola finally asked, somewhat curtly.

Nick was at a loss and could only turn to his bride. "Come on Sara. Let's go sit down. They are waiting for us."

Sara turned from the fountain, still visibly traumatized, and followed her new husband to the satin-wrapped chairs awaiting them at their table.

After everyone was settled, efficient servers placed expensive plates of lobster and prime rib onto linen covered tables. It appeared that Sara was beginning to recover from the startling episode and was seemingly coming around.

While they dined, the band ceased playing and rounds of sentimental toasts circulated the room. Rolling laughter and tears swept through the crowd as tender endearments emerged from the hearts of the wedding guests. It had become a jolly event, bringing a rapturous grin to Lola's face.

It was time to prepare for the final act and while the newlyweds shared their first dance, Lola went to work. The crowd looked on, engaged in romance as the young lovers twirled together as one. Elegant music and candlelight served as a delicate backdrop, spotlighting the floating figures on the floor. When the waltz ended, the crowd clapped with sincere emotion and enthusiasm. After Nick danced with his mother and Sara danced with her father, all returned to their seats for the slide presentation.

Lola turned on the projector and watched the unsuspecting audience. The guests expressed their delight as images of the young couple's youth illuminated the wall. Candid moments, belonging to Sara and Nick during their innocence, trickled from the projector as Lola crept gently toward the rear door, ready for a brisk exit.

The moment Lola had waited for was finally upon her, promising sweet retribution. Closer, she backed up to the door, ready for her escape, but not before she claimed her revenge.

Suddenly, the crowd gasped when a shocking image appeared on the wall, clearly illustrating a recent and sordid affair between Nick and Joya. The color of bare flesh reflected on all of the viewers' astonished faces as Joya and Nick's depravity was unmistakably defined. All were appalled by the revolting picture appearing on the wall, but most couldn't look away from it.

Horror-struck, Joya looked past the condemning glares that started to cross her table. Quickly, she jumped to her feet and fled the scandalous scene.

The music had fallen silent and drumsticks had hit the floor. Without moving, Sara remained stiff in her chair, staring at the hideous figures upon the wall. Her eyes were enormous and her body began to shake with an unfamiliar fury. She turned to Nick and slapped his face hard, knocking him to the floor. Debbie's mouth hung wide open in disbelief and Shaundra's blazing eyes remained steadily on Nick, burrowing her rage in him.

"Just wait, Shaundra," Lola whispered. Nobody could move as they were still seized by absolute shock and then another bright flash went off and suddenly there was a picture of Sara on the wall. She was fully nude and brandishing a lewd act with two men. Again, the shocked spectators sounded in horror.

Sara's father shook his head violently while he demanded, "Somebody turn that damn thing off!"

The captive audience was paralyzed by their astonishment. Nobody was spared the despicable scene. Countless witnesses, consisting of friends, family and business associates babbled on in confusion while trying to make sense of it all.

Shaundra could take no more and fainted as the vulgar image of her daughter remained on the wall. Pandemonium had overtaken the hundred-thousand-dollar wedding. It was beautiful chaos.

Sara bolted out of her chair and screamed, "Lola!"

Chapter Twenty

Lola laughed all the way to the car rental agency as the many rewarding images replayed inside her head. She had accomplished what she had set out to do. Sara was publicly humiliated, her new marriage of only two hours was already in jeopardy and her very expensive wedding was a sham.

When she stepped up to the counter, she brandished a bright smile, like that of the *Cheshire Cat*, when she handed over the Mercedes keys. She was so happy for what she had done, but she couldn't tell a single soul; the only disadvantage to her plan.

A taxi took Lola to her hotel and on the way over, she continued to whirl in pleasure as the scenes of the day bounced around in her head. She had taken her revenge and soon her pain would subside. Sara and her friends got what was coming to them and, finally, Lola could close that ugly chapter of her life. Or could she?

A new pair of silk pajamas waited for Lola on the luxurious bed inside her suite. She had bought the pricey loungewear especially for this night. After her bath, she waited for her celebratory meal to arrive, which consisted of a rare steak, salad, baked potato and cheesecake...because her ravenous appetite called for it.

With another glass of champagne, Lola moved out onto the balcony that overlooked the town. The storm had cleared and left a bright moon and twinkling stars to keep her company. "Somewhere down there is turmoil and heartbreak. I have finally conquered you all," she shouted in victory.

By the midnight hour, came another tumultuous storm, leaving Lola restless. She flipped and flopped in the bed that had turned to stone somewhere in the night. Thoughts of Mike seeped into her head. Until this time, she had been fairly successful in keeping him at a safe distance, fearing his memory would consume her. After his death, Lola had shut the door to her heart where his memory remained in isolation. And there, he would stay.

Ironically, for her own salvation, Lola had learned to cling to the effects of Sara's poison as she knew no other way to live. Vengeance gave her life and excused her from facing the reality of Mike's death. But with retribution fulfilled, her mind was completely empty, permitting her own dreadful reality to return. No more concocting schemes to occupy her time. Suddenly, she was forced to deal with her own hell. There was nobody left to blame or seek to destroy for all of her pain.

Did my vengeance really justify anything? Lola bolted up in bed with that revelation. "I'm dead," she whispered and then began to cry in deep remorse. Sadly, vengeance wasn't the answer, she discovered too late. "Where did I go? Oh, my God!" She wailed, "What have I done? What have I become? Mike, you were right." Lola sobbed for hours, mourning the death of her own soul and cringing from the truth that she had become a monster. "Mike!" she called out to him as she wept in grave despair. "Oh, I wish I could take it all back. Dear Lord, I'm so sorry for everything. I wish I didn't do all those terrible things to them. Daddy, I'm so sorry, I haven't honored you at all." And with her tear-soaked face, Lola dropped her head on the pillow where she uttered the words, "I forgive you, Sara. I'm sorry, Nick and Joya and Debbie and Billy." She sighed and started sobbing again, "Todd, I really am sorry that you died a young man."

"What did you say, love? Can you hear me? Please, say it again."

Lola's eyes were closed tightly. She wouldn't open them because she had begun a dream where Mike was talking to her. If I open my eyes he will vanish, she convinced herself, struggling to hold on to her pleasant dream.

"Wake up, Lola!"

No, I don't want to open my eyes. If I do, you will be gone and I'll be left here again, without you. Please, don't make me, she pleaded with Mike inside her dream.

"Lola, I love you! Wake up." His words were stronger inside her dream. "Wake up, Lola!"

"I don't want to," she mumbled, "for as soon as I do, you will be gone and I can't bear it. I want to stay here inside this dream with you."

"Lola, you *are* here with me," his voice urged again, this time it was even louder and clearer. "I'm here. I'm not dead, Lola. Please, wake up."

"I'm scared. You'll be gone as soon as I do."

"Lola, this isn't a dream. I'm here. I was only shot, but I'm not dead. You saved us. All of us, you did. We're alive, Lola. Open your eyes and you'll see me!" Mike begged again, squeezing her hand tighter. "I'm really here with you. I promise. You are in a hospital in Hawaii. This is not a dream. Open your eyes, Lola. Do you feel my hand holding yours? Trust me, love."

Light penetrated her eyelids as his voice led her out of her dream.

He was grinning wildly as tears swirled across his eyes. "See? I told you I was right here."

"Mike?" Lola squeezed his hand, feeling his warm living flesh. It was true. He was alive!

"We've been trying to wake you for days. You were stubborn and we thought you might never come back to us."

"Us? Does that mean everybody is all right?"

"Yes, everybody. Thanks to you and they are all waiting to see you."

"They are? Everyone?"

"Yes," he revealed the wonderful truth in his blinding smile.

Suddenly, she became overwhelmed with excitement, alternating between laughing and crying. Mike leaned over her and held her tight, calming her. "Here, drink this." He handed her a cup of water.

"For so long, I thought that I had lost you all," Lola said, looking into his eyes as tears streamed down her cheeks.

"For so long?" He looked at her curiously.

"Yes, I dreamt you were all dead and it went on for months, it seemed." She sighed, still having trouble believing it was all a dream. She put the cup of water down onto the table and noticed her finger that was still bandaged from the fishing incident that occurred just moments before they were attacked. It was still healing…still fresh. She shook her head and looked up toward him again, "I'm so happy, Mike!"

"So am I," he said, leaning over to hug her again.

"Lola, do you remember everything?" asked Doctor Reynolds who had just entered the room.

"Yes," she said, as the ugly scene rushed forward. She gasped at some of her memories. "It was awful. I was so scared and I thought you were all going to die on that boat. Those evil men!" She shook her head to rid herself of the horrific images replaying in her head.

Mike squeezed her hand.

For a moment, she was quiet. "Mike?"

"Yes?"

"Those men...did I really—"

"Yes, Lola, you did. But don't think about that now."

She nodded and stared at his cane. "Are you all right?"

"One hundred percent," he grinned. "I was only shot here," he proudly pointed at his leg. "*Hmpf*, it's a mere scratch."

Lola suddenly remembered Sheila caring for Mike on the other boat. "I remember Sheila was helping you."

"Yes, and we're all fine." Mike hugged her for a long time. "It's going to be all right, love."

"It is, isn't it?" She thought for a moment, "So, when can I get out of here?"

Mike laughed along with the doctor.

"You sustained a bullet wound to your leg, as well. You were very lucky," Doctor Reynolds told her. "It did no remarkable damage."

"Is that the only place I was shot?"

"Yes," the doctor confirmed.

"Interesting," she mumbled.

"Why do you ask?" Dr. Reynolds looked at her.

"I was just wondering," she said, remembering parts of her very long and disturbing dream. She put her hand on her leg that suddenly felt tender. Her memory started to fully engage and suddenly a stampede of memories filled her head, making her a little dizzy.

"We couldn't figure out why you wouldn't wake up for so long. You scared us, Lola." Mike admitted.

Lola nodded, deep in thought. She was remembering the rest of her dream and realized she hadn't done all of those terrible things to Sara and the others. Her soul was free from the binding chains of hatred and revenge. She had been granted another chance to forgive, a gift that she would treasure for all time. She was alive again. Lola looked into Mike's eyes, "I guess I just needed to sort some things out in my dreams," she smiled in relief.

"I'm so glad you're back."

"So, how about getting me out of this place, doc?"

Dr. Reynolds chuckled and looked into her eyes with a lighted instrument. While he spoke to Lola, Mike sent a text to Captain Andre, filling him in on Lola's return.

"Your wound is healing nicely and I see no need to keep you here," Doctor Reynolds stated after examining Lola. "All of your tests are good, no head injuries or anything else to worry about. So, I'd say you are free to go, but let's wait until later this afternoon. Sound good?"

Lola smiled at the doctor as he left her room.

"Your mom is a grand lady, Lola. We've gotten to know each other very well these past few days." His eyes twinkled as if he had a secret. "She's just down in the cafeteria with the others."

Tears returned to her eyes when she learned that her mother was near.

"Everyone has been here every day waiting for you to wake up. They're going to be thrilled when they see you." He couldn't stop smiling at her.

"I want to see everyone right away. But first tell me everything that happened."

"Are you sure you are ready to hear it all? Now?"

"Yes, I want to get it over with and get on with my life," she smiled and wiped away a traveling tear, "I have a lot of living to do."

Mike nodded, "All right. You remember our limo driver?"

"*Uh-hum,*"

"He was the leader and one of our former crewmembers was in on it as well. His name was Morgan."

Lola gasped, "Morgan? Sheila told me about him. I replaced him."

"Yes, that's right. Well, the limo driver arranged it so that Morgan would work for us and gain access and information about the yacht, our routines, arms…everything. It was an elaborate plan. Anyway, a witness identified Morgan as the one who broke into the boat on Christmas. Part of his mission was to disarm us by removing all of the ammunition from our weapons. Because he left the weapons storage locked, we didn't think they'd been tampered with, so we never checked to see if the ammo had been removed." Mike shook his head in regret. "That's why when they attacked our boat, we were unarmed...defenseless! We each had our guns, ready for hell, but there we stood, with nothing. I shot first and when nothing happened, Morgan shot me. I never liked that guy. Anyway, Morgan had keys made back when he worked for us and that's how he got into everything he needed. The cops questioned his girlfriend and offered her a deal if she talked. She said when Morgan broke the window on the yacht, it was by accident. His operation was supposed to be a stealthy endeavor and nothing was supposed to draw attention to the fact that there was an illegal trespass."

Lola nodded slowly, taking it all in, "Which one was Morgan?"

"He was a small guy with long black hair."

Lola remembered the dreadful day on the boat. Morgan was her first kill.

"Are you sure you want to know all this?"

"Absolutely. I remember seeing the limo driver on the boat. He was a horrible man."

"Yes he was. And we all had a hard time on that little boat as it was sinking."

"Oh, I'm sure it was so frightening for you all—"

"No, I mean it was hard on us to leave you on the yacht. Alone. We felt as though we'd abandoned you, but we unanimously agreed to keep you a secret from the criminals hoping that you'd seen what had happened and took proper cover. It killed me to leave you on that boat alone with those men, but we felt that you had a better chance of surviving if they didn't know about you." Mike's eyes misted over, "I'm so sorry I left you there."

"But you did the right thing! Look how it turned out. I'm sure it was hard on you all to make that decision, but I'm so grateful you did." She nodded enthusiastically. "When I heard all of those gunshots, after you were on that little boat, I was sure they'd killed you all."

For a moment, he looked very sad. "That must have been so terrifying for you to be so alone."

Lola nodded and then smiled at him with her bright eyes.

"They thought they were so smart in shooting up the boat to make it sink faster," he chuckled. "They sure weren't expecting you," he shook his head, grinning.

His familiar laugh breathed more life in to her. She couldn't be any happier than at that moment, she thought.

"I've missed you so much," he said, squeezing her.

"And I've missed you more than you realize," she smiled, happy to be awake and in his arms.

"Now…before anything else interrupts my intentions, I'd like to give you that Christmas present." He reached into his pocket and pulled out her ring.

A Note From The Author

Thank you for finding my book. I hope it is what you were looking for.

Currently, I am preparing to jump into my next project and I'll update my website as new information becomes available.

I always welcome questions, comments and feedback. Please visit me at www.kimvantrease.com

Kim Vantrease